continued . . .

The Music of the Night

"Danger, deception, and desire all come together brilliantly in this sublimely sensual historical romance."
—*Booklist* (starred review)

"Complicated, challenging, sexy, and altogether adult."
—All About Romance

"Mesmerizing and fascinating. . . . Dark, intense, and with a surprise ending that will leave you breathless, her latest Gothic makes its mark on the genre." —*Romantic Times* (top pick)

"Refreshingly different from the usual romance book offerings . . . intelligent writing . . . an excellent example of what a talented writer can accomplish if they choose not to follow the pack."
—*The Romance Reader*

The Veil of Night

"Intelligent. Passionate. Filled with dark secrets and illuminating love. This is what romance is about!" —Robin Schone, *USA Today* bestselling author of *Scandalous Lovers*

"The next great romance author has arrived, and her name is Lydia Joyce. *The Veil of Night* is a stunning debut from a young writer who possesses remarkable maturity and style. Every page is charged with sensual energy and confident grace. It is a gorgeous, complex, absolutely riveting novel. If there is only one new author you will try this year, it must be Lydia Joyce."
—Lisa Kleypas, *New York Times* bestselling author of *Blue-Eyed Devil*

"A lush, erotic historical Gothic romance, with just the right dark and mysterious hero and a strong heroine who can match him. Anyone who has ached for the Gothics of the past shouldn't miss this book!"
—Karen Harbaugh, author of *Dark Enchantment*

Also by Lydia Joyce

Shadows of the Night
Voices of the Night
Whispers of the Night
The Music of the Night
The Veil of Night

Wicked Intentions

Lydia Joyce

A SIGNET ECLIPSE BOOK

SIGNET ECLIPSE
Published by New American Library, a division of
Penguin Group (USA) Inc., 375 Hudson Street,
New York, New York 10014, USA
Penguin Group (Canada), 90 Eglinton Avenue East, Suite 700, Toronto,
Ontario M4P 2Y3, Canada (a division of Pearson Penguin Canada Inc.)
Penguin Books Ltd., 80 Strand, London WC2R 0RL, England
Penguin Ireland, 25 St. Stephen's Green, Dublin 2,
Ireland (a division of Penguin Books Ltd.)
Penguin Group (Australia), 250 Camberwell Road, Camberwell, Victoria 3124,
Australia (a division of Pearson Australia Group Pty. Ltd.)
Penguin Books India Pvt. Ltd., 11 Community Centre, Panchsheel Park,
New Delhi - 110 017, India
Penguin Group (NZ), 67 Apollo Drive, Rosedale, North Shore 0632,
New Zealand (a division of Pearson New Zealand Ltd.)
Penguin Books (South Africa) (Pty.) Ltd., 24 Sturdee Avenue,
Rosebank, Johannesburg 2196, South Africa

Penguin Books Ltd., Registered Offices:
80 Strand, London WC2R 0RL, England

First published by Signet Eclipse, an imprint of New American Library,
a division of Penguin Group (USA) Inc.

First Printing, December 2008
10 9 8 7 6 5 4 3 2 1

Copyright © Lydia Joyce, 2008
All rights reserved

SIGNET ECLIPSE and logo are trademarks of Penguin Group (USA) Inc.

Printed in the United States of America

To the teachers who let me grow—
Miss Williams, Mrs. Casey, and Mrs. Pennebaker

And in memory of Mrs. Hutchinson

London
August 1, 1866

Dear Mr. Kelly—

Search harder. Scour every filthy flat in St. Giles if you have to. You must find the girl and bring her to me.

I am certain she is in London. I saw one of the necklaces that you failed to locate dangling from a peeress' neck just two days past. Your failure to produce her is most disturbing, and it makes me wonder where, exactly, your loyalties really lie.

You have two weeks. Either bring her to me, or give me proof of her death. You shall regret it if you fail.

—Olthwaite

Chapter One

Two days before . . .

The smothering velvet curtains were shut against the night, but Thomas Hyde, Lord Varcourt, could feel the darkness pressing against the edges of the crowded parlor, tightening around the silk-shaded gaslights and dimming them from yellow flame to orange. The coals glowed sullenly in the grate as the chill of an early autumn sank deep into the old stones of the city.

In Parliament's new limestone palace, already damp and lichenous where it crouched beside the stinking Thames, debate raged. And so the season limped on, with the endless rotation of dinners, dances, operas, and soirees, accompanied as always by the constant, grating murmur of politics and gossip, marriage and legislation, secret cabals and open scandals that took place in the myriad stifling rooms.

Thomas stood apart in a corner of the Rushworth parlor, watching the currents in the room. Jewels glinted in the muffled lights, on swan necks and wrinkled wrists alike. Shadows in superfine and linen, the men moved among the wide skirts of the ladies, stooping to murmur in a delicate ear or pulling aside a hoary one for a moment's stern exchange. The world was made and unmade in rooms like this, and already, Thomas could begin to read the threads that went into its making. Soon he would have enough gathered into his hands that he could pull them and watch men dance. . . .

Bright laughter rose above the subdued murmurs with the suddenness and clarity of a shattered wineglass. Thomas' twin sisters, ever oblivious to any nuance they did not care to notice, stood by the piano with Mrs. Christopher Radcliffe. They were a false focus in the room, as insignificant as the bustling of the servants. Of more interest to Thomas was the presence of Lord Edgington in one corner of the room: The men around him shifted uncertainly, uncomfortably, for the staunchly Tory if wildly libertine family reputation had been shattered a year ago with Edgington's defection to the Whigs.

It was whispered that perhaps some portion of Edgington's political shift was due to his marriage to the utterly unknown Margaret King two years before. Thomas did not discount it. That tiny woman sat in a chair directly in front of him, her thick black coils of hair framing her delicate face, as silent and unreadable as an exquisite sphinx.

Only one other woman sat as quietly as she—and more still, for Thomas at times wondered if she had breathed since the gentlemen had rejoined the ladies after their postprandial cigars. She wore a dress in a red so dark that it was almost black, a filmy veil of jet lace cascading from a golden comb on the top of her head to fall in folds across her face.

Esmeralda, she called herself, though God only knew who she really was or from whence she came. She was the newest accessory for the fashionable parlor, one of a thousand charlatans who now pretended unnatural powers for the credulous admiration of laborer and monarch alike, a mass continental insanity that Thomas had instantly despised and suspected. It was an unpredictable element. A corruptible element. A potentially useful element, to be sure, but far too fickle to be trusted. She was fascinating. It was hard for Thomas to admit it, but it was true—he was no more immune to her carnal attraction than any of the young men who panted after every enticing twitch of her skirts. He was old enough, at least, to know better.

He damned well should be.

As Thomas watched, his mother, Lady Hamilton, paused by the spiritualist's chair and touched one of the woman's gloved hands, which rested upon its carved arm. The veiled woman bowed her head slowly with her usual vulpine grace and then straightened again, freezing back in position as if she had never moved.

Esmeralda heard the dead, she claimed, and saw visions—and collected like pearls the secrets of the noblewomen who confided in her. Now, a mere year after her abrupt introduction into Thomas' circle, it was a poor party that did not boast of her presence as a statue in the corner, declaring the hostess' connection to worlds invisible.

Whom was she watching from behind that veil? Whose tool was she in this game of empires? And how many of the women present, in addition to his own mother, had already been drawn into her thrall? Not even Edgington, with all his spies, had been able to find out. Not even Thomas, with all his ability to coax out confidences.

Lady Hamilton moved on, rubies glittering in her ears in utter disregard to the dark lilac of her dress and her bold new necklace, which marked her captivity to this Esmeralda. Rubies guarded against harmful thoughts, the woman taught, emeralds against envy, diamonds against the spirits of the other world, and topaz against ills of the spirit. Thomas' gut clenched, but as long as his father clung to both life and the title, there was nothing he could do about his mother's preoccupation with mediums and spirit guides who promised to reunite her with the son she had lost some ten years before.

The son many in that very room thought Thomas had a hand in killing.

Lady Hamilton's hand fluttered self-consciously at her neck. She had been playing with her new necklace all evening, all but flaunting it in front of the other guests. Thomas wondered cynically what charms Esmeralda had said over it, or if her visions had led his mother to a certain jewelry shop where the spiritualist coincidentally knew the owner.

Lady James Ashcroft intercepted his mother as she passed near Thomas without acknowledging him. The countess gave the necklace a near-convulsive jerk, and Lady James' eyes obediently slid downward.

"What a brilliant new piece that is!" Lady James exclaimed, her own hand rising to the heavy jewels hanging from her neck and ears, relics of the Indian mines that had made her husband so rich. "It is so deliciously medieval. Please do tell me whom you had make it."

"It wasn't made," Lady Hamilton said in tones of deepest mystery. "It was found. Esmeralda has been possessed of visions concerning it for weeks, and though she told me the import of each, none of it made sense until she saw what I recognized as a peculiar stone in the round garden behind Hamilton House. I ordered it pulled up, and beneath, in a little casket near rotted with age, was this extraordinary necklace!"

Even as those light words elicited the proper admiring noises from Lady James, Thomas felt a chill cut through him. The necklace—found, not bought? If that great pearl was real, the necklace must be worth three hundred pounds at least. Where had Esmeralda come up with it? Who had induced her to plant such a treasure in their back garden, and for what purpose?

Lady Hamilton turned to display the necklace to its best advantage as she expounded upon the story in answer to

Lady James' inquiries. Its glitter seemed to mock Thomas. It had to be a ruse, a beautiful millstone to tie about his mother's neck in order to drown his family. There could be no good hidden in such a carefully woven plot.

Thomas wanted the thing gone—and with it, Esmeralda.

Lady James launched into the tale of another of Esmeralda's prescient insights, this time about her own youngest daughter, whom she had hoped would be wooed by a gentleman—who, as it turned out, had been in the midst of a secret and passionate affair with a married lady. With Esmeralda's delicate hints, the signs had been clear enough for anyone to see, and Lady James had driven off his first tentative overtures toward the young Flora.

Thomas suppressed a bitter smile. He knew whom Lady James must mean: Lord Gifford, and the prediction that the earl's son had a married lover—or two, for that matter—was no prediction at all, from what Thomas knew of the man's predilections.

Lady James was distracted by her eldest daughter's signal from across the room and soon left in a miasma of rosewater to whisk the shrinking Flora from her care and press the unpretty girl upon the nearest suitable man. Thomas took the opportunity to intercept his mother.

He stepped forward, taking her elbow in his hand. Lady Hamilton started when he touched her, and he tamped down a surge of anger against the statuelike form of Esmeralda.

"Madam," he said quietly, "you did not tell me that Esmeralda had given you that necklace."

His mother looked confused, the dark, painted lines of her brows drawing together. "Given me it? No, I had the gardener dig it up—"

"Nevertheless." Thomas cut her off. "It is a gift. Her visions led you to it, you say—how easy would it have been for her to remain silent about them and keep the necklace for herself? No, she wanted you to have it, and I mistrust her reasons."

Her face grew stony. "You are simply speaking from your prejudices."

"I *simply* do not trust a stranger who has no reason to be generous and may have motivations you know nothing of," he returned, forgetting in his annoyance to pander to the illusion that the spiritualist possessed supernatural gifts. "Did it not occur to you that the piece might be stolen? Imagine the damage it would do to your husband in Parliament if our family were connected to a theft. Madam, I would ask you to remove the necklace and to conceal it until we reach home. Then put it away and pretend it was never found." He looked down at her, ruthlessly exploiting the uncertainty in him that Esmeralda had fanned into fear. "Do not wear it— or even refer to it—until that spiritualist is gone."

The color drained from her cheeks, and with it went the traces of her girlhood beauty. "You are punishing me," she whispered, "for not getting rid of her as you told me to."

Thomas stretched his lips in a smile he didn't feel. "No, madam. I am trying to save you." And with that, he let her go, praying that she would accede to his demands.

He turned to face the woman who sat so still across the parlor, who had been sending shadows for him to duel for the better part of a year and who had insinuated herself so fully into society that her presence had become well nigh inescapable.

He had never spoken to her, never acknowledged her, knowing that she would, in time, be tossed away like last season's fashion in hats. That had been a mistake, for society had not tired of her quickly enough—a mistake he would commit no longer. Even so, he had felt her presence at every dinner and soiree like a brand across his brain, enflaming him, goading him. She must know how tempting and infuriating she was to him—for she was, quite clearly, a woman who at all times was exactly as she meant to be.

He closed the space between them, weaving between belling skirts and the archipelago of chairs. The air was heavy with the sickly sweet scents of sherry and sweat, cologne water and drooping flowers, the stench of tobacco hanging upon the coats of the men who had indulged themselves over the supper table after the ladies had retired.

Esmeralda did not stir in her corner, though he would have sworn that her eyes were fixed upon him as he drew near. He stopped so close to her chair that his boot tips creased the stiff dupioni of her dark crimson skirts. He could tell almost no more about her from that vantage than he could from across the room, for she was still just as motionless, the fabric of her veil revealing nothing but a hint of the shape of her face beneath. Her high-necked dress ended far beneath its edge, her tight sleeves coming down over her wrists to meet her short black gloves. She was slender but tall for a woman—he had seen her rise from a chair and use that height and her eerie quietness to silence a room. She could be any age, any woman, really, beneath the armor of silk. Why, then, did she set his blood to racing? If it were not for the small movement of her chest as she breathed, echoed by a flutter of her veil, he could almost believe that she was not even alive.

But she did breathe—and he could feel the tension radiating from her body as he stood over her, looking down. She was afraid of him. It made him fiercely, spitefully glad that he could provoke a response in her as primitive and insuppressible as that which she had caused in him over and over again.

She said nothing, so neither did he. Instead, he walked slowly, deliberately around her until he stood in the gap between the corner of her chair and the wall, directly behind her left shoulder and just out of her peripheral vision.

"We need to talk, *Esmeralda*," he said, saying her name like an insult. "I think I should like to have my palm read." He put a hand on her shoulder. Through her silk dress he could feel the rigid muscle above her collarbone.

"I do not read palms," she said. It was the first time he had ever heard her voice, and it sent a shock through him, for it was neither the exaggerated Gypsy accent nor the cronish cackle he had expected. Instead, it was low and melodious, with the merest trace of an accent that he could not place. "I read souls."

Tamping down the lingering thrill of reaction, Thomas tightened his hand upon her shoulder. "You lie."

"You sound so sure." The reply was swift, practiced; she had met doubters before.

"I am sure," he countered. "If you could read my soul, you would be trembling now."

She gave a swift intake of breath—whether it was a gasp or a kind of laugh, he could not tell. "Reading souls is not as simple a matter as seeing a face."

Thomas refused to continue to be drawn along that track. "You have been giving audiences all evening long. I ask for one now."

"In private." He detected an unmistakable tremor of fear.

Exploiting it, he leaned on her shoulder slightly, deliberately. "Most assuredly."

"And if I refuse?" she asked, unbending even though the fear still lay underneath her words. He did not want to admire this woman; she did not deserve his admiration.

He stooped so that his mouth was level with her ear. "How mysterious do you think Esmeralda shall be once she has been unveiled?" He wound the fabric of the veil around his hand.

"I will come." The words were unhurried, but he felt for the first time that he had found a weapon to use against the knives of words she wielded.

"I am pleased," he said, and he shifted his grip so that he held her arm, half lifting her from her chair. "Do lead the way. I shall follow."

The veil was smothering her, and the man's hand on her arm felt like a vise. Em forced her breathing back under control, willing her racing heart to slow. She had watched the exchange between Lord Varcourt and his mother—had watched Lady Hamilton's hands flutter to the antique necklace at her neck, had seen the terror on her face as her son stalked toward Em. Stalked—not the vain, preening walk of a peacock but the deliberate movements of a predator.

She had now seen him exactly six times. The first had been when he had thrown open the door in the midst of a séance at Hamilton House, causing half the women present to emit faint shrieks and reach for their smelling salts. Then, he had simply called from the doorway, "My lady mother. Mary. Elizabeth." And the giggling twins had been instantly silenced, following their ashen-faced mother from the room.

That had ended that afternoon's session, but she had received a letter—and a payment—the following week to continue to meet more privately with Lady Hamilton. Em had been glad enough, for large shows were only good to entertain an audience. It was only the small sessions in which her skills were put to best use—and her patron could be convinced most thoroughly of her powers. Still, whenever Em mentioned any sense that she had received from the events following Lord Varcourt's interruption, Lady Hamilton would grow pale and nervous and would bring the subject firmly around to her dead son, Harry.

At first, Em had given her the usual palliative communications, feeding the poor woman a constant stream of reassurance about her son's happiness beyond this vale of tears. After that scene, though, a sense of self-preservation and a bone-deep dread had caused her to let doubt about the countess' surviving son seep into her communications, how much out of fear for herself and how much out of a genuine concern for her patroness, she didn't know and preferred not to consider.

Since then, Em had only seen Lord Varcourt across a parlor or a dinner table, as she had begun being included in social invitations during the past two months as a kind of joint entertainment and curiosity. When he had looked at her, she felt the animosity of his eyes boring through her, and she had grown cold inside to think that those eyes might have been the last things that his brother had ever seen. Now she was walking beside him, her arm in his hard grip as everyone in the parlor stilled to watch the two of them—the spiritualist and the skeptic—leave the room together.

No one asked whether she was going willingly. It would not occur to anyone that she was a being whose will meant anything at all.

The man walked a foot behind her so that she could not look at him without turning her head, and that she refused to do. She could feel him, though, a massive shadow that seemed to dim the gaslights as he passed.

They stepped out of the parlor. The footman inside shut the door behind them, leaving them alone in the shadowed dining room, the broad, polished table dully gleaming in the light of the single sconce that burned upon the wall. Em stopped.

"Go on, then." Lord Varcourt demanded. His voice was rich and mellow, which somehow made it far worse than if it had been monstrous.

"I can give your reading here," Em said, knowing that he would reject the possibility as soon as she offered it but making the attempt, anyway.

His hand tightened on her arm. "We shall hold our session where you held your others—in the library."

Em closed her eyes for a moment, swallowing hard. She had chosen to hold the few sessions she had done that evening in the library for precisely the reason that the idea of it now sent a chill of terror through her. It was the farthest public room from the parlors and the dining room, the most insulated from the lights and sounds of the party. *He cannot see your face,* she reminded herself. *Control your voice. Read his tells. All shall be well.* But her own body was strung so tightly that she could spare no attention to read the subtleties in his.

Without speaking, she stepped forward.

Toward the library.

Chapter Two

The half-lit hallways, which had been friendly coconspirators in the creation of a proper atmosphere only an hour before, were now oppressive, mocking the abrupt reversal as Lord Varcourt conducted Em to their interview. She was the one nominally in the lead, for he stayed just behind her with a hand on her arm, but his firm grip left no doubt as to who was truly in charge.

Em walked with a steady, unhurried step, forcing her movements to resemble a natural stride, fighting joints that felt like they had been replaced with rusty clockwork. She wanted to run from the bulk of the man who strode so close to her, but she had nowhere and no one who might offer her refuge.

The climb up the stairs seemed to take forever, time stretching thin, their steps echoing in the shadows of the ceiling high above. Yet it was not nearly long enough, for all too soon, Em found herself standing before the tall, carved door to the library.

"Let me go," she said. The words came out in the perfectly even, perfectly practiced accents she used in all her professional dealings, as she had intended them to. She marveled that her tongue was still under her own control.

The hand on her arm released her. She almost swayed with relief at being free from that grasp, but steeling herself, she pushed the door to the library open and stepped inside.

The room was long and narrow, a central table down its length the only furniture, while tall bookcases rose to the barrel-vaulted ceiling on either side. Allegorical figures smirked down at them from their plastered coffers, their faces pasty in the shadows cast by the small, low fire in the grate along the center of one long wall.

She walked to the massive fireplace before she turned, trying to put as much space as possible between herself and Lord Varcourt. The man was facing away from her as he closed the door, and he paused to examine the knob. The key Em had borrowed felt suddenly heavy in the pocket against her thigh. He contented himself with shooting the bolt home before turning to face her.

His act of straightening reminded her, once again, of exactly how powerful a figure he made. Em had to stop herself from backing up into the mantel. He chose her side of the table and began to walk toward her, his movements easy and dangerous. Between the distance and the shadows, her veil hid his face from her as effectively as it hid hers from him.

"I do my readings across the table," Em said, the words coming out slightly strangled.

He ignored her, coming nearer until she had to close her eyes to force herself to hold her ground. Her crinoline pressed backward, toward her legs. She could hear his breathing.

"I believe you are frightened of me," he said. There was no hint from his tone how such a discovery made him feel. "As well you should be. For I am either a bloodless fratricide, or I am a man gravely wronged. And I am not sure which would be the more dangerous."

Em steeled herself and opened her eyes to find herself

staring into his black gaze. He was not, she thought, a handsome man, with features too rough and a hawklike nose that dominated his face. But the intensity of his gaze and the strength of his jaw gave him an attractive quality that was almost like a sinister sort of physical beauty. Her stomach tightened, fluttered in a betraying reaction. Was he a killer? she wondered. Would she survive if he were?

"I have wronged no one," she said. "My visions are not clear—"

"Do not speak of visions to me," the man spat, his bottomless eyes flashing with a rage that disappeared as quickly as it came.

Em rocked, tensing her hands into fists at her sides to stop their trembling. "I have not said that you are a fratricide."

"You have fostered fears," he shot back, "in order to manipulate my mother. You know no sacred ground, no sanctified memory. You would do anything for a little more influence, a little more power, a little more knowledge. Now you have arranged for a remarkably singular necklace to fall into my mother's hands. And I want to know why."

The enormity of his announcement shook Em—the thought that someone could stand back and see past the pound notes pressed into her hands, ignore the little rewards of money and inexpensive jewels, and look for the pattern she was working so diligently to weave. Part of her cried out against the injustice of his accusations of heartlessness, but that was something she could not defend herself against without revealing far more than she cared to.

"You have forbidden me from mentioning my gifts," she said instead. "I do not see what kind of answer I can give you."

"The true one," he said. "For whom do you work, and toward what aim? Why do you seek to tie so many to you?"

That question was easier, at least, to answer in a way that

he might find palatable. That she could give at least a half-truth in reply that had no bearing on her plans. "I work for no one but myself. I must eat, as others do, and the more who ask for my talents, the better my meals become."

Lord Varcourt snorted, his mouth compressing for an instant. "I shall not stand by as you pluck apart my family for your amusement. From all accounts, you have bedded half the men and dazzled half the women in society. Let our family be one of those you leave alone."

A flash of anger overrode Em's fear in a torrent of heat and shame. *You know the men talk, Em,* a part of her warned helplessly even as she formed her retort. *You know that men lie. You rely on that—you cannot be angry when it happens.* "I am a woman alone in the world, sir. I do what I must. As would you."

Lord Varcourt's body blocked the shortest path to the door, so she spun away to circle the table in the other direction. But his hand snaked out and caught her wrist, and with a sudden jerk, he used her own momentum to turn her back around and pull her to him so fast that she fetched up against his body, her skirts swaying wildly. He lifted her wrist above her head so she could not pull away, holding her neatly against him without even bothering to pin her with his free arm.

Fight, kick, scream . . . But she knew that none of these things would help her here, on the empty first floor half a house away from the party below. So instead, she tilted her head back and met his eyes squarely, though he could not see it, struggling to force her traitorous, panicked breathing back under control. *Your virtue can only be lost once,* she reminded herself ruthlessly. *You have nothing left for him to steal.*

"I, too, do no more than I must," he said, looming over her. "You do not yet seem to comprehend what that means."

Fear and anger battled inside her, tangling with the

white-hot memories that would not stay buried. "Lordling," she said, the word coming out with such bile that she hardly recognized her voice. "Petted heir. Favored brat. What *must* you do? What obligations do you have except to outlive your father and find a willing broodmare from the proper stock to add another degenerate generation to your family? It is all your kind has done for centuries, all you are good for anymore. You aren't even choosy about what holes you put your cocks into as long as they hit the right ones often enough to beget an heir."

The words came out in a breathless rush. Only Em's training allowed her to catch the flash of startlement in the man's eyes, the tiny wavering in the grip on her wrist, before he recovered himself. He lowered the wrist that he held, placing it crosswise against his chest and allowing her to take half a step away. She could still feel the heat of their contact in the warmed wool against her arm, and the solidity of his chest beneath his evening coat frightened her. But the space was enough, and she felt her sanity—and control—returning.

"Who the hell are you?" he asked.

Em found herself laughing, and she bit off the sound before it turned hysterical. He could not know how apt the question was. "Who do you want me to be?" she returned. "For some, I speak to the dead, who dwell on higher planes. For others, I see visions of the past. For others still, glimpses of the future. And then, for some, I have been a very earthly kind of paradise." She, who studied small betrayals, could hide the mocking bitterness of her own words—when she chose. She did not do so now. "I am Esmeralda."

"You shall leave my family alone," Lord Varcourt's mouth said, even as his eyes flared with a very different message.

Em read it with a kind of victorious despair. *You may wish me to leave your family alone, sir, but you do not want to leave me alone.* "I harbor no more ill will toward you than I do any other man of your caste," she said. "I do not seek to harm your family."

"What is it that you want, then?" he demanded.

A place. Images of Lincroft filled her mind, the airy rooms flooded with amber afternoon light, the lawn so green it almost hurt the eyes. . . . "What does anyone want?" she said roughly. "The impossible dream. The world on a string. I already have your mother and sister on one, and half of society, as you call it. And you, too."

The man's eyes narrowed. "I suppose your control of me is why I am the one holding you here by brute force."

"It is why you will not leave before committing at least some minor violation upon my person. Out of your own free will, of course," she replied, stepping closer to him again, using her body like the weapon she had learned it could be. He would rebel against whatever she asked of him—she was certain of it. If she wanted to escape with identity and veil intact, demanding of him precisely what he wanted of her at this moment might be her only recourse.

"Do you believe that?" he said. She could feel the tension in his body.

"I know it," she shot back, goading him. "I knew it when you demanded that I bring you here. Whether you call it my visions or the testimony of your own body, it is equally true."

His black eyes narrowed. "I have heard that you never remove your veil," he said, a dark note that she did not care to examine lurking in his voice.

"You have heard the truth." Had she misjudged him? She had the sudden, breath-snatching fear that her gambit was actually encouraging him.

"You could be horribly deformed beneath it," he said, his voice pitched to bite, "or very old."

"I could indeed. Does it matter? It never has to anyone else," she retorted.

"Do you want to be . . . violated?" His lip curled in disgust even as his eyes grew more hooded, stirring up an instinctive thrill of fear and anticipation.

"Does it matter?" Her echo was a mockery of her own last question.

"I think that it does."

If she told him that she wanted it, he might not believe her—and so he would not be turned away from doing just that. Instead, she temporized, "Sometimes, it is hard to know what one wants."

Lord Varcourt took her hand from his chest. Slowly, watching her intently, he turned her hand palm up and began tugging off the glove, loosening it one finger at a time.

Was this some sort of signal? Was he going to do it, then, force himself upon her right here? Em held her breath, her heart pounding, as he slipped her glove from her hand and dropped it disdainfully upon the floor. Only then did he look down at her hand.

"You are not old," he said.

"No, I am not," she agreed.

"Nor have you ever used these hands for labor."

"I have had no need."

He rubbed a thumb, still gloved, across her palm. Em shivered.

"You do want this," he said, his tone split between vindication and anger.

Em did not answer, swaying slightly with the force of his vehemence.

He lifted her palm to the level of his face. She did not resist. Holding her gaze with his, he touched it against his lips. Her mind froze. His breath was hot on her hand, the faintest traces of stubble above his lip a strange counterpart to his hard, silken lips. Then he moved his mouth against her palm.

The damp intensity of it sent a shock through her, curling hard in her center and running in small jolts along her limbs. Her breathing grew faster despite the iron control she tried to clamp down on herself. His teeth and tongue played across her skin expertly, calculatedly, and she had to fight the contradictory urges to curl her fingers closed and to give herself over to his touch like the lost woman that she was.

Just as she could bear it no longer and felt that she must do something, anything, he pulled away, stepped back, and dropped her hand. In her surprise, she let it fall limply into her skirts.

He looked at her intently, his eyes glittering. "Leave my family alone."

And then he turned on his heel and strode from the room.

Em was left staring at the empty doorway, struggling to regain her composure. *What could he do to me if I don't?* she wondered. *What couldn't he?* She bent slowly to retrieve her glove and pulled it on. She had a gnawing feeling that this encounter, as brief as it had been, was a momentous event in the shaping of her plans. And she was certain that it was not the last time Lord Varcourt would be angry with her, for she had no intention of following his orders. There was far too much at stake.

Thomas paused outside the library door, getting his breath back. He had not intended to kiss the woman's hand, had not planned to touch her at all. Something about her shook the iron control he had kept over himself these past twelve years, tested it like nothing had since the fateful day that Harry died. He'd had to escape—even without the answers he had demanded of her—before he slipped further into her thrall.

He shook himself and started toward the parlor again. He'd gained nothing from that encounter. Certes, he'd frightened a woman a little, but he'd come away with no promises, no information. He'd had all the power in that room, and yet he couldn't help but feel that it had been she who had determined the course of their encounter. . . .

Edgington was waiting in the empty dining room when Thomas reentered.

"I've news of Olthwaite," Edgington said before Thomas even gave him a cautious nod of greeting.

Thomas stopped. In the dimness of the lowered gaslights, he could not make out the baron's expression across the gleaming expanse of the mahogany table.

After returning from his French honeymoon with his new bride, Edgington had changed from Conservative to Liberal and had suddenly become the most knowledgeable man in England about the doings of every MP. Several scandals later, the conservative Tories cobbled together their own network of spies and informants. Even though his own Whigs still held the upper hand, Thomas could not help but ask himself if the edge they had gained was worth the precipitously rising stakes. Their current subject of interest was the Tories' Lord Olthwaite, the self-indulgent new baron whose profligate lifestyle had already attracted almost as much attention as his brilliant speeches.

"I hope it is not reports of more visits to whorehouses and gambling debts."

Edgington smiled tightly. "It is both more troubling and more interesting. It concerns those men he hired."

Thomas' attention sharpened. Lord Olthwaite had, with the clumsiest and most transparent attempts at secrecy, hired a number of street toughs to search for some information for him. What it was they wanted, Edgington had not yet found out the last time they had spoken. "Yes?"

"They're going to every fence and pawn shop in the city, looking for a list of items. Decorative trinkets, jewelry, silver plate—the description was always the same."

"It sounds like a robbery," Thomas said.

Edgington raised an eyebrow. "Then why not go to the magistrate?"

Thomas frowned. "I was hoping you could tell me."

"Would that I could, old boy." The jocular familiarity turned ironic and chilly on his lips. "It could just be the leverage we need." With that, Edgington turned away and stepped, silent as a shadow, back into the parlor.

Thomas stood for a moment, dissecting their exchange, trying to find any hint that Edgington was holding something back. He could come up with nothing of more significance than the man's bald words. He needed to know what Olthwaite was up to—the Whigs needed to know. Olthwaite was an unpredictable element. Erratic, perhaps not entirely sane, and certainly dissipated to the point of self-harm, he was also a brilliant speaker on the floor of Parliament and from one of the most politically influential—if not wealthy—families in all Britain.

There was, however, nothing to be done about it at the moment, as loath as Thomas was to admit it. He squared his shoulders and reentered the parlor.

Half a dozen people turned as Thomas opened the door, their eyes full of hard-edged speculation. He returned to his place in the corner, weaving through the chairs and drooping palms, neither meeting nor avoiding anyone's eyes but looking about with a calculated blandness that made the other gazes drop. The air was stifling after the coolness of the library, hot with the press of overdressed bodies and thick with scent and dying flowers.

There was Lord Olthwaite, sitting between Grimsthorpe and Lord Gifford, his jowly face flushed with heat and alcohol. He was one of those men who looked forty at twenty and would look the same at sixty, if his habits didn't kill him first. He was smiling now, his chest and belly thrust out expansively as he leaned back in his chair. His ease irritated Thomas. What was he smiling about? A crude joke? His new pet light-skirt? Or a new twist to the Reform Bill that he wished to spring upon the Whigs at the next meeting of Parliament?

Lady Hamilton was sitting in another group next to those men, near enough that she might listen to their conversation, if she chose. But Thomas' mother never chose, and at that moment, Thomas was doubtful that she was even capable of carrying on a coherent conversation herself, much less eavesdropping on her neighbors. She sat with the Duchess of Rushworth and Lady James, but the expression on her face was glazed and distant, her fingers worrying with something half-concealed by the reticule in her lap, something that gave the flash of jewels when the orange gaslight struck it obliquely. The necklace. Thomas' lips twisted in displeasure. Esmeralda's claws had sunk deep, indeed.

Lady Hamilton looked up then and saw him standing in the corner, her pupils dilated and gaze unfocused, the telltale marks that she had buried her anxieties in a laudanum haze. Dreamily, she stood, ignoring Lady James and Lady Rushworth, who stared in confusion at her sudden movement. Thomas felt the muscles knot along his back. His mother took one tottering step forward, pressing among the tangle of chairs into Lord Olthwaite's group. Her lips parted as if upon the verge of speaking, and then her expression went abruptly blank, her legs gave way, and she crumpled.

She landed half in Grimsthorpe's lap, and that gentleman grabbed her—reflexively, it seemed, for his expression betrayed more surprise than intent—and kept her from striking the floor. Slowly, fatalistically, her reticule fell from her nerveless fingers and slid down her skirts onto the Axminster carpet, the necklace spilling from it to lie in a glittering heap, a sudden garish interruption to the monochrome of the rose and lark pattern that twined across the floor. It came to rest against the well-polished shoe of Lord Olthwaite.

Lady James gave a little cry, and the Duchess of Rushworth's swollen knuckles tightened around her fan. Silence spilled outward, muffling the room in sudden, thick expectation even as Thomas began elbowing his way across the room to his mother's side. Lady Hamilton blinked slowly, glassily at the winking jewels. Beside her, Lord Olthwaite made a strangled sound. He reached down an unsteady hand and plucked up the necklace.

"What's this, then?" he said, squinting at it with drunken uncertainty. "Where did you get it?"

Lady Hamilton, still sprawled vacant-eyed upon Grimsthorpe's lap, said nothing. Lord Olthwaite appeared not to notice.

"Hey, now. I know this one," he continued, as if to himself. "I do know this little bauble. . . ." The man's expression changed from suspicion to realization, and then, all at once, the color drained from his face, a dramatic change from red to white that sent a chill up Thomas' spine. "She's here! She's mocking me! The little bitch . . ." The words came out in a harsh whisper. Olthwaite recoiled, dropping the necklace as he looked wildly about the room.

Thomas reached out and neatly caught the tumbling piece of jewelry in midair, slipping it into his pocket and out of sight. Olthwaite gave a shudder and headed for the door, barreling past the avid guests in a blind charge. Thomas fought the urge to chase him down and demand what he meant. Instead, he lifted the still-limp figure of his mother from Grimsthorpe's lap and cradled her with as much dignity as possible. Her hoops stuck out ridiculously from her waist to her knees, where his arm supported her, drooping abruptly beyond that point to conceal her calves and preserve what little remained of her dignity. She stirred and plucked weakly at his jacket. Bile in his throat, Thomas freed a hand long enough to give her the necklace. His mother sighed and twined her fingers around it, slipping into a more natural sleep.

"Excuse me," he said, bowing crisply to Lady Rush-worth, and he traced Olthwaite's path out with a good deal more composure, followed by the speculative eyes of the gathered company, his sisters unfreezing to flutter after him.

In the front hall, he set Lady Hamilton, now snoring gently, onto the nearest chair. The rubies that dangled from her ears winked balefully at him, and he turned away abruptly from her limp form, leaving her to the attentions of his sisters and in the unflappable hands of her lady's maid. Turning to the closest bland-faced footman, Thomas ordered the Hamilton coach to be brought around.

He burned with the knowledge of the rumors that would have already begun to fly behind the parlor doors—and he burned even more knowing that his family was at the center of a web of intrigue whose pattern he could not see.

Lord Olthwaite. Esmeralda. Thomas' mother—his entire bloody family. How were they connected, and who was drawing the threads together? Thomas had a sick, lurching sensation that he was as central to someone else's plot as Olthwaite was to his own.

The necklace must be one of those jewels that Olthwaite had been looking for. Then again, Olthwaite hadn't taken it with him in his precipitous flight, and he looked more hor-rified than pleased to see it. Maybe Thomas was inventing connections that weren't there, or drawing the wrong ones. Esmeralda—and whoever was behind her—tied this to-gether. She was the linchpin, and he'd had her at his mercy and had come away with nothing except a sense that she had somehow manipulated him rather than the other way around.

No more. He had to get her alone again—had to get her to tell him what the hell was going on, whatever the cost.

Thomas stepped outside, too impatient to wait for the footman posted at the door to inform him of his carriage's arrival. He was relieved to find that it was already rattling slowly up the street, the gaslights glinting dully off black lacquer, yellow brass, and the glossy sable hides of his four matched horses. His attention was diverted from the welcome sight of his equipage by a swirl of movement at the corner of his vision, and he turned to see a crimson skirt disappearing into a hansom cab directly in front of the Rushworth house's steps.

His breath caught. Esmeralda. It must be. Thomas set his jaw, and in sudden decision, he turned to the footman at the door.

"Summon a cab for my mother." With that curt order, he strode down the stairs, dodging between the waiting carriages to the street, where he met his own coach and threw open the door before the driver had a chance to pull it to a stop. Stepping over the raised iron steps, he leaned out toward the gaping driver. Pointing, he snapped, "Follow that cab. I don't care where it goes—follow it!"

He would catch the woman—make her explain herself and, if necessary, pay for what she had done.

Chapter Three

Thomas watched the street facades pass from between the half-drawn curtains of the carriage. He was no longer sure of where he was. The carriage had swiftly crossed the Thames, and it still moved through the thick miasma that had risen from the river to sink in dank pools among the low parts of the city. It wasn't yet Southwark, but cobbles had given way to rutted dirt, and the streets had an alien cast to them.

The carriage approached a group of black-haired women who lounged on the stoop of a tenement in the yellow glow of a streetlamp, their dresses declaring their foreignness even before he drew close enough to hear the heavy rhythms of their peasant Italian dialect. The area door was open under another block of flats, leaking a sullen light and the dream-thick scent of opium. A minute later, Thomas saw a door that bore the Star of David and two lines of text, one in Hebrew and the second in neat Cyrillic letters.

The streetlamps became fewer and fewer until they disappeared altogether, the only light in the black night coming from the four lamps at the corners of his carriage. Thomas could not see the road ahead of them from his seat in the

back of the closed brougham, and he was beginning to wonder if his driver had gotten lost when the carriage began to
slow. It came to a stop, and Thomas opened the door and
leaned out, peering against the glare of the lamp that stood
between him and what lay before.

There, a few houses down, sat a hansom, its coach lamps
glowing like two bright eyes. There was a movement, and a
wide-skirted silhouette climbed out.

"Wait here," Thomas ordered his driver. He stepped
down, his shoes silent upon the dirt road.

As the cab rattled away, the woman continued walking
down the street, and Thomas picked up speed to close the
space between them. The only light spilled through an open
door halfway down the street, which emitted bursts of rau-
cous laughter at irregular intervals over the wild whirl of
Eastern music. The woman paused at the doorway, and
Thomas made out the shape of a veil in the light. He could
have sworn that she cast a look behind her before she turned
and stepped inside.

Thomas followed and found himself in a low-ceilinged
taproom that was wreathed with tobacco and coal smoke and
crowded with rank bodies. The women sat apart, their heavily layered skirts sewn in brilliant calicos and their hair hidden under kerchiefs. The sober clothing of the men made a
darker shadow on the other side of the room. The chairs and
tables had been shoved back to make a small dancing space,
where four young men leapt and kicked to the music of a
concertina while the audience clapped and shouted encouragement, half in a canting English and half in an unintelligi-
ble tongue.

Gypsies. A tavern full of Gypsies on the outskirts of London. But where was the woman he had followed? What had
happened to Esmeralda?

Thomas scanned the room with narrow eyes. There. He
saw a flash of deep scarlet skirts disappearing around the

corner at the edge of the room. Keeping a firm hand on his money pouch and pocket watch, he pushed through the women to the foot of the stairs. Most of the Gypsies appeared to ignore him even as ghostly hands grazed his pockets, but some looked at him and spat while making signs to ward off evil. Thomas allowed himself a small smile. He supposed he did look rather like a devil, at that. Too bad his appearance had proved so ineffective against Esmeralda.

Thomas reached the corner and discovered a staircase going up into darkness. A boy leaned against the edge of the dividing wall, his expression set into insolent lines that sat uneasily on a face so young.

"Did a woman in scarlet silk and a veil just go up?" Thomas shouted above the uproar.

The child gave him a sneer. "It may be dat she did, or it may be dat she didn't."

With a sense of inevitability, Thomas took out a shilling and tossed it up. The child caught it neatly out of the air.

"Aye, a woman by dat description passed dis way," the child said, polishing the silver coin on his sleeve. "She lets the garret. She ain't no Rom, but her coin's as good as any, though she only gave me a half-bob to send you off."

"Thank you," Thomas said, and he passed the boy to mount the stairs.

The staircase was narrow and dark, the only light filtering around the corner from the tavern's taproom. Thomas' shoes followed a silvery path of bare wood up the center of the steps. The walls were crazed with cracks that spread like spiderwebs across the plaster. The noise below faded as soon as he reached the first floor, and so did the last of the light. There was a shelf for a candle or a lamp at the turn, but it was bare, and when he touched it, his fingers came away grimed with dust.

In the blackness above, he could hear the distinct click of a door being closed—and then a second *snick* as the key

turned in the lock. The garret. However Esmeralda was
using the money that the ladies of society showered upon
her, it wasn't for accommodations.

Thomas took the turn and continued upward, the last
glimmers of light dying away behind him as he passed into
utter blackness. He listened to the muffled cheers from
below and counted the steps. When he put his foot out for
the twenty-third, his leg came down fast and hard, jarring his
knee. He'd reached the landing at the end of the stairs.

He stared in the blackness for several seconds, trying to
get his bearings before proceeding. But the darkness seemed
absolute, offering nothing with which to orient himself. He
extended his arms outward. He had got no more than halfway
when he struck the sides of the walls. There wasn't another
turning here, at least. He stepped forward carefully—once,
and then a second time.

What is that? As his eyes became accustomed to the
darkness, he thought he could make out a brighter glimmer
at the level of the floor. He held still, waiting.

Yes. He was certain that he saw it now. There was a
lighter line along the floor, exactly the width that he'd expect a door to be. He held out his hand and stepped forward,
and his palm came up against a flat surface—wood, not
plaster.

He slid his hand down the paneled surface and found a
knob. Was it still a little warm from Esmeralda's hand, or
was he imagining things? He grasped it, turned—and nothing happened.

It was locked. "Esmeralda," he said. "I know you're in
there. Open the door."

Silence met him from the other side of the door, and after
a moment, the light underneath dimmed.

That removed his last doubt. "Esmeralda!" he repeated,
growing impatient. He rattled the lock. "Open it now."

No response. The knob felt flimsy in his hands. The

woman was a nobody, an insignificant parlor decoration
who was being used as someone's political tool. Her behavior was as nonsensical as if a hammer or a poker had defied
him. And yet there was still silence from the other side of
the door.

He took three careful steps backward, toward the edge of
the stairs. Then he braced his shoulder and ran.

He hit the door with all his strength. The lock simply
snapped, the frame not even splintering at the impact, and he
surged inside.

He found himself in a small parlor with a sloping ceiling
and caught a glimpse of swishing scarlet skirts as they disappeared into the adjoining room, carrying a faint light with
them. He pursued. In seconds, he was upon her, catching her
free arm and spinning her around. Esmeralda came, swinging the lamp in her free hand with the momentum of her
turn. Thomas dodged. The lamp struck his temple a glancing blow before flying from her fingers and hitting the
ground, where its chimney shattered and it began dripping
paraffin onto the floorboards as the flame danced upward
from the wick.

Thomas struck out instinctively, scarcely pulling the
blow in time to turn the punch into a shove. The woman was
flung across the room, sprawling against the side of the bed,
where she collapsed into a chaos of silk and hoops.

Instantly, she struggled to rise. Thomas watched her as he
righted the lamp with the toe of his shoe, fiercely suppressing his urge to help. Chivalry be damned—she'd tried to
brain him.

She still wore her veil, though there was a tear in its hem
and the gold comb that held it in place was askew, and
gloves still covered her hands, disappearing under the edge
of her sleeves. A woman so concealed should have invoked
nothing within him at all, but he remembered the elegant,
fine-boned hand under her glove, the taste and heat of her

palm, and the tense rush that their confrontation had stirred slid into a very different kind of reaction. She was every bit as tempting as she had ever been, if not more.

Control, he told himself. He was in control—of her and himself, both.

"Sit down," he ordered, hooking a ladder-back chair and shoving it toward her.

She finally disentangled herself enough to rise. She stood, immobile, her face invisible and her posture utterly unrevealing of her thoughts. She was tall for a woman, made taller still by the neat little shoes he had glimpsed when she fell, their square heels raising her another two inches. But he was taller, and broad, too, and he used his height to full advantage as he stood between her and the door.

She half turned toward the chair, and he saw her hesitate.

"If you are thinking to pick that up and to use it against me, I will truly strike you this time," he said, putting ice in his voice. "And men stay down when I hit them."

The woman stopped for a moment, and Thomas could have sworn that he felt her gaze searching his face. Then, slowly, she sat.

"There is nothing that you want here," she said, her voice carrying the same melodious timbre that had made him take leave of his senses in the library. "You have invaded my home and attacked me. Leave before I have you arrested for assaulting a defenseless and fatherless woman."

"Where did you get that necklace?" Thomas said, ignoring her.

"I had a vision—" the woman began.

"Enough of your visions!" Thomas cut through her answer. Taking advantage of the rumors that swirled around him, he said, "If you truly had visions, then you would know what happened to my brother, and you would be desperate to tell me what I want to know."

She was silent for a long moment. "Would you kill me, too, then?" she asked finally.

"I will do whatever it takes to get the answer I seek," he said. "*Whatever.* Who gave you the necklace?"

Em stared at the man in front of her, the hard, rough lines of his face set in rage, and she believed what he said. *Survive,* she told herself. *All I have to do is survive.* She could not give him what he wanted; he would not believe her, and the stakes were far too high, for she could hang for what she'd done, however unjust such a sentence might be. She had to deflect him—somehow, anyhow.

She could still feel the heat in his eyes when he looked at her, but it was sharper now, wilder. His eyes raked across her close-swathed body, burning into her. Their confrontation had shaken loose some part of his control, even if he didn't realize it yet—a part of it that she could turn to her own advantage. *Or at least to my own survival,* she amended.

She could not bait him now and step away unscathed, but she would step away alive. Her heart beat faster at what she planned to do—in terror and, yes, raw animal lust, which was so treacherously akin to fear. The cold, hard part of her sneered at that eagerness; she had fallen so far that now a part of her welcomed the risk of failure as much as it did the rewards of success. *Whore,* she mocked herself. *Go ahead. There's nothing left to lose.*

Swallowing down the turmoil that rose from her stomach, Em pushed to her feet and closed the two steps between her and Lord Varcourt. "Do it, then," she said, speaking with the reckless anger that threatened to choke her. "Kill me now, and get it over with. But you don't really want to kill me, do you? You want to throw me on my bed and shove your swollen cock between my legs until I scream for mercy." The coarseness of her words scraped her throat, but she pushed herself onward mercilessly. He wanted her—she could feel it in his body. Right now, his desire for her was the only power she had over him. The only thing that could save her, for what he sought was surely her destruction.

She dropped her voice to a whisper, not trusting herself to speak aloud. "And you know you will." She was a breath away from him now, her skirts pressed against his legs. He stood frozen, his face fixed in a terrible mask. She put her hand on his chest lightly and felt the shudder deep inside him. With great deliberation and every ounce of self-control, she made her hand slide down, across the superfine merino of his coat and below, where she found the erection that his coat had hidden.

Varcourt hissed, his hand snaking out to catch her wrist in a crushing grip. She let go, making herself laugh, a sand-papery sound through her dry throat, and he twisted, forcing her arm straight and pulling her body against his.

"You think that you are a woman of the world, don't you?" he said, the words pouring ice into her bones. "You think that you know everything. That you have done everything, survived everything. But I am telling you that you are just a babe in the woods. You have no idea whom you are dealing with."

His head was bent over hers as he stared furiously down at her. In answer, she tipped her head back, angled it toward him, and kissed him through the fabric of her veil.

If some part of her had desperately hoped that the fabric would provide some barrier to the sensation of his mouth against her, she was badly mistaken. He reacted instantly, completely, crushing her against him as his lips scraped hotly against hers. There was nothing of finesse in his kiss. It was a battle, a struggle, his will against hers. She could taste him, could feel the texture of his lips through the web-thin weave of the veil, could sense the power in his mouth and body. It sent a rippling shock deep into her, pooling heat between her legs even as she fought his assertion of control with every fiber of her being.

Varcourt broke away with a curse. He twisted her arm again, shoving his hip against her at the same time to force her to turn away from him. He lifted her arm, bent behind her back, so that she was trapped, immobile, standing on her tiptoes against the sudden pain in her shoulder as he crushed her skirts against the back of her legs. She was panting— with terror and a lust so frank that it frightened her.

"I can show you entire worlds that you have never dreamed of." His breath was hot and rasping in her ear.

"You don't know what I have done," Em returned. Her heart was beating so loudly that she could scarcely hear her own words.

His hands jerked at the lowest buttons of her bodice at the small of her back, and the buttons popped out of the button-holes. He shifted his hand through the opening and yanked at the ties to her petticoats until they were loosened and shoved out of the way. Em could feel his hand working on her crinoline. The tapes gave, and he hooked his foot some-how in her skirts and jerked the cage down, clattering it to the floor.

"You're a regular courtesan, aren't you?" he sneered. "You know what you're doing, seducing a man into your bed. Charming him with your wiles and drawing him into your confidence." He pushed her to the side, and craning over her shoulder, Em saw him flip up the lid to the box that sat on her night table. He gave a dark laugh at what he found there. "A regular courtesan," he repeated with sarcas-tic satisfaction. He plucked the lamb-gut sheath from the box and held it over her shoulder so that she could look at it squarely as it lay across her chest. "You bring your lovers—your patrons—here, do you?"

"Every night," she ground out. "They line up at my door, and I take them in one by one and teach them tricks they have never imagined."

"Do you tie it on for them? Do you wash it when they

leave, turning it inside out to spill their seed from it? My adventurous courtesan, you are simply too tame."

"I am not an idiot," she hissed back. "And if you want to put your cock where theirs have been, you'll put it on, too."

"I think I can do anything I want with you right now," he said.

Her heart accelerated. This was a contest she could not afford to lose, for losing it could make surviving this night meaningless. She had to force him into acceding, force him into proving his power over her some other way. "Considering the fate of your brother, *anything* can be deadly," she retorted, choosing the words that cut the deepest.

Before she knew he was going to make a motion, she was hurtling toward the bed. She scarcely had time to put her hands out to catch herself before she struck the mattress stomach-down with a force that knocked the breath from her lungs.

"If you know what's good for you, you will not move," Varcourt said, his voice full of a distant calm that sent Em's heart into a panicked tattoo. She held perfectly still, sucking air through the quilts.

"You can have your lambskin," the man said, and Em bit back a sob of relief. If she had miscalculated, provoked the wrong response and become with child . . . The memory of the muddy Thames came to her, swollen and turbid below her toes as she balanced on the parapet of a bridge at high tide and made her decision to live.

A decision she fully intended to keep.

"You have quite the collection here, Esmeralda," Varcourt said in a conversational tone. "Esmeralda. That is such a silly name for a plain English girl like you. I think I shall call you . . . Merry. Esme is nearly as bad as Esmeralda, Essie sounds like someone's cow, and Alda is simply ridiculous, but Merry has a nice ring to it, don't you think? It's so *joyful.*" There was a rattle as he dug deeper into the box.

"You seem to have asked for one of everything. Do you even know what half of these things are, or are they just for show, to impress the callow young men with your sophistication?"

Em's breath choked in her lungs. *He can't know,* she told herself. *He might guess, but he can't know*. "There's an easy way to find out. What did you want to try?" she returned. She wondered, exactly, what he might know—and whether she was more tantalized or terrified to find out.

"I don't need any of these trinkets to expose your pretenses. False spiritualist, false demirep—you are very good at the game, but not good enough. All I need to expose you is this."

Em tried to turn around, but his hand came down between her shoulder blades, more of a warning than an actual blockade, but it halted her nonetheless. "You'll find out soon enough, Merry."

She felt him begin to push up her skirts, and she made fists in the quilt to force herself to hold still, to keep from turning even as hot anticipation twisted through her center and set her limbs to buzzing. She'd taken on too much this time. Lord Varcourt was no boy to be overawed by her assumed sophistication. She knew, with a clarity that sent a panicked awareness through her, that he was what she had pretended to be—exactly the kind of person she had avoided more than a flirtation with, for he was exactly the kind of man who could see her for what she really was.

But what she said was, "Show me the world, then, Lord Varcourt—if you think you can."

Her skirts piled upon her back in a froth of linen and silk. She risked turning her head, but she could see nothing but rumpled crimson fabric. She felt his hands at the back of her waist, following the seam of the pantaloons downward from her tailbone. He had stripped off his gloves—she could feel the texture of his skin through the thin linen, and she suppressed a shiver. He found the slit where the two legs of the pantaloons met. His other hand joined the first on either side of the slit, and Em braced herself.

But a jerk of his hands followed by a ripping sound took her unprepared. She stiffened and forced herself to try not to scramble away. She felt the fabric tear, and after a few jerks, the legs of the pantaloons slid down her thighs, leaving her buttocks bare to the room's cool air. She squirmed automatically.

"Do not move," Varcourt said. His words were roughened with his need, and they sent a tremor of heat across her skin, leaving it agonizingly sensitive in its wake.

She suppressed a gasp as he grasped her knees and began to pull her by the legs toward the edge of the bed, taking the counterpane with her. "Turn over now," he instructed, and again the dark intensity of his voice went through her.

"Whatever you wish," she made her lips murmur, and she turned.

Lord Varcourt had tossed his coat and waistcoat to the side, and now he stood at the side of the bed in his shirt-sleeves, revealing a width of shoulders and solidity of chest that had nothing to do with the tailor's art. She could see the shape of the muscles beneath the fine snowy linen, and she wondered, half desperately, why he could not have been one of those yet-unformed youths who still hovered on the cusp of manhood. They were tamable, controllable—and he was neither of those things. Almost more ominous, though, as her fear that with this man, she would not be able to control herself. His shirt was untucked, hanging over his waistband but doing nothing to conceal the bulge there.

Just do it, she told herself. *Don't think. Don't feel.* But she was already feeling far too much.

Varcourt hooked his hands under her knees and pulled, bringing her legs up on either side of his hips, the movement simultaneously tilting her up and opening her—to his sight, to his taking.

As her mind was still clamoring from his last action, he reached over to the night table and picked up the jar of scented oil. Not even glancing at her face, he opened it with a single twist of his wrist and then, using his hips and his free hand to push her hips upward, he poured a neat line of it from the base of her curls to her tailbone.

Em gasped as the cool liquid struck her heated skin, sending reaction shuddering through her, but he did not give her time to catch her balance. Instead, looking at her intently, he said, "The interesting thing about these rubbers is that they make certain possibilities suddenly much more appealing."

And then, before she could begin to decipher what he meant, he tossed the bottle on the bed and shifted as he took her legs so that his erection was there, pushing against her curls. He slid it back on the oil, toward her opening. Em braced herself, the heat of him impossible, but he pulled back before he was halfway in and shoved her knees up, making her corset bite into her as he slid farther down. Before she could even cry out, he pushed, overcoming the resistance that came too late and filling her hard, leaving the other place clamoringly empty.

Em cried out as her body shuddered, twisting hard in horror and, almost worse, lust. She knew what he has doing— she'd read about it in the pornography she'd bought to learn to play her part, but she hadn't believed it, hadn't thought such things were possible, thought them beyond bearing. And it was beyond bearing, but not as she expected, for it sent jolts of pleasure through her deeper even than the shame, shooting all the way through her palms and the soles of her feet even as she tried to shunt her mind away, somewhere else where he could not touch her.

Looking straight into her eyes, Varcourt reached down and yanked off her veil.

Chapter Four

"You have never done it like this before," Varcourt said hoarsely, his smile like a lash. His body was tense, his face glistening with sweat. He pulled part of the way out of her, and Em shuddered against the slick friction, pushing against him automatically even as she tried to school her body to compliance.

"You can't know what I've done," she panted. She wanted to make herself believe it. "Come on, then. You know you want it. Take it." Take it and be done, for she felt herself unraveling at the edges, and if he did not finish soon, she might disintegrate completely. . . .

"Push against me, then," he said through clenched teeth as he surged into her again, sending the tumult of sensations through her. "Do it."

She did, her hands contradictorily clinging to fistfuls of his shirt, but he just slid in more smoothly, her very pressure shaping her body to him.

"I now know two things about you," he panted, holding himself so deep inside of her that his body ground against her buttocks. "You are not the jaded woman of the world that you pretend to be. And you want this every bit as much as I do."

Em bit her lip around a protest as he pulled himself back for another long stroke, but she whimpered, anyway, the hard knot of flesh below her curls throbbing with need.

"Tell me that you want it." He pushed into her again, and she swallowed her cry. "I will not stop until you tell me!"

Em clenched her teeth and clasped her veil against her chest as he thrust into her again and again in slow, merciless strokes, and she tried to keep back the cries as he drove pleasure through her body like a sword, shattering her into dazzling, sharp fragments that blinded her mind with a feeling so intense that it was almost pain. She tried to force herself to be motionless, but her hips surged against his thrusts, coming up to meet him despite herself.

"I want it," Em gasped when she could not stand it any longer. "I want it."

His fingers tightened around her thighs. "Now I will watch you come." He freed a hand and pushed two fingers inside her, into the empty place, rubbing his thumb hard against the aching knot of flesh. His fingers pushed her one way, his erection another, dragging her up and into a place where her mind rushed with speed and her body screamed as pure heat. She forgot herself—forgot her own existence— for an instantaneous blinding whiteness, shot through with streaks of black as her lungs, somewhere far away, fought the imposition of the corset.

The darkness overcame the light, swallowing everything in nothingness, and when she came to herself, she saw the sheath turned inside out on the bed next to her as Varcourt gave a shuddering thrust, loosing his seed inside the proper place.

"No," she whispered hoarsely, the world dropping out from under her. But when he pulled away, she saw that he'd put on her reserve sheath, and Em almost sobbed with relief.

Realizing that she was free, for the moment, at least, Em yanked down her veil and rolled swiftly across the bed, pulling her skirts down as she stumbled to her feet. Her mind still reeled from what he had just done to her, her body trembling in reaction as it burned with his assault, but Em tamped it down fiercely. She could package it up like she had everything else—set it aside upon the shelf in her mind where things she did not want to look at were placed. Already, she pushed the raw memories away before they could settle upon her mind, stopped her ears to the parts of her brain that were clamoring and shaken, and narrowed her world to cold logic and a single goal: escape.

He knew her face now. Replacing her veil could do nothing but perhaps make his memory of it less precise, but she was under no illusions that he would not recognize her again. He did not know—yet—what terrible significance that had, what power it gave him over her, and all she could do was hope, desperately, that by the time her plans came to fruition, she could have some equal hold over him. She was lucky he had not recognized her instantly when he snatched off her veil—or, perhaps, not so much lucky as insignificant in her prior life. Even if he had remembered her, she was no more ready to answer questions about the necklace than when he cornered her in the library. The answers that she had might just end with her neck in a noose, doing the oak fandango. For now, she must concentrate on getting free, if only from his immediate physical control.

As Lord Varcourt was buttoning his fly, she reached down and pulled the torn legs of her pantaloons off over her shoes before lighting a candle from the lamps and turning to her dressing room door.

"Where are you going?" Lord Varcourt demanded, his words harsh with the remnants of lust.

"I need to step into my dressing room," she said coolly, opening the door. "I can clean up in front of you, but that rather destroys the delicate mystique of what we shared, don't you think?" She made the words acid, calculated to bite.

His face set into lines of suspicion, Varcourt stepped between her and the door, opening it. He scanned the interior of the small room, with its heavy-draped windows and the rows of hooks and shelves for her clothing that surrounded the dressing table. He nodded shortly, and her heart in her throat, Em entered and shut the door.

Moving swiftly and quietly, she set the candle on the table and wedged the chair under the doorknob to the bedroom. Thanking his haste, which had left her mostly clothed, she pushed aside one of the pairs of curtains to reveal not a window but a second door—to the back stairs that ran down the exterior facade of the building. She threw a cloak over her shoulders, opened the door, and ran.

Chapter Five

Ten seconds after Esmeralda closed the dressing room door, Thomas realized he'd made a mistake. There had been so many things to send his mind into roiling disarray—the incredible intensity of her response to him, his confirmation of her limited experience, the mere discovery of the woman in such surroundings. And, of course, when he had yanked off her veil . . .

Ash brown hair, luxuriant even pinned against her head, framing a face of such porcelain luminosity, he feared it would break . . .

That such words, such a voice had come from those lips and that face—it wasn't to be believed. That he was now taking this ethereal being in the most thorough way possible almost seemed inhuman. And yet with her face contorted with all of the emotions he'd hoped to see—shock and fear, horror and deep, deep pleasure—he could not imagine himself doing anything else.

He'd hoped, perhaps foolishly, that he could somehow expunge her influence from his mind by giving in to the dark impulses that she so consciously stimulated in him. He had been wrong. He burned with a desire for her that was deeper than ever, now tempered with an irrational certainty that there was far more to her than he had guessed—something that he wanted, needed to know.

Shaking off those thoughts, he strode to the dressing room door, turned the knob, and pushed. Instantly, the door struck something, the knob jumping in his hand. His stomach lurched, and he jerked the door back and forth. On the third contact, the object behind the door slid out of the way with a protesting scrape. Thomas surged in to be met with an empty room and a swaying curtain. With a sick feeling, he yanked the drape aside.

Another door. The woman had run for it. Thomas struck the doorframe with his fist as he opened the door to reveal an exterior staircase crisscrossing down the back wall of the building to a stinking yard—and there, at the edge of it, he thought he caught a glimpse of movement disappearing into the night.

Thomas reacted, vaulting over the edge of the railing and catching the edge for just long enough to slow his descent and swing so that he landed lightly on the stairs the floor below. Once more, and he was on the ground, something rotten and soft beneath his shoe almost sending him sprawling. He caught his balance and began to run even as he strained through the fog of the black night to make out the vague outline of a gate in the yard, still swinging slightly from the force of the last person's passage.

He pushed through and found himself in a back alley. *You'll be lucky if you don't get knifed for this,* a cynical part of him thought, but he pushed it aside as he swiftly looked around.

There—there was movement down the alley. Thomas veered right and began to sprint. He made out the shape of a human silhouette. He caught up to it, reached out for an elbow but encountered a shoulder, and swung the figure around.

"Can I 'elp ye, sir?" The voice was old and quavering, with the lilt of Devon, the body small and frail. "I got nothing to vilch."

Thomas made out the creased face in the faint light of the cloud-filtered moon. Whether it belonged to a man or a woman, he could not tell. "A woman—did she come by here?"

"Mayhaps," the figure said, then shut its lips tight.

"Thanks," Thomas muttered, and he pelted down the alley, looking for any branches or open gates where she might have turned. The alley jogged, and he barely slowed enough to take the corner—and slammed into something so hard that it took the breath out of him.

There was a cry of pain as the thing—the person—he had struck went sprawling hard across the packed dirt of the alley. Esmeralda. Thomas staggered forward as she lay gasping. His lungs struggled to reinflate. He didn't dare trust himself to bend down to pull her up, so he put a foot on the center of her back to immobilize her until he could get enough air back into his body to steady himself. If she thought him a beast, all the better, he told himself harshly.

"Do not ever try to escape me," he said, forcing his voice to not betray the greed with which he was sucking in air. "I will hunt you down and make you pay for your defiance with interest."

He removed his foot and reached down to take her arm—and had to jerk away as she rolled instantly onto her back, swinging a broken board at his head. With a curse, he kicked the makeshift weapon from her hand, then wrenched her to her feet with a force that pulled another cry from her as he yanked her against him, giving her no room to fight.

"I do not recommend hiding in corners in order to brain me, either," he hissed into her ear. "I will hit anyone who is assaulting me." Her breathing came in panicked, ragged gasps; he could feel it against his chest. Her face was invisible, hidden again by the veil. Why did she have such an effect on him? Why, now that he had slaked his lust, did he want her more than ever—to know the delicate, fey thing behind the act?

Stupid. He took her by the upper arm, hard, his anger at himself redoubling as he realized he was taking it out on her. "You still have not answered my question. It is a very simple one. I will ask it again: Where did you get that necklace?"

"I saw a vision," she insisted.

"No, Merry, I will not take that answer." He turned and began striding down the alley, pulling her after him.

"Where are you taking me?" Her voice held a note of panic, the first sign of unadulterated fear he'd seen from her since taking her veil from her face.

"Wherever I wish," he replied, "until you give me the answers I seek."

"I don't know what more you want!"

"The truth would be nice." He found a narrow opening between two buildings, and they emerged on the street that ran in front of the Gypsy tavern, only a few steps away from the Hamilton brougham.

"My carriage," he said. "Get in."

Thomas could feel the tension in the woman's body as she sat across from him in the dark carriage. He'd pushed her into the rear-facing seat, like a servant, but she had not protested, her wild resistance sinking into an eerily calm acceptance.

An acceptance that he did not for one moment believe.

"Take off your veil," he said.

"No." The reply was swift and unambiguous.

"I have already seen your face."

"Then you must forget it. You have seen the face of a dead woman." The bitterness of her words made him pause, made him consider for the first time that he did not merely have another man's tool here, dressed up to play a role it was not made for, but a person with a separate life, with dreams and memories. And regrets . . .

"What is your real name?" he asked.

She was silent for so long that he thought she would never answer. "It doesn't matter," she finally said. Her tone had changed, moving away from the rough, confrontational words and into something soft, yielding in a way that made him seem like her one last hope. He had the sense that, behind her veil, her eyes still glittered, yet he cursed himself as he stirred involuntarily at her words. "I like Merry. That works as well as any other."

"As well as Esmeralda?"

Her reply was laced with sarcasm. "Better, if I am a good English girl, as you say." She lapsed into silence, and then, in a voice so soft he could scarcely hear it, she whispered, "Heaven help me." The words lanced straight to his groin.

Just then, they arrived at his Piccadilly flat. The driver opened the door, and Thomas stepped down, offering his arm to her with a coldly ironic smile. She knew it for the trap that it was—how could she not?—but she took it with the grace of a lady accustomed to such niceties. Thomas wondered where she was from and what twisted path had led her here, to his doorstep.

He gave the doorkeeper orders to be carried down to the kitchen, then guided the woman up the stairs and opened the door to his flat. He shoved her firmly inside, being careful to keep her within his line of sight as he locked the door and slipped the key into his pocket.

"My valet is visiting his sick mother in Lincolnshire," he said. "Convenient for us, is it not?"

"For you, certainly," she replied, the words cool and crystalline. "There will be no one to betray that you have kidnapped me. It is a hanging offense, you know. I suppose that makes us even, in a way; we can now each blackmail the other."

He cared nothing for her threat. He knew she did not mean it, even if she wished him to believe that there was some force in it, for she could make no more threats as long as she clung to her false persona and the anonymity of her costume. No, it was the necklace he cared about. Her presence in his room would be, at most, a scandal, and he had weathered far worse. The necklace, though, could be used to create the appearance of a crime.

Thomas stepped up to her, and she held her ground, holding perfectly, unnaturally still. He reached out and grasped the edge of her veil. She raised her hand, then dropped it, making no move to stop him. He lifted it slowly, revealing her narrow, high-boned face that glowed with a pearlescent luster. Her eyes seem to look right through him, a green so pale that they looked blue. He had the sense that if fairies— not tiny, sprightly elves but the noble and unearthly creatures of fairy tales—were real, they would look like her.

He swore softly. "A woman like you should not be allowed to hide her face."

"Perhaps it is more important that a woman like me do so," she countered, the throaty earthiness of her voice a strange counterpoint to her ethereal face.

He reached out his hand. "Give me your cloak."

"Why did you bring me here?" she asked, unmoving.

"Because it suits my pleasure. Now give me your cloak."

"Becoming the next Duke of Norfolk might suit your pleasure, but it will not happen," she countered. "Why did you bring me here?"

"Because you have not told me what I seek," he said. He untied her cloak with a single tug, catching it before it hit the floor.

She neither protested nor reacted. "You cannot keep me here forever."

"But perhaps I can keep you long enough." He nodded toward the small, round table where he took his meals when he was home. "Sit, and I will ring for a late dinner." He paused. "I will not tell you to do it twice, and you shall not like the consequences if you disobey."

She turned her pale eyes on him, her expression a waxen mask as they searched his face with an intensity that seemed to burn through him. Slowly, she turned to the table and sat, removing her gloves and dropping them onto its surface.

"You have just returned from dinner," she said, a colorless observation.

"I do not eat much at parties." He tugged the bellpull, summoning the servant with his dinner that had been kept warm in anticipation of his arrival.

"Those who eat do not watch," she said. "You are a watcher. I have received many messages of you."

"Received? From the spirits? Pardon me if I disbelieve that and give stronger credence to the possibility that you were watching me watch the others," he said. "You did not eat much, either—and a meal such as that must be a rare thing in your experience."

"I am rarely hungry," she said, her expression and tone entirely bland. "I live on light and air."

"You are made of rather solid stuff for such a diet," he said.

She made no rejoinder, merely saying, "You are used to watching alone. You do not like for there to be another who watches as you do." Though her face betrayed nothing, he could feel her attention becoming keener.

Thomas hid any reaction. Why did he want to tell her she was right? It must come from the same urge that possesses a person, at the edge of a cliff, to jump off. He strolled over to the side of her chair, so that she had to crane her neck up at him, exploiting the fact that he stood as she sat.

"I do not like games," he said, leaning over her. "I do not

like someone pushing a new pawn onto the board, especially when I cannot tell its color."

The woman's expression turned shrewd. "You live for games. You are a master player. You merely do not like games that you might not win." She shook her head, and her soft hair gleamed in the gaslight. "Have no fear, sir. The game I play is not one that you can lose."

He wanted to believe her too badly. There was something in him that told him she spoke the truth, but he shunned it, instead shooting back, "I need more than your word on that. I need names."

Her lashes lowered, hiding her eyes. "And those I cannot give you, as the only one I have to give is my own, and it is too precious to me to be spent so recklessly." She sounded regretful.

A knock came on the door. Keeping an eye on the woman, who gave him an ironic smile at his attention, he opened it to reveal the neat figure of the kitchen maid.

"Thank you, Peg," he said, taking the tray from her unresisting hands as she stared over his shoulder in surprised interest.

"You're quite welcome, sir," she said, and with one last wide-eyed look, she scurried away.

Thomas closed and locked that door. When he turned back, the woman was lifting her veil.

"You truly do not wish anyone to see you," he said.

"It is better that way." Her pale eyes looked at him unblinkingly. "Your wariness of me is quite enchanting, but I had enough time to brain you with the poker while you were talking to that maid. If I had cared to do so."

"She would have screamed and warned me." Thomas set the tray on the table and circled behind her, taking satisfaction in the tiny shiver of tension that ran through her body. If only he could ignore the reaction in his groin. . . . He took the chair opposite her, sitting with a studied nonchalance.

She looked at him, unmoving, unspeaking, and after a moment, he lifted the lid to the tray. "Veal cutlets, soles la Normandie, and a custard. Quite superb, I might add."

"Your flat is very small," the woman said, ignoring him.

"I am a bachelor," Thomas said.

"Most gentlemen with such modest demands would take rooms at their club," she pointed out. "If they chose not to live with their families."

"Would they?" He set out the extra plates he had told the doorman to order from the kitchen, and when she made no move to play the part of the hostess, he began serving them both.

"Colin Radcliffe, Grimsthorpe, Lord Gifford—each of them took rooms as soon as they reached their majority," she continued. "You, however, did not. I suppose you are not as comfortable among your fellows as they. You watch. You manipulate. You know many but are friends with none."

"I suppose you believe that your keen insights will surprise me into volunteering information that shall give you some sort of influence over me," Thomas said harshly. "So far it has failed. Please continue stating the obvious, and perhaps I will change my mind."

She made no indication that she had heard him. "You do not live with your family, either. You are even less easy with them than with your fellows."

"Why do you seek to antagonize me?" he demanded, pushing her plate in front of her with enough force that she had to put out a hand to keep it from sliding into her lap. "I know that you are frightened of me. I can taste your fear. Why do you then try to anger me?"

"You have strength and society on your side. What have I but words?" she returned coldly. She picked up a steak knife from the untidy pile of silverware that he had made. "And a dinner knife. I suppose I could try to cut you with it." She held it out before her, looking down the length of the blade at him, her eyes as unblinking as a snake's. "I think I might like that. And you might even like me to try it, because then you could hit me and make yourself believe that you had to."

Thomas' hand shot out, encircling her wrist before she could do more than begin to turn the knife toward him. "Do not force me to make you regret it."

"I could kill you," she said, her words almost wistful. "I don't mean that I have the power but that I have the will, a far more difficult thing. People sometimes wonder if they are capable of taking a life. I know that I am; I almost took my own. After that, life itself seems so insignificant."

Thomas saw an emotion behind the glassy clarity of her eyes: pain. It was as distant as a star, and yet he knew that if the distance could be bridged, the vastness of it would dwarf his being, the heat sear the flesh from his bones. It was turned not on him, but inward, and he wondered what stuff she was made of, that she could survive it. Then she blinked, and it was gone. It left a chill in him, though, and an ache that he did not care to analyze.

"What was done to you?" he asked, releasing her wrist and pulling away, as if he could erase the memory of what he'd just seen.

Her eyes dropped to the knife, and she turned it in her hands, watching the gaslight play across the steel blade. "You don't care," she said. "Why would I open myself to you to satisfy your idle curiosity when I have no intention of answering the question with which you have a more pressing interest?"

"You shall answer it," Thomas said flatly. "You shall not escape it."

"Or what?" She didn't look up. "What will you do to me, Lord Varcourt? Some new violation, I suppose. Your cock cannot coax it from me, so perhaps you will turn to more direct violence. Perhaps you shall beat me." The disinterested way in which she pronounced those words sent a shiver through him.

"Perhaps," she mused, "you shall even cut me." She placed the edge of the blade across the meat of her thumb, watching at it indented her flesh. Thomas found himself holding his breath. "You said you would do whatever it takes. Would you do that, Lord Varcourt? I don't think you have the stomach for it." Her voice dropped to a whisper, her eyes growing dangerously bright. *"But I do."*

Before Thomas could react, she drew the edge of the blade across her hand, a thin red line appearing as the flesh parted in its path.

Thomas cursed and struck the knife from her hand. It fell with a dull clunk to the Turkish rug. The woman stared with rapt attention as the blood pooled in the center of her palm.

"Are you mad?" Thomas yanked a handkerchief from his pocket and stood, crossing to her side. He grabbed her wrist and pulled it up roughly. She made no sound and offered no resistance. He wiped the blood away so he could examine the cut. It was long but thankfully shallow, though it bled freely. He pressed the handkerchief into her palm and let her hand drop.

"Hold that, you fool," he ordered. Silently, she cradled her hand, watching the makeshift bandage turn scarlet.

It's an act. It must be. She's been living alone for months and hasn't done herself any harm, he told himself roughly as he got the brandy decanter from the spirits cabinet. But it didn't seem like an act. His mind replayed the scene, her terrible pale beauty transfixed in unholy fascination as she drew the blade across her hand. . . .

He turned back to her abruptly, trying to shut away that image. She had stood while he was turned away, the legs of her chair silent upon the rug, and she was now stooping, reaching with her blood-streaked hand for the knife that lay upon the carpet.

56Lydia Joyce*

"Damnation, woman," Thomas snapped, setting the decanter on the table with a thud. She straightened quickly, turning with the knife in her hand, but he was already lunging for her. He caught her wrist, his body weight driving her back until she hit the wall. Her hand, pinned up against it, loosened slowly, the knife dropping from her fingers. His body pressed full length against hers, holding her to the wall.

She gave a kind of ragged laugh and turned her face up toward his. Their lips met, and instinct overwhelmed him. He took over the kiss, pushing her back to the wall, his knee pressing between her legs and up, hard, against her. Her mouth was hot and hungry, taking everything he gave her and demanding more, her hips grinding against his thigh.

His brain finally battered a message through to his body, and he broke away, staring at the woman as she leaned against the wall, her chest moving against his as she gasped for breath. Her eyes glittered, but no color had reached her cheeks.

"You are mad," he said. He was mad, too, for his strongest urge was not to pursue the woman's revelation of weakness to get the answers he must have. Instead, the most fundamental, irrational part of him wanted to do nothing more than save this strange woman—from what, he didn't know, but he had a sudden, ludicrous conviction that she was in need of salvation, and that she offered him in return a salvation of his own.

"Would that I were," she said. Her eyes strayed to the knife at their feet. "I was only picking it up, you know." Her face was utterly, chillingly expressionless, the porcelain features seemingly painted on.

"Do excuse me if I don't have full confidence in that," he returned.

"Why would you care, anyway?" she asked. "Wouldn't it be easier for you if I simply . . . disappeared?"

"Cutting your own throat on my Turkish rug is not *disappearing*," he said.

"Ah. I see." A ghost of a smile flickered across her lips. "Do release me, Lord Varcourt. Unless of course you still believe you can beat an answer out of me."

Thomas stepped away and retrieved the knife and his handkerchief. She remained against the wall, watching him as he wet the handkerchief with brandy and brought it back.

"Give me your hand," he ordered.

She did so, and he cleaned the cut carefully, uncertain whether he wanted to be harsh or gentle. She stiffened slightly the first time the alcohol touched the wound, her fingers reflexively curling, but almost immediately she relaxed and submitted wordlessly to his ministrations. He bound the wound with his second handkerchief and tied it into a neat knot. Then he turned back to the decanter, returning it to the spirits cabinet and taking out a tumbler. His hands trembled with the effects of adrenaline, rattling the decanter against the rim of the glass.

Bloody hell. That woman had shaken him. He had her locked in his own flat, and yet he felt less in control of the situation than ever. He wasn't even sure that she wouldn't try to kill him—or herself—right there in his parlor.

Thomas set his jaw and poured a generous two fingers into the tumbler, swallowed it in a single gulp, and then poured two more—as indifferent as she appeared, she must be suffering from some invisible disturbance to have done that to herself. In the back of his spirits cabinet, he saw the tiny bottle of laudanum that his mother thought she had hidden there. If the brandy didn't calm the woman from her dangerous state, that should.

How many drops did his mother usually give herself? These days, she had given up on drops and simply tipped a healthy measure into her drink—equivalent to thirty drops, at least. Lady Hamilton was a smaller woman than Esmeralda, but years of abuse surely had dulled the effect of the drug. Thomas blocked Esmeralda's line of sight with his back, for he had every reason to expect that she would protest the brandy, never mind an added dose of opiate. He carefully removed the dropper and watched cautiously as a few drops dissolved into the brandy before replacing the stopper and putting the laudanum and the brandy back into the cabinet together.

He brought the tumbler over to the woman. "Drink," he said, pressing it into her uninjured hand.

She took the cup, the facets of the Austrian crystal glittering in the gaslight. "I hope that you are not trying to get me drunk."

"I am trying to get some sanity into you," Thomas said. "You are the strangest hysterical woman that I have ever seen."

She smiled at that, the curve of her lips not reaching her eyes. "I assure you, Lord Varcourt, that I am quite calm." Looking at him steadily, she drank the brandy in two quick swallows, her head tilting back to reveal the long curve of her neck.

"Now," he said, taking the drink from her fingers, "let us talk."

Chapter Six

Lord Varcourt guided Em to a low sofa before the fireplace. She offered no resistance; she knew that for now, at least, the direct threat of violence was averted. She had shocked him from behind his mask through the trick with the knife—though how much of a trick it had really been was not something she cared to examine too closely, for there had been a kind of exultation when the blade bit into her flesh—

She pushed that thought aside, grounding herself in the dull throb that now came from her hand. There was nothing heady about that, at least. She had chosen life, and she had no mind to change her choice.

She sat at his wave of invitation, and he stood over her, his powerful frame silhouetted by the firelight that gilded his dark brown hair with red. Her heart increased a little at the memory of that hard chest pressed against hers, his mouth devouring her own. . . .

She could sense a need in his body, one mere copulation could not fill but that his spirit was straining for anyhow. Everyone had a weakness, a place that they could not guard, and this need was his. All she had to do was to find out what it was and to get him to believe she could fill it, and he would be as much hers as his mother was. She should strike at the most obvious point first and feel her way from there.

That was, however, much easier said than done.

"I do not believe that you killed your brother," she said. If it had been a séance or a reading, she would have added a reference to the spirits and their messages, but as it was, she spoke the words swiftly, boldly, without any mystical trappings. She did not know whether it was true, but such an assertion, made without warning, had a very good chance of eliciting a response that would tell her more than his words could. It would gain a truer reaction than an accusation, which he had probably heard so many times that he had become numb.

He grew very still, and she struggled to read an expression among the shadows of his face in the haloing light from the fireplace. "You were pleased enough to let my mother believe otherwise."

"It was in my best interests," she said callously, and with some degree of dishonesty. "You would like to be rid of me. If she suspects your concern is not without personal cause, she will not allow you to drive me away."

"And so you fed her doubts. My own mother, who had the doubts to be fed." His smile was hard and ironic.

"She seems to have ample reason to believe that your brother's death wasn't an accident," she said quietly. It was only a half lie; Lady Hamilton indeed seemed more convinced of *someone's* guilt than mere uncertainty of her surviving son could account for. But Em was far from sure just who that someone was.

"No." His response was low and fierce and, Em was certain, unintentional. "When I left Harry at the streamside, he was alive." He shut his mouth a little too fast. He had given her too much, betrayed too much with those words, and

though he quickly pressed his lips together in a hard line, he could not take them back.

She had scored on her first attempt. It was almost laughably simplistic, if this were anything to laugh about. His innocence, if it was that, in doubt—that was his weakness. Had she misjudged him, then? Were those the words of a truly innocent man or of a man ridden with guilt? It hardly mattered. What he hated was others suspecting him. That was enough knowledge to draw him in, against all reason and all sense.

Em pressed home the advantage. "She saw something— heard something. . . ." She trailed off, as if she were searching for the words. She was, she knew, a despicable person, one who traded on the secret pains and longings of others. But she had no other currency with which to make her way in the world. "Your mother has a terrible secret, one that has caused her to doubt you all these years."

"Tell me." The harshness of the words seemed to shake him.

Em knew then that she had him in truth, though he would not know it yet. She shook her head. "I do not know. I never tried to find out. It was not my concern."

"I don't believe you." He stepped closer, so that he was standing upon the edge of her skirts as he loomed over her.

She kept her voice steady with effort. "I told you I was not playing a game that you could lose. I do not care what demons lie in your past, and I did not hunt them."

"What is your game, then? Who is your master?"

"I have no master." She feared she would have to invent a plausible one, and soon, if she was to divert Lord Varcourt. She must hold out a while longer yet—if she confessed, it must appear to him to be in extremis.

Lord Varcourt's jaw tightened, and the tension radiating off his body made her stomach clench. "Why did you give my mother that necklace?"

Now was the time for her most desperate ploy: the truth. "So that she would believe me, know my powers to be real."

"And what do you gain from that? A greater ability to separate mother from son?"

"You might as well accuse me of separating her from the moon," Em said bluntly. "It is no more remote. My goals have nothing to do with you. All I seek is to secure my future."

"With a gift worth five times what she could have possibly given you," he said.

"Three times more," she said quietly. "Your mother has been very good to me. I am not a dog that bites the hand that feeds me."

He stood, swaying slightly in front of the fire. He did not seem to know whether he could believe her, though now she had some hope that he wanted to. "Where did the necklace come from?"

That ground was far too dangerous for her to tread. "What does it matter? It will do her no harm. You cannot keep me here forever," she said. It was beginning to sound like a pitiable refrain. *You're giving him too much,* she warned herself. But he didn't know that yet; he wouldn't know how to exploit it.

"I can keep you here long enough."

"Long enough for what? For the police to come after me? For my belongings to be pillaged by the Gypsies, leaving me with nothing?" She added the bait. "For your mother to lose faith in me, making it impossible for me to ever find the answers that you seek?"

"The only answer I want from you is a confession of where you got that necklace and a full account of your purpose in giving it specifically to her," he said. Those were his words, but the sudden tense lines in his face when she hinted at investigating his brother's death revealed that she had struck home.

"It would not serve you any good to know it," Em said

firmly. "But I can discover other answers, if you wish. You know in your heart that it will be the only way you will ever find out."

"I wish you to be out of my life—out of my family's lives. Why would I encourage you to even greater intimacy with my mother?" he demanded.

The question, as sarcastically as it was framed, did not seem to be as rhetorical as perhaps he had intended it. Em said, "You shall allow me because I can find out what she has never told you—and never will." That neither committed her to his innocence nor accused him of guilt. "Then you will know on what grounds she mistrusts you, that my slight influence could so increase it. And you will know what else she believes about her first son's death, and why she believes it." She met his eyes steadily. "I will swear on anything you name that I have no ill intent toward you or yours. I will pledge my life. You may kill me with your own hands if I lie."

He made a gesture of rejection. "That is not good enough."

She pressed, "I offer you assistance in return for a mere suspension of your antagonism. Can you not give me something so slight?"

"No," he said, the shake of his head like a spasm.

Oh, he wanted to take her offer—he wanted it intensely. He would cave, she was certain of it, but not yet. She'd given him the bait; now was the time to snatch it away and make him believe that he had lost the chance. Once he'd had time to mourn the lost opportunity, she knew that he'd grab for it if given it again. She found that, against all sense, she wanted to help him. As foolhardy as it was to pity such a man, she wished to see his anguish eased, even though she knew that with it would wane her own power over him. She could not feel any real sympathy for him, she told herself, no matter how demon-hounded. No, this desire was born from her guilt about how much she took in her role of Esmeralda and how all she gave in return was empty reassurances. For once, she wanted to give something that was real.

She was finding it increasingly difficult to keep all the levels of the mind going at once to separate memories and intentions, analysis and words. She was exhausted and had eaten almost nothing since luncheon.

"Then you shall have nothing," she said, with every ounce of finality that she could put into her voice.

"I will have you," he said roughly, almost desperately, "any time I please."

Em's pulse sped up, and she allowed her eyes to grow heavy lidded as she looked up at him. "That goes without saying, as I would not deign to negotiate over such a trifle."

"You are not as cold as you pretend," Lord Varcourt said harshly.

"I have never pretended any such thing," Em returned. "I may have promised carnal pleasures, but never did I say that I was cold."

"That is not what I mean, and you know it. I mean, cold in here"—he brought a finger against her forehead— "and in here." He moved the finger to her left breast, just over her heart. "You have not been unmoved."

"What would you know of the workings of my heart?" Em scoffed, even as it squeezed inside her chest. "According to your testimony, I have none, if you remember."

"Where are you from, Merry?" he said, as if she had not spoken. "You are ill-suited to play the role of world-weary courtesan."

"I am from nowhere," she whispered, shutting away thoughts of Forsham, dreams of Lincroft, the golden days that had ended in darkness. Her head seemed to swim a little with those memories, and she gave it a shake, pulling it back to the here and now.

"Your hands are soft—they have never done rough work.

Your face echoes that testament to a gentle life," he said. "How did you fall so far?"

She laughed humorlessly, and she decided to trade him confidence in exchange for confidence, to give him a tiny piece of the truth that would make him believe that one day, she might offer more. "I did not fall as far as you might think. There were many who would say that blood showed true, in my case." There was little difference between a bastard and a whore, and it was as a bastard she had been raised. The knowledge of how unjust that label was had come far, far too late to save her.

Standing between her and the fire, Lord Varcourt extended his hand. Em stared at it, trying to determine the impulse behind the action. He didn't move, and eventually, reluctantly, she took it.

He pulled her to her feet with a kind of steady insistence. She was tall, but he was taller still, so that at such a close proximity, she had to tilt her head back to meet his eyes. What she saw there made her wish that she hadn't looked at all, especially not without the protection of her veil to hide her face and her reactions from the intensity of his gaze.

"You are not going to let me go home tonight," she said, the calm of her words belied by the rapid acceleration of her heart.

"No. I will not," Lord Varcourt said. The heat of his body seemed suddenly unbearable to her, and she had to force herself not to step away.

"I am a madwoman, you know. I very well might murder you in your bed."

"I sincerely doubt that."

"You don't doubt," she countered. "You try very hard not to think about it, because you still want me."

A ghost of a smile flickered across his features. "You are astute. I am not letting you leave this place tonight, and so why should I not indulge myself?"

She did not think she could survive a night of his attentions with the integrity of her mind still intact, yet she dared not overtly rebuff him and lose the modicum of leverage that she possessed. And a part of herself, a part that filled her with shame and fury, did not want to reject him at all. That part of her seemed stronger than it should be, disjointing her thoughts and forcing her to assemble her ideas through sheer will.

She pitched her voice to bite. "You may mock what you believe are pretensions to experience, yet one taste was nowhere near enough for you." She tilted up her chin, making herself step closer to him, so that her breasts brushed his chest through their clothes. "You should be afraid."

"Why is that?"

"Even as you mock, you lust. Against all sanity. You can't resist me." Her smile was hard. "Your rough wooing did not convince me to give you what you sought. Why would a softer seduction?"

"Why can't it be just for my pleasure?" he countered. Yet there was something in his gaze, in his eyes, that made her wonder. . . . It was getting hard to think through the haze that veiled her mind, and Em felt a spike of alarm run through her, its artificial dullness doubly frightening.

She pushed away from him and turned to the looking glass that hung over the chimneypiece. Her own face stared back at her, her irises reduced to narrow green bands around the black wells of her pupils. She had seen that often enough in Lady Hamilton to recognize it for what it was.

She'd been drugged.

"You bastard!" she hissed, snatching a candlestick from the mantel and whirling with it raised to strike. His body weight hit her first, knocking her backward, her skirts swinging into the coals with the stench of scorched silk. She brought her arm down, hard, and it met his head with a satisfying solidity. His weight driving against her went suddenly slack, and he crumpled into a heap upon the hearth rug.

She stepped away unsteadily, prodding him with the toe of her shoe. He didn't move.

"I hope you're dead," she said down to him, but the fear that gripped her stomach told her that wasn't true. If he were dead, there was a good chance that she would hang for it, and even if he wasn't . . . Well, the man was certainly an unprincipled boor, but he hadn't done anything that she probably wouldn't have done in his place. She would, in fact, have done far more—from such a position of power, she would not have let her guard down so far as to let herself be overcome by someone so insignificant.

That's because you have no breeding, she told herself with the deepest irony. It was, in truth, because she was desperate—far more desperate than such a privileged man could understand. She bent to feel a pulse. It was there, strong and steady, and though a quick check of his head revealed a rising lump, she doubted that she'd broken anything.

Em rifled through his pockets swiftly and found the key to the door. She palmed it, and as she passed the spirits cabinet, she paused long enough to look inside. Yes—there it was. Half a bottle of laudanum. With an unholy pleasure, she opened the stopper to the brandy and emptied the laudanum into it, watching as the paler cloud of liquid dispersed into invisibility into the golden alcohol.

"You bastard," she repeated to the man slumped on the floor. Or rather, she tried to, for the words slurred on her tongue. With a sudden surge of fear, she put the laudanum and brandy back, her hands and eyes refusing to coordinate movements. She got the decanter in place and swung the cabinet shut, and then she turned on increasingly unsteady legs and walked toward the door. Distantly, alarm bells were going off in her brain, but they were growing more and more muffled in the fog wrapped around it. She grasped the doorknob and pulled. Nothing happened, and she stood, swaying and staring stupidly at it for a moment.

Must get out. Those words came through the fog. Then *Key.* She looked down at her hand. It was wrapped in a hand kerchief, and there, upon the handkerchief, was a key.

She held it clumsily and tried to put it in the door, but she couldn't see the keyhole. She realized that she was sliding down, and after a moment, her perspective canted sideways as her face came to rest against the floor. She breathed the resiny smell of the floorboards and thought muzzily that this wasn't what she was supposed to be doing.

"Oh, damn," she said distinctly.

And then blackness washed up through her mind and dragged her down.

Chapter Seven

Thomas opened his eyes to see the turned mahogany leg of a chair a few inches from his nose. It took a moment to put that together with his throbbing head and the memory of the candlestick.

He surged to his feet—and immediately regretted it as a wave of pain and dizziness overtook him. Fighting back the urge to vomit all over his rather expensive French shoes, he grabbed the chimneypiece and checked his pocket for the key. Gone.

Silently cursing the pounding of his head, he started for the door, determined to catch up with Esmeralda, whoever she was. So intent was he upon reaching the door that he almost tripped over Esmeralda's crumpled form before he saw it, lying upon the rug. For an instant, he was confused—had she been struck on the head, too? But then he realized that the combination of laudanum and brandy on an empty stomach must have done its work as thoroughly as a candlestick to the skull.

He hadn't meant to knock her out. He hadn't even meant to dose her very heavily. Nevertheless, he snorted at the mental image of both of them slumped unconscious upon the floor, causing a new wave of pain to pass through his head. Poetic justice, but whether it was responsible for his unconsciousness or hers, he couldn't say.

Thomas picked her up with a grunt, and she lay limply in his arms, her head lolling and limbs dangling. The helplessness of her body sent a stab of guilt through him, but he suppressed in fiercely. He stood for a moment, deciding what he was to do with her. He settled on his valet's room—William would not be needing it for some time.

He pushed the door open with his foot and set her down on the bed. Her face was perfectly smooth in unconsciousness, and Thomas realized with a small jolt in his gut that she was not as old as he had assumed. He had assumed she was . . . what? Twenty-eight? Thirty, even? The bitter cynicism of her words and the chilly, jaded expression she affected made her seem as if she'd seen some of the world, at least. But now that she lay there, without the animation of consciousness, he was barely able to believe that she was much more than twenty.

At least she was no child, he thought with a shiver of self-disgust. He didn't know what he would have done if she had been sixteen. And yet she could have been, under her veil, and he wouldn't have known it until too late.

"Who are you, Esmeralda?" he whispered, and for the first time, the answer mattered to him.

She would awake in pain if she spent the night strapped into her corset at the constriction appropriate for a dinner party. The hard logic of that thought wriggled into his contemplation of her still form. Part of him considered his throbbing head and accounted it as no more than she deserved. It was, he thought, singularly foolish of him that the thought of this discomfort should bother him so much when he had done nothing but try to cause her discomfort since he had pinned her in the library. But the feeling remained nevertheless.

He rolled her onto her side and unbuttoned the back of her dress—or rather, the rest of her dress, for the bottom part still had not been buttoned—easing her limp arms out of her sleeves and steadfastly ignoring the warm pliability of her body.

The frame that the silk enwrapped was fine-boned, for all its length, undeniably feminine and fragile enough to make him grit his teeth against the feeling that he had brutalized her—was brutalizing her still. Trying to shut his mind to the delicacy of her porcelain skin, he maneuvered her petticoats off her limp figure. It didn't work, for his brain, denied of considerations of what lay before him, conjured up instead lurid recollections of the softness of her thighs against his hands and hips, the heat of her welcoming him half-unwillingly, tightening around him until he came without thought, without control.

Resolutely, he turned to remove her shoes, but even the narrow bones of her ankle seemed determined to keep him from regaining his equilibrium. Setting his jaw, he unfastened the two buckles that tightened her corset without the need for a maid. His hand brushed one high, well-formed breast as he eased it off, and he burned with the memory of what he'd done and the desire to do it over again.

The warm, pliant flesh beneath his hands as he rolled her faceup again seemed to taunt him with his own need. She had been teasing him, leading him on. She had offered herself to him, not once but multiple times. She deserved it. She had wanted it.

She was lying unconscious on his valet's bed, looking lost and innocent.

Damn her.

For seventeen years, he had ruled himself with unrelenting control. This woman may have made him forget himself to the point of tricking himself into believing he was in good judgment making a choice that was really no more than a lapse, done in the heat of the moment for the basest of reasons. In his mind's eye, he saw Harry's face, thrown into lines of shock, fury, and pain, the wide welt already spreading from lip to temple. That had been different. That had been a true mistake—Harry had to know that, God had to know, the universe had to know. . . .

Stoically, Thomas pulled his necktie from his collar with a swift hiss of silk, taking up the woman's wrists in one hand and tying them to the bedstead, the tightening bonds flaking some of the paint from its cast-iron curlicues. He was aware of the deep irony of his care with her comfort and now his actions of restraint, but he was far from done with her yet, and he was not entirely certain that if he left her free that he might not be murdered in his bed before morning. He must stay in control—of himself and of her both. Whatever ludicrousness that fact caused.

He gathered her clothes in his arms and stepped back. She was as pale as a vision as she lay there, her arms stretched up above her head, their white lengths cut by the black slashes of his necktie. The golden comb was still shoved into her coiffure far back on her head, the pushed-back black veil making a backdrop beneath her for the wisps of light brown hair that curled from its pins to cloud around her face. The dark crimson of his makeshift bandage across her palm drew his eye. What could have driven one so young so far into the darkness of the mind?

The last look of a doomed brother as he was left behind forever. No. Those were his demons, not Esmeralda's.

He pulled a blanket over her, then turned away without answers and shut the door, troubled by the person of this strange woman who had burst so unwelcomely into his life, not merely by what she had done. It was becoming increasingly evident that she was more than an enemy's pawn, more than someone to bend to his will.

He dropped her clothing on the parlor sofa. *It does not*

matter what age she is or how vulnerable she looks, he told himself as he retrieved his interrupted dinner and began to eat with swift, mechanical bites. *She is a dangerous woman.* Dangerous to his peace of mind, dangerous to his family, and, perhaps, dangerous to his future.

It did not matter, either, what promises she held out to him—of information or reparations. But, oh, how he wanted to believe, to believe in anything when she looked at him with those too-wise, translucent eyes. . . .

He stared blindly at his plate, focused instead inwardly, on that fateful summer day and the stream, dark and swift with rain. It focused on the memory of Harry's face, as white as a lily petal as the void of his mouth opened to scream his fury at his brother and at the world that had broken him even in his mother's womb.

The idiot, other boys would call him. *The lunatic,* even. An inadequate heir—even in their father's most optimistic moments, Lord Hamilton never doubted that. *Thom, you must watch out for Harry,* Lord Hamilton would say. A dozen instances out of hundreds crowded in on Thomas' mind: his father in front of the fire in his study, in the school-room, at the dining table, walking the grounds. Any time Harry's weaknesses left him unable to carry out a task, Lord Hamilton's eyes would turn to his second son, and he would say, *You must watch out for Harry.*

When Thomas was very small, he'd wanted to cry, "But who will look after me?" As he'd grown, that feeling had transmuted into something quite different—a sense that he was doomed to be no more than an extension of his brother, to fill in the pieces that had somehow been left out. He was to run the estates, stand at Harry's elbow in social occasions, sire the heir. There was not enough in Harry to make a proper heir, and after Thomas finished filling in the holes, there would be not enough left of him to make a person of his own.

Thomas swallowed the last of his wine in a single gulp. He held the faceted glass up to the light so that the gas' flame fragmented into a thousand shards of amber. He considered pouring himself more. No. The last thing he needed was too much drink on top of a concussion. He set the tumbler down and pushed his chair from the table, his footsteps heavy across the muffling wool of the rug.

In his own bedchamber, he stripped dully in front of the cheval mirror and draped his clothes over the back of a chair. Holding the blankness of his mind like a soap bubble, he cleaned his teeth with tooth powder, splashed water on his face, and lay down. But as he began drifting off into sleep, the images of the woman's body and his brother's face pushed against the edges of the bubble, shrinking it as they tangled and merged into dreams in which his hands kept turning to claws.

Em woke to a dim, bare room and the rush of memory of her last waking moments. *Where am I?* she thought, a thread of panic wriggling through her mind.

She sat up—tried to sit up, for instantly, her arms were caught up short and she was yanked back down again. She paused, gathering her breath as she assessed the situation. Her wrists were tied to . . . something above her head. She craned her neck and caught a glimpse of black silk and a white bedstead. Her wrists were not protesting the tightness of the knots—at least, not yet—but an experimental tug convinced her of the futility of trying to fight against them.

Her tight nipples rasped across the linen of her shift with that movement; she had been stripped to her chemise, and the chill of the room had seeped into her bones, for the only blanket that she could see was now tangled around her feet. She took stock of her body. She ached, yes, but not unexpectedly. She came to the conclusion that Varcourt had limited his improprieties to removing her clothing, a discovery that gave her relief and unease in unequal measures, for in some ways, it was easier to control a man who was not in control of himself.

By the light of a single narrow window, she surveyed the room. The bedstead was iron, the mattresses of good horsehair and feather, though the coverlet under and quilt over her were plain. A small clothespress and a high, utilitarian chest of drawers completed the furnishings, and the rag rug on the floor was the only element of the space that might betray some personal taste. There had been two doorways off the parlor, one presumably leading to Lord Varcourt's bedchamber, and the other . . . here? It could be a servant's room. It could be anything.

Wherever it was, she wanted out. She turned on her side so that her back faced the wall and began to kick it, slowly and steadily at a pace that she could maintain for hours.

She didn't have to wait that long. After her fourth kick, she heard the sound of footsteps across the floor on the other side of the walls. She tensed and froze, staring at the door as the seconds drew out like spider's silk.

It opened. Lord Varcourt stood in the doorway, wearing a dressing gown, his hair disheveled and black eyes burning. Over his shoulder, she could see the parlor of his flat, and a small bit of the fear loosened inside her. He had not absconded with her to some secret bolt-hole or hideaway where he took women, never to be seen again. And yet that relief was only momentary, for standing there, he looked capable of anything.

"Does your head hurt?" she croaked.

His dark eyes narrowed. "Most abominably last night, though it is a little better now."

"More's the pity." His feet were bare under the hem of the dressing gown, and so were his calves. Her heart beat a little harder even as she told herself that he was wearing a nightshirt beneath, that he must be. "You drugged me," she said aloud, the words too flat to be an accusation.

"It seemed the thing to do at the time." He raised the corner of his mouth—his incongruously sensual mouth—at her. "Would you care for a drink? To . . . relieve yourself?"

"I would care to be untied," she replied curtly. "My hands are falling asleep."

"Untied," he repeated. "No, I would really rather not untie you at the moment. I quite enjoy having you in a position from which I know you can neither run away nor brain me." He paused. "Nor do both in succession, I suppose."

"You can't keep me here," Em said, hoping that the confidence in her voice would somehow make the words truer.

"So you keep saying, but I don't see why not." He pushed off the edge of the doorframe and walked to the side of the bed, looking down at her as she lay there.

Anger, fear, and a hot awareness that was neither battled inside her, but she kept them firmly tamped down as she returned his look, stare for stare. She couldn't bear it if he repeated the things he had done to her in her bedroom—but part of her wanted nothing else.

He reached down, and she stiffened, but he was only pulling something—the comb—from her hair. He came away with it in his hands, and the veil came, too, sliding roughly between her body and the sheets underneath her. He dropped them beside the bed.

"You don't need that here," he said.

"I need it everywhere," she returned, attempting to test again the bonds that held her wrists while appearing not to move.

He laughed, the harsh sound sending a chill through her. "Merry, I do believe that you are frightened of me."

"You haven't got the stomach I have for pain," Em returned. "What could I be afraid of?"

"Perhaps not of me, then," he amended. "Perhaps of what I can make you do."

Em tilted up her neck even as her legs instinctively curled toward her stomach. "You've done your worst already. If I left you panting for more, then take it, take whatever you want. But do not pretend you are intimidating me by it or that it will get you closer to the answers to the questions you continue to stubbornly ask me."

His smile was feral. "You don't think so?" he asked. "How odd. Because I do." He pulled his dressing gown loose with a single tug of the tasseled sash, and it fell open, revealing nothing but hard flesh beneath. He pulled the sash off entirely and looped it around her neck, watching her face with a keenness that seemed to cut into her.

Em schooled her features into perfect stillness even as the silken cord caressed her neck. *Did I miscalculate?* a part of her brain demanded. *Was this the fatal gamble?* But another part of her, dark and black, said, *If he tightens, it will all be over soon.*

Survive. She had made that decision months ago, and she would not take the coward's way out now. She would survive—she must survive. She knew with suddenly clarity what had gone wrong. They had come too close the night before—not only had Varcourt stolen from her the composure and indifference that she had clutched so dearly to herself, but he, too, had drawn too close, intolerably so. And unless she restored that distance, he would try to do so, his own way, to try to save himself.

So when she opened her mouth, she said, "Do it. You know you want to. You know you've wondered what it would feel like, to wring the life out of someone."

With a curse, Varcourt yanked the cord away so fast that the friction burned Em's throat. Her success proved her right. Ignoring the sting, she narrowed her eyes at him in an expression of contempt. "Coward," she said, goading him with careful calculation. "I know why you didn't kill your brother. It isn't that you didn't want to—oh, no, everyone knows just how you felt about poor little Harry, the idiot heir. It is because you couldn't."

The slap caught her off guard, filling her brain with a blinding flash of pain and making her head ring. He'd pulled most of the force of the blow, but she still blinked back the tears that sprang to her eyes as she stared up at the man who stood over her, his hand still raised, his eyes dark and wild with anger and a blossoming self-loathing. *"My brother was not an idiot."*

Em laughed at him, pitching the sound to be low and biting even as his words pierced her. "No, you couldn't kill your brother. But you can hit a woman who's tied to your bed. Do you feel like a man now, Tommy boy? Are you proud of yourself? You will still hate me every time you see me, but now you will also hate yourself."

"You meant me to do that." The words came strangled from his throat as his hand dropped.

"I play your mother with promises of messages from her dead son Harry," she said, making her words cruel. It hurt to do it, but she ignored it. She was used to pain. "I play you with words that burn in your heart. Yes, Lord Varcourt, I am a fraud. The only spirits I hear are people's own demons, whispering to me through their words and their actions."

"Why?" he demanded. He leaned over her and planted a fist on either side of her head as if that were the only way he could trust himself not to strike her again.

"You ask me that while I'm strapped to your bed with knots you tied with your own hands?" She shook her head, rocking it from side to side on the mattress. "What else do I have, Lord Varcourt?"

"Your patron," he said.

"I have none." Her smile was bitter. "I do not understand

why it is so hard for you to believe that I am alone in this world."

"Someone gave you that necklace," he insisted. "Someone told you to get it into my mother's keeping. It is not a mere scrap of paste and base metals. Lord Olthwaite recognized it—he went half-wild when he saw it."

"Did he, now?" Em asked. The events since the dinner fell into place—why Lord Varcourt had pursued her after she left the library, why he had been so insistent upon knowing the origins of the necklace, why he would not be distracted as he had been in the library. The stakes had risen—for everyone. "Why don't you ask him where it came from, then? I'm sure he'd be pleased to blubber everything upon your strong shoulder. That, or you'd drive him to madness. Either way, no harm done, yes?"

"I think I have a very good idea of where it came from," Varcourt said. "I want to hear it from you."

Em looked at him steadily and granted him a truth he would not believe. "Trust me, Lord Varcourt, there is no one so inextricably involved in this as Lord Olthwaite. There is blood that cries his guilt out from the earth, and it will be heard, one way or another."

"Damn you, woman," he snarled, pushing away from her. "You make my palms itch."

"Every time you strike me, you give me a little piece of your soul," Em said coldly. She knew him so well already—so well it almost frightened her. "There are men who beat their women for evening exercise, but you are not one of them. Your rage is your demon, and I have him by the balls. But I must be careful, for he's a dangerous little beast and would kill either one of us, given half a chance."

His jaw tightened, its muscles forming hard bulges along its edge. "You are mad."

"And you want me nevertheless," she returned. "Don't deny it—I can feel it in your body from here. Unless you have a sheath of your own with you, you'll have to rape me to get what you want, and I don't quite believe that you're willing to live with the consequences you will exact upon yourself if you do that."

He stared down at her. "I have one."

"Then you brought it with you because you knew what you were going to do even before you opened the door, didn't you?" Em said, a sick, shivering satisfaction in her belly.

He hissed out a ragged breath.

"I thought so. In the library, I knew you wouldn't give me the satisfaction of showing the weakness of lack of self-control. In my rooms, I knew that you couldn't refuse. And here . . . well, once that barrier had been broken, you wouldn't be able to stop yourself from doing it again, would you?" she said. "Not even when I was drunk and drugged, so certainly not now. Such a gentleman you are."

He raked his fingers through his hair. "This isn't about being a gentleman."

She pushed on recklessly. They were getting too close again, her words striking like lashes instead of merely driving him back, but she could not help herself. "No, this is about getting answers. What answers do you think are hiding between my thighs? None about me, Lord Varcourt, I'll tell you that much. But you might just find some about you."

"Shut up," he said, the words grinding out of him. "Just shut up."

Em smiled even as she ached. "Make me. I know you will."

And he did, his mouth coming down hard, crushingly against her own. His lips moved insistently, his tongue pushing hard between them and against her teeth. She opened, letting him inside. *I could bite down,* she thought, but she knew she did not want to. Part of her—too much of her—reveled in the hot demands of his mouth, the bruising force of it, reveled in the release, reveled in the self-punishment of the pain. . . .

She pulled against the silken bonds that held her, but they only cut into her wrists. Varcourt pulled back, giving her a narrow look.

"It will not give," he said harshly. "I am not letting you go. I want those answers."

"Shall you keep me tied here for days, then? For weeks?" she pressed. "I can tell you no more."

"I shall keep you for now," he said. It seemed like a meaningless statement, but Em recognized it as the admission of defeat even if he did not. He would keep her tied for now to convince himself of her helplessness. And then he would let her go. The very fact that he needed convincing told her the level of influence that she already had over him.

For once, she held her tongue.

He stood as he pulled something from the pocket, his dressing gown falling open at the movement. He looked even more powerful half naked than he did dressed in all the trappings of influence that were an aristocrat's wardrobe. He was tall, certainly, but broad, too, the width of his shoulders tapering to hips that were narrow in comparison but still had a heavy-boned, hard-flanked heft that made her feel almost insubstantial. From it jutted his erection, disproportionate even on his hard body, inherently threatening and ludicrous at the same time, though Em could find nothing funny in it at the moment. Did she truly expect to channel the forces behind that strong body? she wondered as her heart accelerated, her certainty dissolving. How could she hope to not be overwhelmed?

Varcourt opened his palm, and on it sat the orangey rolled form of a rubber sheath. "It's not lamb's gut, but I assume it will serve your purpose just as well," he said. "Tell me, what did you say to the young men to get them to wear it? I assume you didn't claim to have a disease, nor did you accuse them of one."

He was too clever by half. "I said that a man's seed would affect my powers."

"And why should they care?" Varcourt looked at her skeptically.

Her lips twisted. "Because of the nature of my powers. All of them."

He let out a bark of laughter. "You're a sharp one." He held the sheath out to her. "Lick it."

She just stared at him.

"Now," he said, and his tone brooked no argument. She put out her tongue and licked the small, hollow bubble in the center of the rolled disk. It tasted of rubber. "More," he said. She did it again.

"Novice," he said in a tone of satisfaction. "I'm surprised you even recognized a rubber, since it wasn't in your bag of tricks."

"Novice? You just asked me what I'd told the men—"

"Men, yes. But how many?"

"Plenty. You cannot refute that."

"I can refute it by the most reliable means possible," he retorted. "Your reactions betray you. They did last night. They did just now. And they will continue to do so."

"So I lied," Em said, tugging again futilely against the bonds that held her. "I claimed to have slept with every Member of Parliament, but the truth is that I only took the less adventuresome half into my bed."

"Three," he said.

Em's blood froze in her veins. "What?" she said through her suddenly dry mouth.

"Three men, or perhaps even two," he repeated. "Four at the outside, though I sincerely doubt it." He sat down on the bed next to her, the sheath disappearing into his pocket, and she automatically slithered away, as far against the wall as she could with her wrists affixed to the center of the bed. He rustled in his dressing gown and drew out the knife she'd used to cut herself the night before. He looked at her steadily for a moment, then took the edge of the neckline of her chemise firmly in one hand and notched it swiftly with the knife. He took hold of the fabric on either edge of the cut and pulled. It tore neatly down its length, exposing her from neck to navel.

She refused to give in to the temptation to twist to her side to conceal her nakedness, even though his hungry eyes on her body made her burn with shame and need in equal measures. What did he see in her bare flesh to make him look at her like that? She had, at times, loved her body, and at others hated it with the passion of self-destruction, but she had never seen anything in it to warrant such scorching intensity.

"I spoke with each of the men who claimed to have shared the pleasures of your . . . bed," he said, shifting his grip along the cloth and tugging again. The rest of the fabric gave way, and Em didn't dare voice a protest. "Most of them were simply lying. Of those who weren't, most were callow youths who admitted, blushingly, to have been so . . . overwhelmed by your presence and, shall we say, style that they got decidedly different results from their trysts than they had expected, and in their embarrassment, they embroidered the results."

"You knew that before. . . ." Em had to force herself not to gape. "Before you came to my rooms." He had done that to her—all that, knowing that she had experienced so little, with the full knowledge of exactly what he was using to call her bluff. She'd had no idea that such sensation could exist, that things like that could really be borne by a body.

"That I did," he said. "I had thought that you would change your mind about your offer before the act was completed, so to speak. I had not counted upon your determination. Or was it recklessness?"

Her smile felt like a rictus. She wanted to hate him, but the same intensity that angered her made it impossible for her to break past that intimacy to hate. "Insanity. Desperation. Indifference. There are so many possible causes; how can you presume to choose one?"

He put a finger on her lower lip, his touch drawing downward, across her chin and along the line of her throat. Her skin prickled in response, sending shivers of reaction through her. "I presume everything," he said quietly.

"What do you hope to gain by this?" Em tilted her head to take in the entirety of their situation. She suddenly needed to hear him admit the futility of his position. "You have no reason to believe that you would be any more successful than last night in wresting information from me."

"You are quite right. I have none," Varcourt said.

His heavy features were inscrutable even to Em's skills, but she pursued a growing certainty. "You came in like that because you wanted to settle the score, didn't you? To prove to yourself that you were still in control, that last night had been your own idea." A spasm passed across his face, gone so quickly that she almost missed it. Em weighed her choices, forcing herself to be dispassionate, and she suppressed the surge of relief as she decided upon telling the truth. "Last night was my idea. No amount of revision can change that. Even though you took advantage of the range and limits of my experience, I invited. I initiated. You cannot change that."

That stung him. "You seemed eager enough for it. I suppose that is how you came to be here—couldn't keep your skirts down and so got tossed out on your ear. Who was your first? Was it your dashing tutor? The drawing master? Or was it the gardener's boy? One with little knowledge and no skill, for certain."

Damn him. He knew how to cut, too. The memories welled up—her fear, the man's bad breath and pawing hands. The truth would hurt him as he'd meant to hurt her, and she traded wound for wound. "It was my landlord. I had arrived in London friendless, and I found rooms in an inexpensive but reputable boarding house. I had not been there two weeks when my landlord seized my things and threatened to tell Scotland Yard that I was a thief if I protested."

"Were you?" He seemed unable to help the question.

"Of course not. But who would believe me over a pillar of the community? I did not know what to do. He had seized every source of material wealth that I owned—I didn't even have enough for another meal. He gave me a different option, though: I could give myself to him, and he would return my property. A decent woman would have thought her life was worth her virtue. I did not consider it wise to be decent." Then, when her monthly flow had been delayed, she feared that it had been for naught, that she had merely doomed herself and a babe to an even more miserable death. The sound of the Thames filled her ears, the soft plash of rising tidewaters turning to a roar in her mind. . . .

"And such was your induction into the world of carnal delights," he said, his eyes narrow—narrowed to hide how much her words had affected him.

"It was not as bad, perhaps, as it should have been," she said, pulling herself from those burning thoughts. She had stepped away from that parapet, and the next morning, she had wept in gratitude to find her flow restored—and then constructed the scheme that she was still working within. "He fancied himself something of a Casanova, it seemed, and my imperviousness to his blandishments had provoked him to action."

"And then what did you do?"

She raised her eyebrows. "He returned my things. I left. I came here. I began a new life—in which I played the seducer far more subtly and skillfully than that buffoon could imagine."

Varcourt looked at her for a long moment, his eyes raking across her body. She did not pull at the cords. She had no energy to do so. There had been no reason not to give him that much of the truth, and at this point there were very compelling reasons to try to win over his sympathy by doing so, but she had not anticipated that it would cost her so much. She felt spent, wrung out in a way that the events of the previous night could not cause.

"What do you want?" His voice was so soft that it took Em a moment to realize that she had heard it.

"I want to go home." That, too, was honesty, every word of it aching with desire. Which home, though—that he could never guess.

"And with me? What do you want of me and my family?"

"Faith." The most difficult and intangible thing of all.

Varcourt's heavy features tightened. "So that you can do what you please to us?"

"I want to do nothing to your family. Yes, I need your mother now. But no, I shall not hurt her in any way. I thought I was saving her from you. She's so frightened—"

"She has no reason to be!" he said, cutting her off.

His face was open, pained, and she forced herself to gather her wits to take the opening that offered. "Are you an innocent man, then?"

"Innocent of murder." His voice dropped, his gaze going abstracted. "I must be."

That trace of doubt—there it was, the missing piece. She would use it, but not now. Her own confessions had been water on fertile soil, then; she had not given away those parts of herself for nothing. She closed her eyes to hide the jolt of emotions that went through her.

"And what do you want of this, between us, right now?"

She opened her eyes. His face was close above her, leaning over, his lips a breath away. She knew the answer that he wanted—the answer that, so traitorously, her own baser self wanted, too.

Em knew that this encounter would not be so easily shut away. With her mind rubbed raw, she had no defenses left. It would be a release from the emotions that had knotted them each, separately, into such misery. And it would join them, him to her but also her to him.

But it was also the surest way—and it might be her only way.

She arched slightly against the sheets and brought her lips up to meet his.

Chapter Eight

Thomas took her mouth, pressing her head back into the pillow. He had starved for this—for days, months, years. The carefully controlled, carefully managed affairs he'd had left him empty in a way he had not quite understood. Her lips were soft, but her mouth was not. It took, and just as insistently, it gave, demanding that he have her there, now.

Heat seared through his body, through his spine, sending more blood to his erection. He yanked the sheath from his pocket and broke the kiss long enough to spit into the small well at the tip. Esmeralda's eyes had opened as he pulled away; she stared at him, transfixed.

"This is why I had you lick it," he said, and he put the wet side of the sheath over the tip of his penis and rolled it down the shaft.

"What does it do?" She look startled as soon as she uttered those words, her green eyes widening—she had not meant to ask such an ingenuous question.

He smiled tightly. "Lubrication."

Her lips formed a small O, and he stifled them with his own, moving half over her, half next to her, ignoring the part of him that warned that he was sealing his fate. He kissed her mouth again, whether to stop her or himself from speaking, he did not know. He cupped a breast, teasing it with his fingers. He felt her catch her breath against his lips, sending another spike of desire through him. The skin of her throat was impossibly delicate under his lips and teeth, and she shuddered against him as he moved downward, arching against the bonds that held her fast.

"If you tell me to stop, I shall," he said. "Say it now, for I'll not flagellate myself with having forced you later. This is your only chance."

"If I were going to, I would have done so already," she said.

"Good," he said, and then he covered her naked breast with his mouth, pulling on her nipple with his teeth until it grew as hard as a pebble. She gasped and moved against him, and he would swear that this was the first time she had experienced such sensation. Thomas' mind swirled with all the things he would do to her, show her, teach her—the first rough lesson was just the opening to a new world. But he slammed a door on those thoughts as soon as he recognized them. He would share nothing with this woman except what he must.

What he must—and what they had right there, at that moment.

He released her, moved to the other breast. Thomas rounded it slowly, working his way in. He could feel her pulling against her silken bonds, the muscles beneath her breasts tightening helplessly as he moved across her delicate flesh with his lips, teeth, and tongue. Her nipple hardened, formed an impossibly tight bud. He teased her pale pink areola with his tongue, circling the knot at the center as she panted and strained.

He could do anything to her, he thought with fierce satisfaction. Anything at all, and she could not stop him.

He wanted to make her scream.

He took her nipple hard in his mouth, his tongue scraping across it as he suckled it. Her back arched, pushing toward him, and a strangled whimper came from her throat.

He pulled back far enough to see her face. "You can stifle it now, but I will have you crying out in pleasure before this is over."

"Why?" she panted, rocking her head against the bed.

"Because I can," he said.

"You could just take, too," she said. "That would prove your power just as well. Why do you care what I feel—or don't? Are you doing it to please me or punish me?"

God, how much of an innocent was she? No virgin, certainly no virgin, but neither had she ever had the enjoyment of a sensitive lover. Was frank coercion the closest she'd ever come to a proper seduction? His stomach tightened at that thought. But he would show her no mercy. She deserved no mercy. "Because," he said, an answer that was a nonanswer. "Just because." Because yes, he wanted to prove his control—but his need to see her pleasure, to see her soul stripped bare to his, was just as strong. He needed to know what it was in her that drove him to need her, to make him desire so fervently to believe in and save her. Then maybe he could break free.

She shuddered again, but her expression was of sensual anticipation rather than disgust.

He held two fingers up to her lips. "Second chance to prove yourself," he said.

She looked like she wanted to ask another question, but her jaw tightened for a moment, and she kept her silence even as her gaze remained riveted upon him.

"Aren't you even going to ask what I mean?" he said. He moved the two fingers across her lips. "Lick them. I know you know how to do that. Show me how you undid the untried youths."

Green sparks flared deep in her eyes. "Your spies."

"Indeed." He raised an eyebrow. "Your talent with your tongue had me fooled for a while. I've heard you brought men to their knees. Wherever you picked that up, it is a trick that has served you well."

"You heard an exaggeration." But gently, with acute self-consciousness, her gaze moved from his face to his hand. The pale pink tip of her tongue parted her lips, then flicked out delicately, moving across his fingertips. With an expression of complete concentration, she moved down the length of his fingers, sliding along the outside and then pushing them apart to rasp against the delicate webbing between them. Did she have any idea what that did to a man, where else he imagined that little pink tongue moving, tasting? Lust heated him, tightening his loins and sending throbbing heat to his erection. He could not hold off from taking her much longer. Her eyes went half-lidded as she worked, and Thomas found himself almost mesmerized against his will. She changed the position of her mouth, and suddenly, she was drawing his fingers into it, sucking against them as she moved her tongue around and between, using her breath to cool him before taking him again into the soft heat.

Finally, he drew back with a long, shuddering breath. She tugged at the bonds that held her to the frame.

"That is the best I can do without my hands," she said, her gaze veiled behind her eyelashes.

"It is plenty," he said with a swallowed curse.

"And that was . . . more lubrication?" she asked, her voice so small and soft that it was almost a whisper.

"Yes," Thomas said. "Oh yes."

He slid his damp hand down across the valley of her small, firm breasts and her tight belly, then between her thighs, which loosened at his touch. Most of her skin was still chilly against his own warm body, but between her legs, she throbbed with heat. Her short, springy curls were still damp with the perfumed oil he had put on her the previous night, its scent mingling with the heady smell of her femininity to send hot jolts of need spearing through him. His torture of her was turning into torture of himself—but he would press on for a while yet.

His wet fingers parted her curls, separating her folds. He shifted his hand. Her thighs tightened momentarily before opening under his touch.

"Lubrication for this," he said. And he slid his fingers in with a strong stroke, down to the third knuckle.

Her hiss of breath had a moan in it, and her hips tilted upward, toward him. He thrust his fingers into her again, moving them against the slick walls, and her body jerked. She moaned again, more loudly, clamping her jaw down on the end of the sound to muffle it. He moved his thumb up, against the hard knot of flesh just beneath her pale curls. She whimpered through closed lips as he set his thumb against it. Her vulnerability drove him onward.

"You shall scream," he promised, and then he began to move it in rhythm with his fingers, testing her, pressing her, until he found the rhythm that forced her breath into more and more ragged gasps, her hips thrusting mindlessly into his hand as he watched her through narrowed eyes. The rush was incredible, watching her pant and writhe against the white sheets, her head arched back and eyes staring sightlessly at the ceiling. *She* was incredible, like no woman he'd known, fighting her body with every ounce of her will while her very resistance sent it even more precipitously toward the edge. In this moment, he owned her, controlled every ragged breath and whimper. But a part of him feared that in his very possession of her, he was in danger of losing himself.

He took her with his mouth, sliding from her lips to her body, moving against her neck and breasts. His erection throbbed in rhythm with her shuddering body, clinging to the edge. Mercilessly, he pushed her over into the climax, and she made a thin sound that started as whistling air but ended in a ragged, choked scream.

"Just like that," he ground out.

He could wait no longer. He moved to cover her, his hips pushing between her thighs as he rose, his erection following the slick path of her wetness up and into her so that he was sheathed root deep. Her body arched hard toward him, her fingers tightening impotently in their bonds. With her thighs, she urged him harder into her, until she lay spread and panting with her hips ground up against his.

She was so hot that he was almost undone at once. The damp, muscular walls inside her still pulsed with the tremors of her last climax. He rode them, finding the rhythm that made them continue, reinforced them as she rocked, gasping and whimpering, beneath him.

Her thighs came up to clasp him to her, then slid nerveless from his flanks as a new wave of contractions within her gripped him, pulling at him, urging him to spend himself. She arched hard and cried out again as she came, the fine muscles under the thin skin of her upper arms standing out as she strained against her bonds. She pulled away, fighting the intensity of what he was doing to her, fleeing the unremitting power of the climax. But he could feel in her body how much further she could go.

"Not yet," he said through gritted teeth, denying her relief, and he pushed her harder, further, until tears mingled with her inarticulate cries of pleasure and her body felt like a furnace around him, so tight that he could not think, so slick that he forgot the rubber that clung to him. Only then did he let himself go, coming hard, the force of his climax jolting up through his spine to the top of his head until blackness closed in at the edges of his vision.

Then he was kissing her, her mouth, her forehead, kissing the tears from her cheeks, babbling nonsense in a low, intense murmur as she lay with sudden complete limpness beneath him. *Idiot,* his mind railed against him. *Fool.* But in stripping her control, he'd sacrificed his, too, and it was a full minute before he could wrest back conscious command of his own body and roll sideways, off her, so that he was balanced precariously on the edge of the narrow bed.

"What was that about?" she finally said, her voice trembling and breathless.

"Just what I promised," he said. He stripped the sheath from his penis and let it fall damply to the floor. Some remaining insanity made him add, "And just the beginning." But it wasn't the beginning of anything. It couldn't be. There was nothing between them except opposition.

"But I don't understand," she said, and her voice was so pathetic that Thomas rolled over to look at her.

She lay bonelessly against the bed, her skin so pale that even the white sheets could not make it seem dusky, except for the feverish pink of her cheeks and lips, echoed in the brightness in her eyes. Dried tear tracks ran down into her hair, but her eyes were clear and bright—the tears of ecstasy did not leave the same bloodshot traces as pain and sorrow.

She was, he realized abruptly, the most heartrendingly beautiful woman that he had ever seen. And she was his enemy. He must remember that.

"There is nothing to understand," he said aloud. "There is nothing to be understood."

She just shook her head slowly from side to side. "Let me go, Lord Varcourt. I don't know what you are looking for, but you shan't find it between my legs."

The words were far too close to the warning that the more practical parts of his own brain had been trying to telegraph him for the past hour. *I can't. Not yet,* said one desperate corner of his mind, and he didn't know what it wanted more—answers about her purpose with his family or her body. Aloud, he said, "I know."

Then came a knock on the outer door.

Chapter Nine

Thomas pushed off the bed and pulled his dressing gown around him. With a quick look at Esmeralda, whose face was once again expressionless, he tied the sash around his waist and stepped out of the room, shutting the door behind him.

The knock came again, more sharply this time. He strode to the outer door, scraping the hair from his eyes. He tried the knob, then remembered belatedly that his key was missing. He spied it, lying half under the edge of the door, and retrieved it, opening the door just as the man on the other side raised his hand to knock again.

It was Lord Edgington, as cool and impeccably groomed as always.

Thomas tensed and stepped aside. "Come in, Edgington. I wasn't expecting a visitor so early." He did nothing to hide the edge in his words.

Blithely, Edgington crossed the threshold, removing his coat, hat, and gloves. "Varcourt." His golden gaze raked Thomas up and down. "Where did you put the chit?"

"I haven't the slightest notion of what you're talking about," Thomas said, folding his arms across his chest.

Edgington just snorted. Dropping his outerwear upon the console, he strode across the room, throwing open the door to Thomas' bedroom. Unabashed by the lack of discovery that it yielded him, he crossed to the door to his valet's bedroom. He swung the door open, took one look at the woman on the bed, and then closed it again.

"Untie her, please, Varcourt, and tell her to dress," he said, returning to the middle of the parlor, where he planted himself in front of the hearth. "The constable will be coming soon, and the more decent the front you can give, the better it will go for you."

"Who the bloody hell has called the constable?" Thomas demanded.

"How should I know?" Edgington said, raising an eyebrow. "Gifford? Colin Radcliffe? Half the dinner party knew you went haring off after that spiritualist when Lady Hamilton collapsed, and when you brought her here . . ." He shook his head. "You must be mad, man, with the debate on the Reform Bill as hot as it is. It's even keeping the season alive past its time."

Thomas did not ask how Edgington found out that he had taken Esmeralda to his rooms. He had a very good idea.

Thomas grunted and turned his back on the man, retrieving the woman's clothes from the sofa before entering his valet's bedchamber. He shut the door behind him. Esmeralda lay naked as he had left her, curled upon the bed with her face buried in the mattress.

"It is I," he said, setting the clothes down on a chair and stepping toward her.

She turned to look at him.

"I apologize for Edgington's intrusion," Thomas said stiffly, feeling it was necessary to say something. "There didn't seem to be a discreet way to stop the man."

"I heard him coming," Esmeralda said. And she had hidden her face, as if her nudity otherwise meant nothing.

Thomas compressed his lips. There had been a time, he was certain, when she had possessed a full measure of natural modesty. Had her coercive landlord taken that much from her, that she no longer cared who saw her body displayed before him? Or had it been more insidious? He took his knife from his pocket and began to cut the bonds around her pale wrists, working carefully to keep from cutting her or further tightening the silk.

Most girls he knew would have chosen the path of virtue—not from an excess of delicacy but because such a proposition would have shocked them so deeply that they could not have managed to imagine that they could accept it, even if they might later bitterly regret such temperance. Something, though, had broken through the gentle, sheltered life in which Esmeralda had certainly been raised. And if someone else had broken it, Thomas must have ground its shards to dust. . . .

He cut off that thought.

"I overheard your conversation," Esmeralda continued.

"Then I shan't be obliged to summarize it. Why did you not scream for help when I first let him in? Modesty forbid you?"

She cocked her head to the side. "I assumed whoever it was would be your associate."

He paused as the first knot gave under his knife, freeing one of her wrists. She pulled it loose and instantly began working on the second with her fingers.

"And because you don't want anyone to see your face," he guessed. "How can it be that important to you?"

"It is that important," she said tightly, and he noted the missing words of the echo. Not just important to her— important in an absolute sense.

"You don't want anyone to know who you are," he prompted.

She smiled toothily as her other wrist came free. "Three

cheers for milud!" She adopted a clumsy cockney accent. "He's uncovered a true mystery, he has!" She sat up, rubbing her wrists.

Thomas ignored her. "Your clothes," he said, nodding to the pile as he rose.

"I'm surprised you didn't burn them, just to make sure I couldn't leave." She pulled the ragged remains of her chemise closed. "I can get dressed on my own. Go see to the baron. I don't want any more trouble from the constable than you do."

Thomas hesitated, wondering if she spoke the truth.

She picked up her corset, and her smile had a feral edge. "I would give my life for the game I am playing. The small satisfaction of seeing you taken away in a Black Maria is a paltry thing next to that."

Thomas gave her a curt nod and left, shutting the door behind her.

Edgington was sitting on the sofa, turning his cane between two flat palms and watching the brass eagle upon its handle twirl. He looked up as Thomas entered the parlor.

"I don't know what you were doing with her in there, but I do not like it," he said flatly.

Thomas glared at him, leaning against the chimneypiece. Edgington had never been a friend of his, not even in boyhood, though now they were at least nominal political allies. "It's a private matter. She's dragging my mother into something deep."

"Things can become a matter of public interest with remarkable celerity these days, particularly when those things are sufficiently tawdry," Edgington returned.

Thomas snorted. "And who began that?"

Edgington ignored him. "I fail to see the connection between your mother and what I saw in there, and I don't doubt that any other impartial observer would share that particular blindness, never mind those who wish you ill." Edgington's hand tightened, and the cane abruptly stopped whirling. "What did you do? Yank her into your carriage, take her back to your flat, tie her up, and have your way with her?"

Edgington's tone betrayed nothing, but Thomas had the sense that his answer could end up being very dangerous indeed. He tamped down on an angry response. "I swear to you that I did not rape her," he answered tightly.

"And the ropes were her idea too, yes?" Edgington said with deep sarcasm. "Never mind. It is enough for you to know that my wife has some interest in the welfare of Esmeralda."

"Her name is not Esmeralda, and you know it," Thomas returned.

"Nevertheless," Edgington said evenly.

"I haven't seen Lady Edgington even speak to the woman. What interest does she have in her well-being?" Thomas pushed.

"My wife does not believe in spiritualists. However, she does believe in desperate—and reckless—young women. Suffice it to say that the baroness has invested some resources in keeping the girl safe. She seems to be convinced that Esmeralda is harmless. Mostly harmless, at any rate," he amended. "That is enough for me to take her interests somewhat to heart myself."

The implied warning was clear. "I see. What if, by some chance, she were threatening Lady Edgington rather than inciting her pity?"

Edgington smiled the disconcerting smile of which he was a master, golden charm and bloodless ice in equal parts. "That, old boy, would be an entirely different matter."

There was another knock on the door.

"I believe that will be the constable," Edgington said easily. "I will try to forestall him for a while so that you may at least get some pants on. Protestations of innocence are so much more believable when one is fully clothed."

With that, Edgington crossed to the door, leaving Thomas to duck inside his bedroom before he heard the latch lift and the baron issue a cool greeting as the rough tones of the constable identified him.

Thomas started to pull on a fresh shirt and trousers—and then, after a moment's thought of how Merry must look in her own bedraggled gown, chose last night's attire instead. It would be harder to assert the innocuousness of their activities if he looked freshly changed while she was in the wreck of her clothing from the night before.

He paused at his dressing mirror long enough to comb his hair back into place. As he did so, he heard the door to the bedroom next to his swing open, and Merry's voice came, speaking in chilly tones.

"Good morning, officer."

The constable said something indistinct, and she replied, "I met a misfortune on the road, and Lord Varcourt was kind enough to rescue me. He requested a number of readings of me, which I was glad to give in return for his service—I am a spiritualist, you see—and I am afraid that we rather lost track of time. Only when Lord Edgington came did we realize that morning had come."

Thomas took that as his cue and stepped out of his bedchamber. Esmeralda was standing with her back very straight, her torn veil falling to her breasts and covering her face and the ruin of her hair. The dupioni was wrinkled and stained, but she looked as much of a lady as his own mother ever did. The police officer wilted before that chilly regality.

"May I help you, constable?" Thomas asked with every demonstration of politesse.

The man stood near the door, swaying with his hat grasped in his hands. "I'm not very well sure, sir. Is this lady 'ere telling the truth?"

"I believe that she has laid out the main points quite clearly," Thomas said, wary not to be lured into a direct lie.

"Well." The man cleared his throat. "Well," he said again, "the lady looks well enough. Would you like to file a report about your accident, miss?"

"No, I don't think so. I saw nothing of the ruffians who would like to have assaulted me, so I doubt it'd be any use, and it would all be such a bother."

"I'll just be going then, eh?" He hesitated again, looking her up and down as if searching for hidden signs of coercion and distress.

"Let me see you down," Esmeralda said, interposing herself so smoothly that Thomas could think of no reaction before she was halfway to the door. "I was just leaving myself."

"I surely would appreciate dat, miss," the man said, looking relieved. "A bachelor's flat is no place for a lady."

"You're quite right," she murmured, looking over her shoulder at Thomas. "It was quite thoughtless of me to come."

With that, she left, and the constable shut the door behind her.

Thomas let out an explosive breath of air, turned on his heel, and strode into his bedroom.

"You wouldn't care to tell me what this is all about, would you?" said Edgington levelly from the sofa.

"I don't believe I would," said Thomas, throwing off his dressing gown and quickly stripping off the previous night's clothes.

"You're going after her, aren't you?"

"Of course," Thomas snapped. "I wasn't done with her."

"*Be* done," Edgington said. "I wouldn't know where you'd think you were going, anyhow. I doubt she'd return to her flat now."

"She's a lone woman wearing an expensive but bedraggled

evening gown at"—he fished his pocket watch out of his waistcoat pocket—"nine o'clock in the morning. Of course she'll go home."

Edgington looked as if he wanted to say something, and he paused before finally saying, "I hope you know what you're doing."

"So do I," Thomas replied, jerking on a fresh vest. "So do I."

Thomas stood in the darkness at the top of the landing and pushed open the broken door.

Esmeralda whirled away from the trunk she was packing. She wore a light gray walking dress now, with a new veil in a darker gray that was lifted from her face to fall behind her and brush her shoulder blades. Her expression was so weary that it took him like a punch to the gut before he could steel himself. Then her face became carefully bland, and he wondered if he'd imagined it.

"Go away," she said distinctly, then turned back to her task of shoving everything mobile into the trunk.

As he folded his arms and leaned against the doorframe, Thomas took the opportunity to survey the room. The parlor was small, the walls covered with glaringly new peacock wallpaper and hung with curtains in shades of red, blue, and gold that seemed calculated to create a sense of exoticism. The very deliberateness made it fail for him.

Why am I here? he asked himself. He'd given up on the hope that he could somehow wrest the answers he wanted from her at his rooms. Yet he'd been drawn here, so strongly that he hadn't thought to fight it, to question it until this moment, when he stood facing her, and he realized he had nothing left to threaten or promise.

"You don't want to leave this flat," he said eventually.

She snorted, not even looking at him. "Considering where you are standing, that is a very foolish thing to say.

Are you planning on kidnapping me again? I have a feeling that this time, you will have an audience for the act."

Tory spies. Hell, for that matter, Edgington's own spies. Thomas had no doubt that there was more than one person lurking outside the Gypsy tavern, watching for him with far too much interest.

"All the more reason for you to stay," he said. "I can do nothing to you here now."

"I have told you all I can," she said.

"I doubt it," he returned flatly. What was the motivation for some cast-off, gently bred daughter to play games with his mother? Esmeralda was all show and dazzle—there must be some darker substance behind the puppet that she represented that was directing it all.

Her face betrayed no reaction, which he took as a bad sign. He was beginning to wonder if she herself weren't her own puppet master, as she claimed. But if so, to what end? He could not wrap his mind around it. She turned back to her packing, her movements stiff.

"That doubt was not the only reason you followed me," she said finally.

He straightened. "What other reason could I have?"

"Reasons. Two of them. First, you are interested in my offer of assistance concerning your brother's death." Her voice was completely level, but Thomas' heart squeezed hard inside his chest. "Second, you are yet hungry for me. I suppose there is a self-destructive streak in you that I did not anticipate, as you will find nothing but your end in me now."

Thomas ignored her second assertion, unwilling to examine it. "What could you possibly discover about Harry's death that I do not already know?" He made his words flat and ugly. "On the day he died, I left him at the streamside, screaming his head off because the horse had splashed water on him. Six hours later, he was found drowned one hundred yards away. Everyone knows the story. At a distance of twelve years, I doubt there is anything more to be discovered."

"Nothing more to be discovered that is not already known, perhaps," she returned swiftly. "But there are secrets that were never spoken aloud. There were many people there that day—you may not have been the last to see him just as you were not the first to find him, after. If different people hold different secrets, as I know your mother does, the pattern of truth may be hidden among them. I am very, very good at getting secrets from people without them ever realizing that they are telling me anything. That is the measure of my unnatural abilities. You may be exonerated by it." She shrugged. "Or damned, as the case may be."

"The truth will not convict me of this," he said, his teeth gritted.

Her light eyes grew frigid, boring into him. "What will it convict you of, then?"

"Many things," he said. "I have committed many sins— but not that."

"Tell me."

He opened his mouth—then closed it again, hard. "It is none of your business."

"If you want the truth, it must be my business. I know scarcely more of your brother's death than the gossipmongers. I must know truth to get more truth." Her face was expressionless. "This is your moment to decide. Tell me and stop interfering with what I do, and in return, I will give you the truth. Or keep your own counsel, continue to hound me, and never know. Choose."

He stood in the doorway, wavering. His duty to the Whigs was clear—he must not sacrifice their objectives to his private desires. But did he belong to them? Was he not his own man, with his own needs? His own demons to be battled? She could be lying, stringing him along for her own purposes. Or she could be offering everything, even though her own intent was far from pure.

He felt the shadows pressing in on him as he had not in a long time, the hard-won control slipping slowly from him and pushing him, inexorably, into chaos. This woman before him was not the ultimate cause, for she had merely revealed what had always been there, lurking. . . .

Choose.

"I accept your agreement," he said stiffly.

There was a tiny movement in her shoulders. Was it relief? Victory? Her eyes only glittered more brightly.

"Tell me, then," she said in a whisper. "Tell me about those sins. Tell me about that day—all of it, for once in your life."

He stared at her, struggling to find the words that he'd never spoken before. . . . To his enemy. For surely she must still be. Was he arming her? Or was he doing what he must to save himself? But he could not be arming her, no matter how much the explanation felt like a betrayal of himself and his family, for he would not tell her anything that anyone could not find out, if they only asked the right people.

"You must understand what Harry was," he said slowly. "Everything he was. He was my brother." That word hurt. "He had always been . . . not right. Not an idiot, though many would have you believe that. He was brilliant, in a narrow way. He knew the bloodlines of every horse in the stables back as far as the records lasted, from memory—he'd taken over the breeding of them when he was eight, and he was amazing at it. He made money, a tidy sum of it, out of what for most gentlemen is simply an expense. In the last twenty years, more than a third of the winners of the Ascot came from our stables. And trains—at seven, he had every train schedule in Middlesex memorized. He'd draw up maps to imaginary countries and spend hours coming up with their train tables." The memories brought back old bitterness, old resentments, as much as it did fondness.

"So he was no idiot," she prompted.

"But he was not right." He scraped his hand through his hair to conceal how unsteady it was. "He could not manage with the world. He had schedules, just like his imaginary trains, and if anything did not fit, he would fall apart. If his breakfast was late, or his socks needed darning, or someone came to visit when they were not supposed to or did not come when they were expected . . . he could not manage."

Esmeralda gazed at him steadily, without judgment. "Many people are inflexible," she offered.

"No. An inflexible person becomes irritated or even angry. He . . . disintegrated. It tore him to pieces, hour after hour. Life isn't predicable, and he could never reconcile himself to that, though God knows almost everyone in the house tried to help him at one point. Mealtimes away from the nursery were a nightmare—his diet consisted of exactly six things."

"Children are often picky."

"*Six* things, Esmeralda. He was eighteen when he died, for God's sake, not four. Father tried to bring him down to the table once a year until he was thirteen. He wouldn't touch anything, and when Father tried to insist, he would begin screaming and throwing things. Father had him locked in the night nursery—he'd tried to move him to his own room, but he'd gone hysterical about that, too—with nothing but a plate of food and water, and he stayed there for five days without touching the food before Father gave up. You couldn't put him into a proper suit. He couldn't talk to someone he hadn't known for a long time, and even then, he didn't talk like a normal person. He couldn't be the earl. He wasn't capable of it. He was brilliant, but something in his head was broken." The words came more easily now.

"What happened the day he died?"

Thomas stopped. There were things he had never confessed, never intended to confess—nor would he now to her. He could not trust this woman, not her or her offer. Even if she was lying, she could at least do little damage with what he planned to say—not with the prevalence of far darker suspicions. It hardly even counted as a risk.

He spoke. "It was a house party. All the young people decided to go for a ride. My father the earl insisted that Harry come, too, and as usual, I was tasked with watching him. At first, everyone stayed together. Then someone declared a steeplechase, and we all strung out along the route. Harry was last. He would not race. We came to a stream that was too big for the horse to jump. The water splashed onto his coat as his mount began to cross, and he started screaming as it soaked through, and refused to continue."

"He was frightened of water?" she asked.

Thomas leaned back against the doorframe. It was strangely like the inquest, all over again. Normal people always asked the same questions and struggled with the answers because they made no sense to anyone except for Harry himself. "No, quite the reverse. He had too little fear of it—he was incapable of judging depth, for one, and once walked off the end of a pier because he saw some floating sticks. He hated his clothes getting wet in some areas and not in others. Bone dry or entirely soaked was fine with him—but the splashing made him furious."

"What happened?"

"I left him. He'd been whining all along, complaining about the heat, the smell of the horse, the food we'd packed for lunch. I'd grown sick of it, so I told him to follow me across or find his own way home. When I arrived back home, he'd not returned, so most of those who rode turned out to look for him. My father found his body lying in the stream. He had slipped and cracked his skull on a rock."

Her gaze was unblinking, a void that sucked at him,

pulling more from him than he meant to say. "The more details of that day that you can give me, the better I can use
them to bring forth confidences in others."

"I understand," he said stiffly, but he added nothing more.

She stared at him again for several seconds more, and he
could almost believe that she could see more than ordinary
mortals. Then she seemed to shake herself slightly. "I shall
also need a guest list, of course."

He inclined his head. "I think I can remember well
enough."

"Then I suppose I shall start tomorrow, at Lady James'
séance."

He frowned. "I've heard nothing of that."

"I doubt you would be invited," she said drily.

Thomas paused. "What do you want in return?"

"It is a bargain, isn't it? My own heart's desire—that you
leave me in peace—for yours." Her face twisted in a bitter
parody of a smile.

"It had better be worth it."

Her eyes were green ice. "To both of us."

"You will not leave these rooms?" he pressed.

She sighed, the brittle mask crumbling, and scrubbed her
face with the back of a hand, the first human movement she
had made since he had arrived. "For now, I will not leave. It
is a truce."

"A truce," he echoed, and he turned and walked out the
door.

Chapter Ten

Em sagged as the door closed behind him. She hadn't believed that he would demand more of her there, not really, but she still harbored a marrow-deep fear of him that she could not escape. What kind of man was he? She could not encompass him, and that scared her most of all. Most people were simple souls, each as individual as a flower's blossom, but ultimately of an easily identifiable type. Lord Varcourt escaped such classification. *Sui generis,* she thought, the Latin phrase curling into her mind from another life.

A life that she was determined to regain. She rubbed her cheeks with the heels of her hands, trying through the friction of flesh to return some blood flow to her sluggish brain. He had shaken her. There was no other word for it. She had hated and feared him, and then she had not quite hated and feared him as her body craved his touch, and now that hatred was twisting inside her, changing even as she tried to keep hold of it.

It was all so simple when she had been able to see him as nothing more than an obstacle or, possibly, an enemy. But the starkness of his face as he told the story of his brother's last day had lashed her like a whip, and it was too hard to keep hold of that simple picture. She kept returning to the memory of his eyes as he spoke those colorless words. . . .

She was committed now, thrown into an alliance of sorts with him, whether she wished it or not. It had been her idea, her decision, and it had seemed so rational at the time. Now she had the sudden sick certainty that getting further enmeshed with this man would prove to be the biggest mistake of her life.

Hamilton House. It lorded over its two acres under a slaty sky, rearing up through the fog at arrogant angles. Thomas rode up to it with a sense of inevitability. The entire neighborhood of Wirthing Green was Lord Edgington's property, and the rents he received from the land must mount to a staggering sum. Farther out from the City than most of the fashionable districts, only now were the first of the garden districts and professional suburbs nibbling at its borders. Yet it was close enough to the heart of London to have lured away those who sought houses larger and grander than the Georgian row houses of Belgravia of their forefathers—often grander even than the new stuccoed mansions of Belgravia Square itself.

Lord Hamilton, typically, had wanted nothing but the best, and upon his father's death, he had found the perfect wife and had built the perfect house in swift succession. Hamilton House was the culmination of everything the man was, with its bleak gray walls and jagged crenellations. Romantics built castlelike homes full of warmth and brave simplicity, but Lord Hamilton's monstrosity was as cold and hard inside as it was out.

The dark gravel crunched under his mount's hooves as Thomas guided the animal around to the mews. The stable boy came tumbling out at the sound of his approach and took the horse's reins with a muffled "Milud," as Thomas dismounted. Slapping his gloves against his thigh, Thomas strode toward the entrance to the conservatory. His father had scorned the delicate glass and iron traceries that most Englishmen now sought, choosing instead a heavy stone design that the broad plate glass windows could do nothing to soften.

He swung open a French window and passed through. In the chinoiserie parlor he stopped as his sisters froze on their perch on a delicate settee and looked up at him guardedly with two pairs of identical bright green eyes.

"Why are you here?" Elizabeth asked, smiling in a way that she probably thought looked adoring. It didn't, and it did nothing to hide the waspishness of her voice.

Thomas feared that he knew the reason only too well. He had always been the only one to exert a restraining influence over the twins. His father scarcely acknowledged the existence of such things as daughters, and his mother simply indulged their every whim. The somewhat ineffectual influence of their nurses and governesses had been little better. At least they were too good-natured to have become brats, he assured himself, though they were well on their way to becoming hellions, instead. "What are you two up to this time?"

Mary blushed bright scarlet, but Elizabeth made a face, edging slightly in front of her sister. "Nothing at all, dear Thomas. I am merely expressing a sisterly interest in your activities."

"You are wondering, rather, if I have a brotherly interest in yours," he said wearily. "Have no fear, Liza. I haven't come to spoil your games this time. At least not until I find out what they are," he added, in order to crush the dawning speculation in her eyes.

"Oh, Thomas, you are such a stick in the mud," Elizabeth said, putting on pretence of a pout.

He snorted. "You forget that you two are grown women

now. The pranks of children are easily forgotten, but a lady who has no discretion can easily shame herself."

"We haven't yet," said Mary.

Thomas shook his head. "Where is our mother?"

"You forgot to ask us to spy on her today," Elizabeth said with a touch of malice, "so I neglected to keep track of her every word and move."

"She hadn't left the breakfast room, last I saw her," Mary interposed before Thomas could respond. "Do you wish to speak to her?" He could hear the muffled hope in her voice.

Speak to her—about what? They'd had nothing to speak about for years now. He attended every family function at which he was expected to come and play the heir, and moved his mouth to make appropriate sounds to his parents, but except for the occasional political strategy sessions that Lord Hamilton assembled in his oak-paneled library, he hadn't exchanged anything more substantial than pleasantries with them in years.

But Mary would not understand what held him back and made him keep his cool reserve. "I shall talk to her later," he said instead, and then he left the room. Upstairs, he opened his mother's door. Her dressing room had spilled over the years from its original confines to completely engulf the bedchamber and sitting room, too, pushing her to move her accommodations to another set of rooms down the hall from the suites of the earl and countess. Thomas walked through two rooms crowded with armoires and highboys to the innermost chamber. There, Thomas found her lady's maid, Valette, straightening her mistress' clothing.

"Excuse me," he said coolly as she looked up with an alarmed expression. He brushed past her to open her jewelry boxes, one after another, searching for the garishly enameled necklace that she had worn four nights before.

Valette stood, wringing her hands and uttering ineffectual phrases, clearly torn between defending her mistress and not interfering with the man who would likely become her master. Strings of pearls, intricate lacework metal set with garnets, black smoked steel cut like gems and adorned with jet and hematite, rubies and emeralds in outdated settings—they gleamed in the light shining in low beams through the window. But nowhere was the necklace that he sought.

"What are you doing?" His mother's tremulous voice sounded from the doorway.

"I tried to get him to leave, madam," Valette fluttered. "He would not!"

Thomas cut off the maid with a glance. With a terrified look at her mistress, she fled the room, sending Lady Hamilton's skirts swaying in her passage.

The air was stifling with lavender and his mother's perfume. The ghosts of a hundred teas, a thousand dinners and balls pressed in on him in the forms of the dresses that hung along the walls. His mother looked at him, her blue eyes wide and faded, her hands knotted at her waist with rings glinting below her swollen knuckles.

"This must be six seasons out of date," he said abruptly, seizing the edge of one of the dresses. "You will never wear it again. Why do you keep it here?"

Lady Hamilton entered the room with the queer grace she had developed years before. When he was five, he had taken a bet with a friend that she had wheels rather than legs under her skirts and had been bitterly disappointed at the brief flash of shoes as his mother mounted the steps into a carriage.

His mother touched the dress, a pale yellow tea gown, with delicate, trembling fingers. "It has memories," she said. "I wore this to the afternoon soiree in which I learned that Faith Ashcroft was engaged. I wore it to a tea at which the Duchess of Rushworth served the most exquisite crumpets, and I had to bribe her cook most outrageously for the recipe."

"Why can't you hold those memories in your head, like most people?" he asked wearily.

"My memory is not as . . . reliable . . . as one might wish," she said, fingering the fabric lovingly. "It gets mixed up in the dreams."

"Opium dreams, you mean," Thomas said.

She shrugged. "If I can touch something, feel it, I know that the memories were real." The gaze she turned on him had none of the vagueness of her words. "What are you looking for, Thomas?"

"The necklace that Esmeralda gave you," he said flatly.

She shook her head woefully, her hand straying to the pouch that hung from her chatelaine. "It is mine. She saw it in a vision. It was meant for me."

Thomas bit back a rejoinder. His mother would not believe that Esmeralda had confessed to being a fraud; she would not believe it if Esmeralda told her in as many words. "I will return it to you, if it is possible," he said instead.

"Why do you want to take it at all?" A querulous note entered his mother's voice.

"I want it examined," he said. "Would you not like her to be exonerated?"

"You are the only one to cast aspersions on her in the first place," Lady Hamilton said.

Thomas held out his hand. "Mother."

She tightened her grip on the chatelaine for a moment, staring at him. Then, slowly, she lifted the pouch and opened it, taking out the necklace with two fingers. "I feel that it is an echo of my soul," she whispered as she dropped it into her son's hand.

Thomas' throat tightened. "I will take care of it as if it were such, madam."

She gave him a long, pained look, then turned and glided out.

"There's rosemary, that's for remembrance," he quoted

softly. "Pray, love, remember." But somehow, he could not shake the feeling that his mother was better suited for the role of Hamlet than Ophelia.

He emerged in the hallway to find his father standing there, like his own black shadow. He was a stooped version of Thomas, his hawk-nosed face carved in lines that held sorrow now as well as hauteur. He seemed out of place in the corridor, for though the house had been constructed after his image, as it were, he had retreated from it into the private world of his study, the saloon, and his bedchamber until he seemed like a snail levered from his shell outside of them.

"Do not upset your mother, Varcourt," he said sternly. "It is not worth it."

"It is so much easier just to let her have her way, even to her own destruction, isn't it?" Thomas could not hide his bitterness.

Darkness passed across Lord Hamilton's face. "This is not about what is easy, Thomas. Sometimes doing nothing is the hardest thing of all. Your mother deserves what peace she may find."

"Peace, yes," Thomas said. "I fear that Esmeralda represents an attempt to hurt us through her."

"We all have our Achilles' heels, do we not?" Lord Hamilton paused. "I think you misjudge the situation. Esmeralda may be preying on an old woman—but she is giving your mother the comfort that no one else has. I shall not intervene on your suspicions alone. If you discover credible evidence to support your claims, then I will put a stop to this. Credible evidence, Varcourt," he repeated firmly. "Otherwise let her be."

And Lord Hamilton turned away, retreating with slow deliberation back into the recesses of his study.

Thomas stared after him. "And there is pansies," he murmured. "That's for thoughts."

Chapter Eleven

The coral parlor glowed with afternoon light that poured through the French windows, their broad panes cut from the clearest and flattest modern plate glass. The women sat on divans and low chairs like scattered flowers, lost in the pale froth of their skirts.

Em sat alone, as she always did. Alone and austere, encased in steely blue-gray that hugged her corseted body and the shape of her hoops, streamlined from the ultimate extravagance of two years before. Two others stood out in the gathering of ladies. The frizzy-haired woman looked like a farmer's wife who'd lost her way, wearing an outdated, frumpy gown and burdened with tasteless gewgaws. The black-haired woman matched her in quality of jewelry, but the effect was quite different, for on her it took the form of hundreds of gold bangles and necklaces that clanged with every movement, the costume of how the ignorant thought that Gypsies would dress rather than how they really did.

Em sat in her corner of the room, statue-still, as her heart beat far too hard. Her time was running out now—she could feel it slipping through her fingers. Society, ever fickle, was growing bored with her, and Lady James had brought in these two strangers to liven up the event. If she did not bring matters to a head soon, it would be too late.

I'm not ready, she thought. How much more time did she have? A week? A month? Let it be a month—by then, everything would be settled, one way or another.

These two women, at least, were no competition for her. The faux Gypsy radiated uncertainty, while the farmwife's blatant avarice made the ladies grow cold, their upper lips rising in dainty sneers whenever they looked at her.

Radiant in peacock blue, Lady James moved to the center of the room and clapped her heavily jeweled hands. Two dozen elegantly coifed heads turned, eyes blinking with the correct mixture of polite anticipation and fashionable ennui. Em knew them each, their dreams and secrets ferreted out through the judicious employment of secret information. That was her advantage over the other two spiritualists—the seeds of knowledge from which a tree might be grown.

Some spiritualists hired spies or bribed servants directly, a dangerous business, prone to error and discovery. Em had come by much of hers honestly; for two years, she had sipped the stories Alice brought back from the London season like ambrosia, reading her letters to tatters, and upon Alice's return to the country, whispering for hours when Alice sneaked into the nursery in the evenings, the two of them curled under the dark tent of the quilts as if they were small children again, hiding from Nursie and monsters.

In those days, it had felt as if Alice had become the elder, for Em had been left behind. There had been a place for her in the nursery, so in the nursery she stayed; not for her were presentations to the Queen, London seasons, or debutante balls. In two seasons, Alice had been married; in one more, she was dead.

Lady James was speaking, attempting to school her voice to the proper atmosphere of mystery, but her innate good cheer made the most dramatic announcements sound quite merry even as the soft-footed servants moved from window to window, drawing the curtains tight against the afternoon and leaving the room in peach-hazed dimness.

Em forced herself to pay attention. There were to be two events: a large séance in which the spiritualists would simultaneously attempt to contact the spirit world, followed by private consultations in different corners of the room. Em must vanquish her competitors in the first before turning to her own goal—two very different goals, now that she was investigating the murder of Thomas' brother, as well.

Why she was taking the second one seriously was a thing that she did not care to examine too closely. She could just lie to Lord Varcourt, as she lied to everyone. If anyone deserved it, it was he, for her bargain had been one made under duress. But she felt spurred to deal honestly with him in this manner, reaching for truth with the desperate relief that she could, for once, be true. She was not sure how much that urge had to do with Lord Varcourt and how much with her own continuing struggle with veracity, invention, and falsehood.

Lady James concluded. Em waited three breaths and rose, drawing her skirts about her in a motion calculated to attract even the most unfocused eye.

"We must form a circle," she said, pitching her voice to carry to all corners of the room. Then, moving with great deliberation, she crossed to the wall, where she turned and resumed her motionlessness.

"Of course we must," the farmer's wife said quickly, clearly annoyed at having lost the initiative.

"Circles mean power," the Gypsy intoned.

Lady Mary, sitting close to her mother Lady Hamilton, hid a smile behind a white glove. Em had scored her first mark of the afternoon.

The ladies rose and moved about the room desultorily as the servants shifted the chairs among the ebb and flow of crepe de chine and book muslin skirts, the circle forming silently. In moments, everyone had taken their seats—everyone, that was, except for Em, who stepped forward so that she reached the remaining chair just as the farm woman sat.

All eyes were upon her when she took her seat, two dozen expectant faces waiting for her to begin the proceedings. Lady Hamilton's eagerness was almost pathetic, and Em had to steel herself against the tightness in her gut that she told herself was mere nervousness. She said nothing, her back perfectly straight, the veil not even fluttering with her breath. Every second was counted off by the cartel clock on the wall, its ticks reverberating against its marquetry case. Even the servants at the perimeter of the room caught the unnatural stillness. Finally Lady James shifted slightly as she realized that she was the nominal hostess. Only then did Em raise her chin and speak.

"I can feel the spirits flocking thick around us. We take them in with every breath. They run through our blood and escape in our softest exhalations back into the room."

"Er . . . very good . . ." Lady James said, looking around with alarmed eyes, as if she might see the ghosts hanging there.

"Madame Violca claims great sensitivity to the world beyond the veil, madam," Em said. She had learned the names of her rivals by eavesdropping on Lady James' conversation with her guests; it was possible that the farmwife Mrs. Meade had done the same, but the fake Gypsy was out of her element, shaken by her opulent surroundings and incapable of keeping her wits about her.

Em suspected that she was an unconscious reader—one who excelled in automatically reading the tiny, flickering expressions that passed over people's faces and responding to them without realizing what she was doing. With her senses so overwhelmed here, the faux Gypsy would swiftly betray her inability to commune with any deeper power, and she would go home convinced that the spirits would not come to her if she strayed from her proper place. "Let Madame Violca do the honor of telling us what spirits visit today," she said.

Madame Violca looked up, panic flickering across her face before she covered it in an expression meant to look otherworldly but in reality appeared merely constipated. The guests leaned forward. "I sense a man," she announced, and a small susurration flowed through the assembled women. Her voice gained a little confidence. "He is an older gentleman. A . . . a husband?"

Em felt a small surge of triumph as a negative reaction ran through the ladies. Madame Violca had erred, and badly. Even a stranger should have known there were no widows among this group—there was no black crepe or even the half mourning of gray and violet among the ladies, and no widows caps.

"Not a husband of someone here," Madame Violca said, but it was clear her confidence was shaken. "No, he was another woman's husband. But related to a lady here. Her . . . father? Yes, I feel that it is her father. I am seeing a letter."

Em tensed. Madame Violca had done this in the wrong order. Every reader knew that one should start with the name and then find the relationship. There were many women here, but even if she chose the letter J, there was a chance that not one of their fathers' names was John.

"I am seeing the letter J," Madame Violca went on. "Or maybe it is merely the sound of the letter J. Who does this mean something to? A father and a J."

"My father's name is James," said Faith Weldon, reaching for Lady James' hand.

Madame Violca took in their clasped hands. "No, I do not feel him on the other side."

Crisis averted. Em suppressed her frustration.

"I feel someone else." Madame Violca was gaining some

confidence now. That was a bad thing. It was time to take over.

"It is not a J," Em interposed. "It is an R. Richard. I feel that someone's father had the name Richard." She turned her head in a calculated manner, moving it slowly until she stopped directly before Mrs. Morel. The blond woman treated her with a cynical smile, but after a moment's hesitation, she decided to play along, as Em knew she would.

"That must be my father," Mrs. Morel said in her light, jaded voice.

From there it was an easy task to shut out Madame Violca altogether. Em gave the usual message of contentment on the other side of the veil and then proceeded to warn Mrs. Morel to avoid black-haired Spaniards on her planned trip to Nice.

Madame Violca's bangles clashed unhappily, but she hadn't the nerve to speak up again. The farmer's wife would not be so easily cowed. As soon as Em paused, Mrs. Meade broke in, singling out Mrs. Morel. She was a skilled cold reader, Em had to admit, but her social clumsiness meant that she had no chance. She began to pursue Mrs. Morel's love life—a topic that, at the best of times, was better left unexplored. Mrs. Morel's expression of amusement swiftly became frigid, and the more that Mrs. Meade floundered around, attempting to recover, the more contemptuous the lady grew.

Finally, with a delicate clearing of her throat, Lady James broke in and suggested that the ladies separate into smaller groups now. Em took the opportunity to select her own audience, leaving the others to sort themselves out. She singled out Lady James and two of her daughters, Miss Hawthorne, Lady Mary and Lady Elizabeth Hyde, and, of course, their mother, Lady Hamilton, who had been watching Em with avid eyes all afternoon.

Em drew her small group aside and led them to the

pedestal table that she had already chosen, nestled away in the corner of the room with heavy draperies swathed around two sides. She always chose a pedestal table when she could; they were easiest to rock and provided a much more convincing, subtle tilt.

Lady Hamilton smiled tremulously at her. Em did not smile back—not that the countess could see anything with her face hidden by her veil.

Em had promised Lord Varcourt that she would investigate his brother's death. With her own plans coming so near fruition, it was dangerous to add a second scheme, but she must make an effort. God only knew how good the spies were at Varcourt's disposal, and even without the fear that she might be discovered if she did nothing at all, she had an obscure feeling that she owed him . . . something.

It was a ridiculous thought. She'd done Varcourt no permanent harm, not even in the eyes of his mother, and he'd certainly meant to do her some. But the pain in his voice as he bleakly recounted the day of his brother's death had struck something inside her; that and the battle she could see in his eyes whenever he looked at her. He had tried to scare her, to brutalize her as far as he had the stomach for it, but she had used him as thoroughly as he ever had her. She recognized in him the same reckless desperation to reach a goal that seemed to hold every hope in it. She knew what her own goal was—as for his, she doubted that even he knew.

She stood as the other women fluttered into place with a rustling of lace and silks. As a mere hanger-on, it was expected that she sit last, but she knew how to manipulate convention so that the others felt, however unconsciously, that they were waiting on her. Eight expectant faces turned toward her, young and old, eager and skeptical. Moving with the unnatural smoothness that she had drilled into herself, she took her chair with silent grace.

"The spirits call loudly today," she said, soft enough that

the women leaned inward. "They swirl about, pressing messages upon me, urging me to impart them to you. But even with such a clamor, the winds of the other world blow between us, twisting the words, muffling syllables, and I must do the best I can with my corruptible body to be open to what they are trying to say."

She looked slowly, deliberately around the table, turning her head in an exaggerated manner so that they could tell what she was doing. "Miss Hawthorne," she said.

The pretty girl jumped and paled slightly. "Yes, Madame Esmeralda?"

"You have lost someone—no, perhaps I should say something of value recently." Good society underestimated what coachmen knew and what harmless bits of gossip they were willing to impart to a cab driver who was sufficiently motivated by a generous tip. "It was a pet. A lap dog?" The question was important, even when she already knew the answer. The hits would cover the misses, and a tone with just the right balance between certainty and doubt allowed Em to assure her clients that whether they said yea or nay, it was in line with what she had already felt from the spirits.

Miss Hawthorne's face crumpled. "His name was Beauchamp. He was very old."

"Of course," Em murmured. The girl had given her more than she'd hoped for. "He is right here. Can you feel him? He is very happy. He no longer aches in the mornings. He can move like a puppy again. There are endless fields beyond the veil, and he has discovered the joy in romping through them with packs of blissful four-legged compatriots, rolling and wrestling in the grass."

"Oh," said the girl, looking pathetically grateful. "He was always so frightened of the outdoors."

"I know. There is no fear in the Elysian Fields for dogs. All sorrow and fright is left behind in their mortal husks. Dogs are true innocents, of course. Men may find pain or fear in death as in life—damnation or ecstasy—but dogs are not so burdened. They cannot sin but that man makes them." She smiled beatifically even though the women could not see her. It was best to be absolutely clear, certain, and convincing, for it bound her clients to her, for they would find any other spiritualist's version of the afterworld unpalatable since it would be incompatible with what she had first convinced them of.

"Oh," Miss Hawthorne repeated.

"The dogs in the fields are waiting for their owners to join them. Then they will be reunited forever," Em explained.

"Oh." This time, it was more like a sigh. The girl settled back, an abstracted expression on her face.

Em waited a moment for the women's attention to return to her, and then she began to sway, slowly, delicately. Eight pairs of eyes sharpened upon her, and she increased the sway and began to whisper, barely audible, so that they were forced to strain to catch snatches of her words. "I cannot understand you. No, no, you must— I cannot. Who? You cannot give me these hints; you must do better. I cannot understand. No, no, not two." She raised her voice slightly. "One is enough. I cannot bear two. I cannot play Fury for every injustice that the world bears. Spare me!" On the last word, she gave the table a violent rock using the metal hooks strapped invisibly beneath her wrists. The women recoiled, Lady James gasping as Miss Hawthorne gave a little shriek. Lady Hamilton just looked at her, her pale blue eyes burning.

Em slumped forward in her chair, going perfectly still. For a moment, there was complete, stunned silence. Then, slowly, the women began to stir. Just as a concerned murmur circled the table, Em gave a little shudder and pulled herself upright. The women instantly hushed.

"They are gone now," Em said, her voice hollow. "I have a message, however—and a new mission. You all know that

I was brought to the English shore by the voices from beyond, drawing me to discover the truth of a great injustice that had been done to an innocent. Now I have a second commission, one I am loath to accept but that carries with it its own urgency, that of bloodguilt."

"What is it?" Lady James whispered.

Em turned toward her. "I do not yet know. But I do know that Lady Hamilton holds the key to it in her bosom."

Clutching at the long string of pearls that encircled her neck, Lady Hamilton sat, a stricken expression on her face. With a sick weight in her belly, Em realized that her faint suspicions had been as well founded as she had made out to Varcourt that they were—the woman did know far more than she had ever admitted about her eldest son's disappearance. Lady Hamilton had been so desperate for messages from beyond, so easily persuaded of anything Em wished her to believe because her need was so much greater than her wisdom.

Em's lips found the shape of the words automatically, and she spoke them even as she hated herself for it, for the exploitation and the presumptiveness of it. "He forgives you."

Lady Hamilton, beautiful, fragile Lady Hamilton, who hid in a laudanum haze so the world could not touch her, dropped her gaze to the swollen knuckles that held so tightly to the thick strand of pearls. And then she burst into tears.

I have needs, too, Em thought, unmoving as Lady James drew the countess into her embrace. *I have needs greater than yours. Your living son, too, has a right to know what you have hidden all these years. I am doing only a little evil to cure a great one.*

Yet self-loathing curled, bitter and cold, in the pit of her stomach, and Em added another sin to her mental account.

* * *

"She's in dere, guv," the urchin chirped.

Thomas looked out of the carriage window at the unprepossessing building and then doubtfully at the child across from him. The filthy creature could have been male or female—its face was indeterminate under the grime, and oddly wizened. Thomas suspected that the child was far older than its starved frame suggested.

"Are you certain?" he demanded.

"I saw 'er go in meself," the child replied. It tugged its clothing. Thomas hoped that it did not have body lice hiding in its ragged wrappings of men's castoffs.

He handed the child a shilling. "Wait outside. If she is really in there, there shall be two more for you where that came from."

The child made a shrugging kind of motion that might have meant anything and took the coin in its grubby hand. Thomas stepped out of the carriage and ducked swiftly into the doorway of the building. He knocked. No response. He tried the door, and a bell jangled as he entered.

A wave of heat hit him. Aside from the bell, there was no indication that the establishment was a business. A woman sat in front of a huge and smoking cookstove with an enormous black boiler tank above it, rocking a cradle with one foot as she darned a sock. Two more small children tumbled on the canvas hearth rug, sooty but stout and hale. The only light came through the windows, covered with greasy oil paper.

The woman's face pinched with suspicion as she surveyed him. "I ain't got nuffink 'ere dat you want," she said shortly, rocking the cradle so furiously that Thomas feared the babe would roll out.

"I am looking for a woman," he said.

"Dis is a respectable 'ouse," the woman snapped. Her knitting needles flashed.

"I am not seeking a baud," he said stiffly. "I am looking

for a woman who just came in. She wears a veil and is sometimes called Esmeralda."

"'Er." The woman looked even angrier. "She pays for a
private bath, she does. She's me best customer."

"Where is she?" When the woman hesitated, he said, "I
will search every room in this place if I must."

"And I'll call the constable on you, even if you is a toff,"
the woman replied.

Thomas softened his voice. "You know you don't want
that. Calling a constable on a gentleman can get you nothing
but trouble. I don't want to hurt her. She is a . . . an associate. I just need to talk." He spread his hands in a sign of
harmlessness.

The woman's expression did not ease. "She's on the second floor, room on the left. Don't you be disturbing 'er when
she ain't decent. I won't have no trouble, now, you 'ear? I'll
send little Jim 'ere to raise the 'ue and cry if I 'ears the least
stir."

"Yes, madam," Thomas said, sweeping her an ironic bow.
He mounted the stairs. The place stank of damp wood and
cheap soap, a sort of very clean hell, dark and dank and dripping with condensing steam. At the top, he chose the left
door and lifted the latch.

A billow of steam enveloped him as he stepped inside the
burrowlike room. Three wooden baths occupied most of the
floor, with a bench along one wall that had a row of hooks
above it. Two of the baths were empty; in the third lay Esmeralda, her hair twisted high on her crown. She turned her
head unhurriedly. If she were surprised, she did not show it
as she blinked her pale, catlike eyes at him.

"Lord Varcourt." On her lips, his name twisted into something unpleasant. "I paid a shilling extra for a *private* bath."

"Don't blame the matron," he said, closing the door behind him. "I threatened her quite unconscionably."

"No doubt," she said. She stood, water cascading from

her supple limbs, and reached for the linen towel that hung on the nearest peg. She wrapped it around her body as she stepped out of the bath, tucking it so that it stayed around her. "What are you doing here?"

"I had you followed," he said. "You shall always be followed." He leveled the words carefully, letting the threat sit unspoken within them. Something of the intimacy they had shared still lingered between them, something more meaningful than the mere sharing of bodies. Thomas had to divorce himself from it. It could mean nothing, in the grand scheme of things. It would be best if he did not pretend that there was anything of significance in it.

"I thought we had decided to become allies," she said. She raised an eyebrow, holding her ground. The words were more of a challenge than an appeal.

He stretched his mouth into a smile. "A truce is not the same as an alliance."

She turned her back to him dismissively and loosened the towel, beginning to dry herself briskly with a show of nonchalance that Thomas didn't believe for a minute. There was too much tension in her body, a visceral awareness of him that made a wholly primal reaction course through his veins.

"What do you want, Varcourt?" she asked.

"Many things," he drawled, watching her softly slender body. Her motions faltered—he caught the tiny shiver that passed through her, and his skin tightened in reaction. When her arm moved, revealing the profile of her breast, he caught a glimpse of a taut nipple.

"I am not interested in games," she said flatly.

"I'd truly be an idiot if I believed that for a second," he said, folding his arms across his chest as he leaned against the wall next to the door. "But I did not come to toy with you. I came so that you might report your progress."

"We could have discussed it at my flat." She dragged her

chemise over her still-damp body and turned around, taking in his position with a flick of her eyes.

"It's being watched," he said.

"By you?" she retorted.

"By everyone." He shrugged.

She snorted and pulled on her corset, hooking the busk closed with fast, jerky movements. Thomas watched her, each motion engraving itself on his brain.

"You can button yourself up to your neck, and it won't stop me unless I want it to," he said flatly.

Esmeralda froze, her hands on the straps that would tighten the corset in two tugs. "We have an agreement," she said. Her voice was steady, but the tautness in her face betrayed her. "You should have no more need to terrorize me."

He regarded her consideringly. "Perhaps it isn't that I need to. Perhaps I want to."

"Ha!" Esmeralda yanked on the straps, and they turned the buckles that tightened the laces across the back. "You can keep telling yourself that. Perhaps you shall even begin to believe it. But there are different kinds of needs."

"There are, indeed," he agreed easily. He stepped toward her, closing the space between them and pressing her back against the clothes that were hung on the wall between two of the baths. "And do you not need it, too? Do you not feel what I do?"

Esmeralda stopped and tilted up her chin. Her pulse fluttered swiftly in her throat. He reached out and touched her face, cradling her cheek with gentle fingers, brushing his thumb across her cheekbone. She recoiled slightly, then stiffened as she controlled her response.

Thomas' lips twisted. "I thought that this was the cue for *la belle dame sans merci* to use her wiles to enmesh the corruptible knight in her web. Aren't you going to tell me that you are dying for my touch? That you dreamt of it? Panted for it?"

"Of course not." Her words fell like drops of crystalline water, frigid and clear. "Quite the reverse. I will tell you that you are dying to touch me."

He started to jerk back. Then, to hide the movement, he changed it midmotion into a kind of slide of his hand around to cradle the back of her head. He moved his mouth down, toward hers, determined to take what he wanted. She stiffened in his arms as if prepared for an assault, and without even consciously realizing it, he changed his strategy.

He met her defiant lips with a touch that was so light that it caught her unprepared. She staggered slightly under it, the swift intake of her breath between their lips sending a startlingly erotic reaction through his body.

He could feel her body's heat through their clothing, still damp from the bath, could taste the faintly salty tang of her mouth. Her breath was hot and unsteady, and he took advantage of her lack of surety with every iota of skill that he possessed. She leaned toward him, the stiffness of her body flowing out with her resistance, and he felt his self-control eroding. . . .

He pulled away, and she swayed, her eyes flying open to reveal an instant's confusion before it was replaced by her normal clarity. He mentally shook the spell of her soft, pliant body from him, forcing himself to smile. "You make a very bad coldhearted whore."

"Or a very good actress," she returned, her voice trembling slightly. "Tell me what you want from me. I will not bandy words with you all day. I have an appointment this evening."

"At the zoological gardens," Varcourt said. His mother had been atwitter about it all morning.

"Indeed." She narrowed her eyes, speculation clear. "Why did you come here, if not to bait me?"

"I want to hear your account of the séance yesterday afternoon." His body still held her inches from the wall, blocking her and forcing her to tilt her chin up to look at him. He exploited that advantage mercilessly.

Her face went set and hard. "I made your mother cry," she said tartly. "I hope that is satisfactory progress, as it is all that I can report. Perhaps if I press her hard enough, I can get her to fling herself into the Thames."

"I already knew about her weeping," he said, keeping his expression blank. It was no business of hers, the contradictory emotions that his too-fragile mother made him feel. After all her flightiness and her retreats from reality, after all her suspicion and her indifferent care, he owed her nothing. And yet she was a rankling sore under his breastbone, and he ached because of her tears even as he knew he'd cause a thousand more if it was the only way to pry her secrets from her.

But Esmeralda—why her bitterness? She was the exploiter of weak-minded old women. Why should the tears of one of them scald her so?

She pressed her lips together. "You heard about the séance from your spies, I suppose? If they tell you all, what need do you have of me?"

"I need your analysis," he snapped. "That is how you manipulate people, is it not? You read their reactions; you ferret out their secrets and weaknesses."

Esmeralda swallowed visibly. "There was not much to analyze," she said softly. "I said, 'He forgives you,' and she burst into tears."

"But what does it mean?" The frustration leaked into his voice.

She shrugged. "It could mean anything. It might mean that she has finally so addled her brains with her laudanum that she is going mad. It might merely mean that she feels desperately guilty about your brother, which I do not think you need me to tell you. Or," she added in an icy tone, "it might mean that she is desperately and directly guilty in his death. She has secrets, of course. Whether they'll be of any good to you is another matter."

Why was she discouraging him? Did she have some other deep plan that made her want to escape their bargain? Or did she truly feel such pangs of guilt?

"Which do you believe?" he asked her softly, running his forefinger down the side of her cheek and along her jaw.

She shivered, her eyes growing murky with a thousand thoughts. Her lips parted, and she blinked slowly, mesmerizingly at him. When she spoke, it was with the conviction of the damned.

"I believe that she knows more about her eldest son's death than anyone has ever guessed."

Thomas' lungs clenched and his lips stretched, a reflexive motion that may have been a smile or a grimace—not even he could tell. He stepped back jerkily from Esmeralda and turned his back to her, pushing through the thick steam of the room and out of the door, away from Esmeralda and her eyes that saw too much.

There were things he did not want seen.

Chapter Twelve

Em exhaled, resting her head against the wall. Slowly she pushed away and pulled her corset and chemise off again, dropping it on the bench.

She should be leading Lord Varcourt onward, down to his own confusion and paranoia, and yet she had to fight the urge to reassure him—or, contradictorily, to tell him that he and his truth can go hang because she wasn't going to play any part in torturing an old woman.

Lady Hamilton's wracking sobs still haunted her. Em had never hurt the woman before. Manipulated her, yes. Capitalized on her obsession about her dead son by offering reassurances that had no real substance—yes, that, too. But Lady Hamilton had always left their sessions with a lighter mind. Em had certainly never provoked the woman to tears. This new task was making her skin crawl in a way that made her willing to do almost anything to avoid pressing the woman further.

Almost anything. But not give up her future.

She eased into the tub again. Her skin stung where it was rubbed raw, but she grabbed the sponge and began to scrub again, scraping her reddened skin over and over as if she could wash away the memory of those frail old shoulders shaking with tears.

Em should be glad. She had Lord Varcourt now, owned him body and soul. But she remembered a silly story from her childhood about a monkey that had ridden on the back of a crocodile out to the center of a swift river. It was a safe ride until the final snap. . . .

Em ignored that thought, ignored the self-loathing that threatened to shred her from the inside. She could not turn back or flinch away—it was a matter of her own survival. Scruples were for those who knew where their dinners would come from in two months. They weren't for a fraud who was already half-whore, poised on the edge of utter destruction. It would all be over soon, and she would have Lincroft and could forget all of this like an ugly dream.

She closed her eyes and tried to erase from her mind the image of Varcourt's dark eyes, piercing with pain and hope. Yes, that, too, must be forgotten. Otherwise, she might never find peace.

It was still three hours before sunset when Lady Hamilton's party arrived at the gates of the zoological gardens. She was gray-faced, her eyes glassy with laudanum. When she smiled at Thomas, it seemed that her mouth might break.

Reactions warred within him as he watched her—protectiveness and bitterness, pity and resentment. He wondered if there had ever been a time when he had simply loved his mother with the childlike openness and reflexivity that his sisters still had, if there had ever been a time when he had not felt her ambivalence toward him, her inability to forgive him for being undamaged when her firstborn so decidedly was not.

He had doubted Esmeralda when she'd told him that his mother was hiding some information about his brother's death. After all, what could his mother think that she knew?

She had been at the house the day Harry died. But Mary's report of the tea with Esmeralda had erased that doubt, and now he didn't know if he should hate his mother for hiding what she knew from him or hurt for her more.

He held out his arm for her when they lit, steeling himself as she hesitated, telling himself that he did not care whether she took it. She stood on the footpath, looking frail and far too old as she made her decision; then finally, she took his arm, leaning on it slightly as they passed through the gates. Behind him, his sisters linked arms and bent their glossy red heads close together, whispering.

"You so rarely accompany us these days, Thomas," his mother said. Lord Hamilton had usually called him Varcourt since the end of the inquest into his brother's death, but his mother never called him anything but Thomas. "Why did you decide to come with us this time? Especially as you were so unkind to me two days ago . . ." She trailed off reproachfully.

"You know I do not mean to be cruel. You have been looking a little under the weather of late. I thought you might appreciate the support of a male presence," he said. He did not even feel guilty for the lie.

"Esmeralda will be there, you know." Lady Hamilton stared straight in front of them as they walked past an artfully wild rock garden.

"Yes. I heard that she upset you yesterday." He watched her closely, but the laudanum deadened all reaction. Impulsively, stupidly, he added, "You should not stand for it. You don't even have to face her. Give me the word and I shall send her away."

Lady Hamilton sighed. "Do you hate her so much?"

Visions of their encounters, all of them, flashed through his head. Hate? He'd tried, but what he felt for Esmeralda was far more complicated—and dangerous—than that.

She'd gotten under his skin, into his blood. "I just don't want to see you hurt, madam."

"Oh, Thomas, you must believe in her. I must believe in her. She sees so clearly. She sees more clearly than even she believes." Her eyes were shadowed.

"She is a fraud, Mother." The words came out blunt, clipped—he had to say them even though he knew it would do no good.

"She might even believe that. I am open to such a possibility. But her sight is still true," she said, her voice imbued with an ethereal conviction.

Thomas smothered his frown. There was nothing to be said to that.

He almost missed Esmeralda when they came upon her. She was sitting on a bench nestled against a backdrop of hothouse plants, the deep green of her dress shading into the fronds of the banana plants that surrounded her. She must have spotted them before they saw her—her face was turned toward them under her jet veil. But she did not acknowledge them until Lady Hamilton addressed her.

"Madame Esmeralda! I am so pleased you could make it." Thomas' mother's voice contained no joy, only an abstracted sense of emotion that might have meant anything—or nothing—under the influence of her opiate drops.

Esmeralda rose and bowed her head, her veil sliding across her breasts. Over that blank appearance, Thomas superimposed the image of the face under that veil, remembered the feel of those breasts in his hands.

"I am always at your disposal, Lady Hamilton," she said. The foreign note was back in her voice; Thomas had not noticed that she had dropped it at some point in her dealings with him.

Esmeralda fell into step beside them as they headed toward the carnivora house. "I fear that I did not sleep well last night. I was plagued by visions," Esmeralda added in a subdued tone after they had gone a dozen yards. "I sense that your dreams, too, were troubled, madam. Can you remember them?"

"Yes." Lady Hamilton's worried mouth compressed briefly, cutting through her drugged indifference.

Esmeralda took her free hand and squeezed it briefly. Lady Hamilton returned with a pressure that looked more like a desperate clutch to Thomas' eye. The younger woman said, "We shall endeavor to see if they were true dreams or false ones, then. True visions come from beyond, but the spirits of those who wish us ill can deceive."

"So you have said. These dreams, though, were true."

What do you mean? Thomas wanted to demand of his mother. But he bit his tongue and waited for Esmeralda's answer. She held his mother's trust far more than he, and however much it rankled, he could not change the facts by mere wishing.

"We must speak on this in its proper time," was all Esmeralda said.

They walked along the length of carnivora house, an incongruity of classical columns and iron bars. The six cages facing them were long and shallow, keeping the animals close to the passersby. One of the tigers slept with its back pressed against the bars.

"It's so close we could touch it," Mary observed.

Thomas turned to look at his sisters. "I do not recommend it."

"We would never, of course," Elizabeth said with scorn. "Do you think us fools?"

Thomas chose not to answer that question. Reckless, they certainly were. They had tumbled up rather than having been raised, his father's inattention giving his mother free rein to indulge them how she chose.

They paused in front of the lion cage—his mother's favorite and always her first stop. Lady Hamilton dropped both his arm and Esmeralda's hand to step forward and survey the four beasts. They were lolling about on the hard cement floor, knots of muscle and sinew visible under sleek fur.

"A lions' den," Esmeralda murmured, so softly that he almost missed it.

"They are such noble beasts," his mother said. "So powerful and brave."

They looked powerful, certainly, but they seemed more bored than noble. "What makes a lion brave when it is locked in a cage?" Thomas asked.

"Is a man braver after he has performed a brave act? Or is he brave because of his character before the act that allowed him to do it?" Esmeralda's reply took him unawares.

"Is a murderous man as evil as a murderer?" he retorted.

Her head tilted to the side. "I wouldn't presume to say. I was asking a question, not making an argument."

"I would not call those lions brave," Elizabeth announced.

"Why ever not?" Lady Hamilton asked.

"They are far too lazy to have a brave character," her daughter said.

"How can you tell?" Mary said. "They haven't got anything to do but lie there. The cage is too small for exertion."

"I do not think that a lion has a brave character," Esmeralda said. Her quiet assertion went unnoticed by the twins, who began to argue good-naturedly.

"Most people would disagree," Thomas said, turning to her. Encased in silk from head to foot, she seemed constrained, oddly diminished despite the circumference of her skirts.

"I know." Her hands tightened at her waist, their fine bones visible through the soft leather of her gloves. "Bravery implies selflessness, or at least some risk of self for a purpose that is greater than mere gain. Lions use teeth and claws to kill animals that have neither to fill their own bellies. They are no braver than butchers."

"You make them sound evil," Thomas said.

Her head turned to face him, and he imagined her translucent eyes fixed upon him. "Not evil. Only men are evil. But neither are lions brave."

He half reached for her, not knowing what he meant by that movement, but she was already turning away. He shook the impulse from himself and looked for his mother.

Lady Hamilton wandered farther down the row of cages, toward the leopards. Thomas noted that her color was better, but her hand still strayed to the pearls at her neck, worrying them as she walked. The twins followed, still wrangling.

"You shouldn't have come," Esmeralda whispered harshly as soon as the three were out of earshot.

"Shall I leave you alone with my mother, then, to do as you wish to her?" He could not hide his bitterness.

"You have up until now," she said, the words pitched to cut. They did.

"Only because I cannot forbid her from seeing you. Yet," he added.

She stilled, then shrugged with an indifference he did not believe for a moment. "I do not wish to investigate your brother's death. If you choose to hinder me, it is your cause that is harmed, not mine."

Thomas muttered a curse under his breath. It was a fool's bargain. He knew it. But he could not let go of the hope, the fantasy that something might be changed after so many years.

"Your mother will not confide in me while you are hanging over her shoulder like a raven," she continued coldly. "You must leave us alone if you wish to learn anything. Depend upon your spies to confirm our conversation, if you must, if they can hide close enough to hear this time." There was a hint of scorn in the last words.

Thomas did not move for a long moment, staring at the woman who stood so close to the lion cage, her dark green walking dress clasping her narrow waist and disappearing beneath the black veil that hung from her hat and hid everything from him.

Finally, he nodded. There was nothing else he could do. "Speak to her, then. I shall go to"—he snorted—"to the monkey house. There is a kind of poetic irony in that, I think." He tipped his hat at her sardonically and left.

Em watched his tall, broad form as he sauntered off, and suppressed a shiver. Even when she had deliberately provoked him, he did not lose control of his expression or quicken his steps in anger. Only when she had taunted him with her body and his own lusts had his iron grip on himself slipped. She was not sure whether that should encourage or terrify her.

He was gone now, though, and she should be relieved. She dragged her eyes away from Varcourt, turning again to Lady Hamilton and her girls and squaring her shoulders. She had two obligations now: one to herself, and one to Lord Varcourt. She just hoped that she could handle them both.

She caught up with Lady Hamilton. The twins had moved on ahead, strolling along the paths with their heads pressed close together. The countess was humming softly, a tuneless and breathy song. Em knew that half the woman's fey quirks were an act, more for her own benefit than anyone else's. Lady Hamilton had the need to play at Lady of Shalott, to cast herself as the doomed maiden too delicate for this world. It gave her a meaning for her life that she seemed to otherwise lack.

For several minutes, Em simply walked beside her, arm in arm, letting the countess choose their path. Finally, Em said, "What was your dream?"

In the cage in front of them, a porcupine, like an overgrown hedgehog, trundled over toward its dish. Lady Hamilton's eyes did not stray from it even as her gaze went unfocused.

"I saw Harry again," she said.

"Ah. That is very serious," Em said.

"He was dead—just as I saw him when they carried him

back home in a litter slung between two horses." She sounded as if she were describing something that happened very long ago to someone else, her tone almost dreamy. "And then he sat up, and he accused me."

"Of not speaking out?" Em hazarded.

"Of letting him die. Because I didn't speak out." She nodded, the movement slightly convulsive. "But he had it backward. He was already dead, and nothing I could do or say would make a difference."

"Perhaps speaking now would give his spirit peace, and he would stop sending you such dreams," Em murmured.

Lady Hamilton looked at her. "You said he forgives me."

"And he does," Em agreed. "But the voice of justice is hard to stifle."

"What of the peace of the living?" the lady demanded. "Don't they deserve a little compassion, too?"

"Mercy is a virtue that cannot be exercised while evil remains hidden," Em urged.

Lady Hamilton looked at her for one agonized second and began to open her mouth. But she closed it with an audible snap and shook her head. "I cannot," she said.

"I understand," Em said. "Whenever you are ready to give your spirit—and Harry's—rest, I am here to listen. I hide secrets within by bosom so that none might find them." Each statement was individually true, and yet the whole was a glaring falsehood. Em ignored the dagger of guilt that slid slowly between her ribs.

"Of course you do," Lady Hamilton said with a tremulous smile, reaching over to pat her hand. "You are my treasure."

Em bowed her head as if humbled, grateful that her veil hid the shame that was surely etched across her face.

Chapter Thirteen

"What did my mother tell you?"

Em turned at the voice. It should have diminished Lord Varcourt to stand there upon the promenade that occupied the flat roof of the carnivora house, with the vast landscape of Hyde Park spreading out in all directions below them. Instead, he looked even more massive and immovable, like a single megalith atop a bald hill.

"We spoke of little of import to you," she said, the memory of Lady Hamilton's pain making her excessively waspish. She did not stir from her bench.

He didn't betray a reaction, nothing that even her well-honed skills could see. Good. It meant that he felt she was dangerous enough to be guarded with—which meant that he would be careful with how he treated her. "We have an agreement," he said evenly.

They did, and she had gone too far. Em schooled her voice and posture. "These things take time."

"Time is a luxury I can ill afford," he muttered.

"Why? What do you think is going happen if you do not have your answers soon?" Em could not stop the question—his statement echoed her own sentiments so closely, and yet with so little apparent justification for it that she was left baffled.

His gaze fell on her, but he seemed to be staring straight through her. He gave a sound that might have been meant to be a laugh. "Nothing at all. I feel rushed and squeezed—I have felt this for days, a change in the air, the coming of something momentous, and yet there is no reason to think that tomorrow will not be just like today." His voice was pitched low, as if it were meant for himself more than her.

Em pursued that line softly. "Why? What is it that hounds you so?"

He seemed about to say something, but then he stopped, his gaze refocusing. "I am suspected of killing my brother. Is that not enough?"

"It seems a heavy thing, indeed," Em murmured. She turned her head away slightly, as if she were looking over the tracery of paths below, but she kept her eyes firmly on Varcourt. "Your mother did speak of your brother today."

"What did she say?" The demand was swift.

"She talked about how he loved trains and potatoes. And how he had a violent temper." She paused, waiting for him to fill up the silence.

"Well, Harry certainly wasn't known for his self-control," he said crisply, then stopped.

Em pressed him. "Did he ever hit you?"

Varcourt's dark eyes grew more shadowed. "Is it important?"

"It might be. The more I can tell your mother that she never told me, the better." This was an outright lie. Lady Hamilton had spent most of the afternoon telling stories, good and bad both, about her dead son. Em had drunk in each detail, knowing that in them were the keys to pursuing the truth that Varcourt claimed he wanted to know. But she needed Varcourt to make the confession, too. It would strengthen the intimacy between them, however false it must be, and thus foster greater trust in her.

Just as importantly, she could check each one's story against the other. People lied, even when they believed themselves to be telling the strictest truth. How they lied and what they lied about was sometimes more important than the truth itself. Em needed to know what Lady Hamilton felt it was worth reconstructing a new truth about—and what lies Varcourt told himself, in the depths of the night.

Finally, Varcourt spoke. "Yes, he hit me." The answer was so quiet she had to strain to make out the words. "When he got angry, he went into fits, and he would hit anything and throw anything. I was hit with a shard of a teapot that struck the fireplace surround when I was two. You can still see the scar above my eye, if you know where to look. After that, I—and later my sisters—had a different nursery and different nurses from Harry."

"You must not have seen him often, then," Em pressed.

Varcourt snorted. "Every day, for play and at our lessons."

"Lessons?" Lady Hamilton had said nothing of her older son's schooling.

His mouth twisted. "We shared the same tutor until I went to Eton at thirteen. Harry was always better than I at maths. Incredible, really. I said he was no fool."

"Yes, you did." Em bit her lip, then forced the conversation back around to its original line. "There must have been many opportunities for him to hit you, then."

Varcourt's jaw tightened. "I was stronger than he by the time I was six, so it hardly mattered much."

An evasion, but a telling one. Em said, "Did you hit him back?"

His chin jerked up, and he stepped back, away from her. "I thought you said you believed that I did not kill my brother. If this is nothing more than an elaborate game to trick me into damning myself—"

"Of course not," Em reassured him swiftly. "Murder is a far cry from childish scuffles."

"Not as far as it should be," he retorted. After a silence, he added, "Yes, we fought, both of us."

Em pursued, "Did others know?"

Again a snort. "How could they not? In some circles, children are kept hidden away in country houses until they come of age. In ours, the children did not often come to London for the season, but country house parties were always an affair for families to strengthen their ties. Children were encouraged to play with one another in hopes of forming bonds that would become advantageous friendships or even marriages as adults. Harry and I fought often enough that it was well-known among our society, children and adult both. If it had not been, I would not have been so suspected."

"I can imagine that did not seem difficult in that case for people to create a scenario in which you might do him harm," Em said. "Perhaps he began to throw things, to strike at you, and you struck back—"

"I did not kill my brother." Each word was like ice. "By the time I was twelve, he'd sufficiently gained control of his impulses to no longer try to hurt me very often, much less when I was sixteen."

She heard in those words what he did not say as well as what he did—he did not declare that they no longer had fights. She gauged him carefully, the gray cassimere and white broadcloth of his coat and shirt stark against the weak blue sky, and decided to bide her time.

"Your mother carries much guilt on your brother's account," she said instead.

"I know that she does, but I wouldn't know why," Varcourt said gruffly.

"What about you? Do you know why you feel guilty?" Before he could do more than frown, Em continued, "She is a mother. I hardly think she needs a reason to feel guilty about her child. You, however, are just a brother, not a parent."

He shook his head.

"But I do still believe that she knows something of the day of his death that she has never told anyone." She paused. "As do you."

Varcourt's black eyes swept over her. "If you believe that I killed my brother, this exercise is pointless."

"Is it?" Em decided to push him. "Perhaps you are cleverer than anyone has ever given you credit for and this is an elaborate gambit to throw me from my main task."

"And what would that be?" His gaze grew narrow.

A miscalculation: she had given him ammunition she'd had no intention of providing. "I've told you all that needs to be said." She stood briskly and made to leave, but Varcourt caught her arm, turning her toward him.

"What if I don't believe you?" he insisted. His grip on her arm was not painful—not quite—but there was the threat of violence lurking in it.

Em stiffened, awareness of him trickling through her. "Then saying more won't change that. You'll just believe that I've told a different lie."

He was unmoved. "I won't be your marionette."

"Of course not," she said scornfully. "You are the puppet master. But you must believe me when I tell you that my strings aren't worth pulling."

He regarded her for a long moment. "You have come here to lure me to my destruction."

Em suppressed a shiver as her awareness turned sharper. "I am just a single small woman," she countered. "I do what I must and no more."

He pulled her closer to him, so that her skirts brushed against the fine gray fabric of his pants. "I do not understand how you can be invisible behind your veil and remain so damned tempting."

"I tempt no one." She willed her pulse to slow.

"You would tempt a saint." His hand slid from her arm to her waist, and he pulled her to him.

Em resisted even as anticipation twisted heavily in her center. "They'll see."

"Who will?" he said, his jaw tightening.

"Their spies. The baron's spies. We could scarcely be more visible," she said tensely. "You do not want to risk your endeavor on this."

"Let them see," he said, a trace of a sneer in his voice. "They will think that I am trying to seduce you to my will."

"And are you?" she asked, her mouth suddenly dry as her heart grew loud in her ears. He was too close—her thoughts were scattering, fleeing from her.

"It's worth a try, don't you think?" He closed the space between them and silenced her with a kiss.

His mouth was masterful, almost businesslike with its thoroughness, neither teasing nor demanding but devastating in its completeness. Em found her body surrendering despite her urgent sense of the danger of giving in. His lips rasped her through the veil, his arms pulling her close so that his body heated her through their clothing.

Finally, she was able to wrest control back from her body. She stiffened and jerked away, backing up against the parapet, struggling to catch her breath. Varcourt's eyes glittered darkly.

"Good," he said. "Now slap me."

"What?" Em gaped at him.

"Slap me," he said, closing the distance between them.

Her mind still reeling, she pulled her arm back. Putting all the force of her frustration and confusion into it, she swung at him.

Her wrist smacked into his upraised palm. Holding it, he smiled humorlessly at her. "Now let the spies report *that*."

And with that, he let her arm drop, spun, and walked away.

"Have you any news?" Thomas asked, looking at Edgington steadily across the man's library desk. It had been four days now since he obtained the necklace and gave it to the baron; Edgington had sent a carefully worded letter asking for this meeting that morning, and Thomas hoped that it meant that he had discovered the source of the object.

They each nursed a tumbler of Jamaican rum, a drink for which Edgington had a distinct if inexplicable weakness. It was good to know another man's proclivities and foibles. The knowledge was almost more important about an ally than an enemy.

"It is indeed the necklace that Lord Olthwaite was looking for, or damned close to it." Edgington pulled it from his desk drawer.

"Where did it originate?" Thomas asked. The stuffed heads of deer and foxes that encircled the room just below the ceiling peered down, glassy-eyed, at them.

Edgington raised an eyebrow. "Discreet inquiries have resulted in nothing definitive, but the most likely answer, based upon an old insurance inventory I managed to obtain, is that it is a family piece."

"A family piece?" he echoed. "So someone burgled Olthwaite's pile of stone, and rather than report the theft, he began hiring thugs to find it? That hardly seems likely."

Edgington appeared to consider. "If it was stolen, it would probably have been an inside job. It usually is, for heists as large and risky as that."

Thomas did not ask how Edgington knew. The baron had been a veritable font of information concerning the criminal classes since he'd joined the Liberals. "So we should look for a servant who left service—when?"

Edgington shrugged. "He's been looking for a month and a half now."

"At least two months ago, then. Any idea of when it was last definitely at Olthwaite's?" Thomas asked.

"His father surely would have noticed it missing, so before his death eight months ago, I can only assume."

"Assumptions can be dangerous, but they are also neces-

sary." Thomas grimaced. "Fine, then. A servant who left between six weeks and a year and a half ago. Why would he
not have pursued this individual to the fullest extent of the
law?" He had his own ideas, but he wanted to know what
Edgington thought.

Edgington laughed humorlessly, holding his tumbler up
to the light. "There are always reasons. Blackmail is the
most likely—with the culprit being in a delicate condition."

"You think Olthwaite put his cock where it didn't belong
and is trying to avoid scandal?" Thomas frowned skeptically.
"That doesn't seem much like him. I doubt the man gives a
farthing for what society thinks. If he did, he wouldn't have
come soused to half the dinner parties this season."

"If only he'd come pissed to Parliament," Edgington
muttered.

"On the other hand, getting a maid in a family way and,
perhaps, tossing her out on her ear so that she felt she must
steal his family jewels in order to survive would be politically damaging on a level quite different from the usual sort
of scandal," Thomas continued. "Particularly for a Disraeli
Conservative who is eager to portray himself as deeply concerned about the common man—and his daughters."

"True enough," Edgington said. "Do you think this is the
origin of the mysterious Esmeralda?"

He snorted. "A maid? Never."

"A middling village shopkeeper's daughter, then, seduced by the local aristocrat?" the baron suggested.

Thomas hesitated. The image of her bare flesh rose in his
mind, the taut white expanse of her stomach, the tightness of
her around his cock. He could not imagine her in Olthwaite's
bed by choice, even if her story of her loss of virginity was a
lie, much less imagine that she had ever been with child.

"I doubt it." He did not elaborate at Edgington's raised
brow. Instead, he said, "It is very distantly possible, but I

would be willing to bet one hundred guineas that she's never born a child."

"Well enough, then," Edgington said. "She isn't a maid, and she wasn't made . . . unexpectedly expectant by him. Blackmail, then?"

"Direct blackmail I think would be well within her capacity." Something made him add, "Or revenge."

"Revenge." Edgington seemed to be tasting the idea. "What a curious idea. Revenge for what? I might ask. What would discourage Olthwaite from pursuing her?"

"The motive for revenge might in itself be a kind of blackmail. Rape?" Thomas suggested, not even certain where such a thought came from.

Edgington tensed. A sensitive topic? "What makes you say that?"

Thomas wasn't sure. "No normal, healthy girl of good breeding does . . . what Esmeralda has done."

"Offer herself to you?" Edgington drawled. "You always claimed that you could seduce them in droves."

Thomas set his glass down on the desk. "What happened between us was no seduction."

"Wooing by force?" Edgington suggested lightly, though there was steel in his eyes. The firearms in the glass cases that lined the room seemed to glint malevolently at him.

"Force was certainly involved, but it wasn't entirely mine." At Edgington's narrow look, Thomas made an irritated sound. "No, not like that. She wasn't trying to fight me off. Quite the opposite."

"Why?" Edgington looked unconvinced.

That was a question that Thomas hadn't sufficiently analyzed. "To win. To make me do what she wanted of me."

"And what did she want?" Edgington pressed.

Thomas shook his head. "I don't know."

"I suggest you find out." Edgington emptied the rest of his glass in one long swallow.

Thomas left the library with the necklace in his pocket, walking through the series of parlors, salons, and withdrawing rooms on his way to the entrance. Gray-clad maids in crisp white aprons looked up at his passage. As he stepped into the grand parlor next to the front hall, he paused. There sat a woman, as small as a child, in the midst of an arabesque of white lace and cerulean silk, her doll-like face framed by masses of thick black hair. Her eyes stared at him piercingly from across the room. Behind her stood a whey-faced woman with red-blond hair, her hand protectively on the smaller woman's shoulder.

"Lady Edgington," Thomas said, giving a nod to the small woman.

"Lord Varcourt," she returned. "I pray you have a good afternoon."

"Indeed," Thomas said. "And you, as well." He nodded again, then crossed the room under her sharp gaze and out into the echoing hall with its great rotunda. He looked up at the fresco of the overblown Europa being borne away on the back of the bull, and he wondered which had truly been deceived. The footman handed him his coat and hat, and he stepped out of the manor into the pale afternoon light.

He needed to find Esmeralda. He had new questions for her.

And he would continue to tell himself that they were the only things driving him back to her door. . . .

Chapter Fourteen

Shopping as Esmeralda was still a surreal experience. Without the need for drama, Em simplified her costume to what any decent widow might wear—a plain black dress with a nondescript bonnet and veil. The local shopkeepers had once pressed her with their sympathies, eager to hear a sentimental story, but her reticence had rebuffed them, and they had gone through stony resentment to unnoticing acceptance in short order.

Still, the entire activity was so foreign to her prior life— her other life—that she hadn't been able to separate the act of buying her food and her clothes with that of her masquerade, and she sometimes felt that she must search within her own mind to find herself during such outings.

She spoke the words she must to get butter, cheese, bread, and apples—her suppers were taken care of for a small fee by Mrs. Grey, the wife of the Gypsy family who owned the tavern from which she rented her flat. Em regretted the expenditure of paying someone else to prepare her meals, but she didn't know the first thing about cooking, and the Gypsies would not allow her in their kitchen because they considered her unclean.

Dodging through the drizzle, Em flagged the omnibus and stepped swiftly on board with her basket over her arm, paying the fee as she worked her way, bent under the low roof, through the maze of knees and skirts to an empty corner. The other occupants steamed gently in the close quarters, the smell of wet wool, manure-stained boots, and unwashed bodies suffusing the space.

Em stolidly kept both hands on her basket, being careful of her healing hand and not allowing herself to surrender to the affectation of sniffing a scented handkerchief under her veil. But she thought longingly of the clean scent of hay-making time and the stronger garden smells of blooming flowers and rich earth. Those were the memories of her girlhood, so muddled and bittersweet.

First came the halcyon days before she had realized there was a difference between her status and that of the Wythe children that was greater than the fact that the man they called Father she must call Uncle William. Then came the realization—not hers, at first, but Edgar's—that her future was to be a good deal less certain than that of the children of the household.

She could still remember the moment Edgar had spoken the words that had seemed to seal her fate: poor relation. She hadn't understood what the words really meant, beyond the tone of contempt with which Edgar had pronounced them, but she had been thrown into a frenzy, perhaps fed by the subconscious knowledge that there was something different about her, after all. She had snatched up his pennywhistle and his lead soldiers and hurled them at him, and one had caught him hard enough on the ear to draw blood. Nursie had come in then and put a stop to the fight, and as one of the nursemaids coddled the weeping Edgar, she had drawn Em aside and explained, not without some compassion, that the boy had spoken the truth. . . . And what that truth meant.

It was many more years before Em fully understood.

The omnibus lurched to a standstill. It was her stop. Em elbowed her way out of the omni and stepped onto the packed dirt of the road. She was a creature reared in the country, her soul rooted in the earth of her home. And here she was, in London, a city of streets and buildings where the soil was dead and trees grew behind little fences or in girdled parks, where she had to wash the soot from her hairbrushes every evening.

She entered the Gypsy pub. She was grateful for her flat. Not only was Mrs. Grey an excellent cook, but the division of the sexes and the preoccupation with community morality and the pollution of women, most especially of non-Gypsy women, meant that the men would never disturb her. Too bad she couldn't say the same for Lord Varcourt. Ignoring the people gathered around the bar, she mounted the stairs to her rooms.

Em knew that she was not alone the moment she closed the door. She could feel Varcourt's presence in the room, an almost palpable force that seemed to overwhelm her small parlor.

"I have no news for you," she said without turning around.

There was a sound near one of the windows as Varcourt stepped away from the draperies.

"The door was locked," she said. She held on to her composure even as her heart began to race, the beats so loud that she could almost not hear the sounds of his footsteps as he approached. She had not been so afraid of him in the park—she had not even been very afraid of him the last time that he had followed her to her flat, for exhaustion had worn out her fear. Now, though, she'd had no time to prepare herself, and she was painfully aware of how little recourse she had.

"I know." His voice was too close, the room too small to hold him.

Em shot the repaired bolt home and turned around. Varcourt seemed more at ease in the room than she'd ever felt. The parlor was Esmeralda's domain, as carefully crafted as the woman herself. The room was swathed in blue and scarlet, swags of cloth hiding how scantily furnished it was so that she'd not had to squander too much money on it. Em always felt like an interloper in it, crowded by Esmeralda, for all that the second woman was an invention.

Much better was the sterility of her narrow bedchamber, which had no personality at all—none of her own to betray her, nor any of Esmeralda's to smother her. That room had been her refuge until Varcourt had invaded it, her seductress prop box kept there so that it could not be found accidentally by any client she chose to take into her front room.

Now even her bedroom did not seem like her own anymore, marked as indelibly as the stain of paraffin on the floor by Varcourt's intrusion. The quiet, good country girl she had been wanted to cling to the belief that she had been scarred by the horror of it; the woman that she had become still savored the terrible climax and wondered if she was damned.

"Why did you come?" she asked the viscount, the words mere noise to break the silence.

Varcourt raised an eyebrow. He was not a handsome man in the conventional way. Fashion appreciated fine lineaments and delicate mustachios. His features were too strong, his brows dark slashes above his eyes, and the bridge of his nose too pronounced. And yet he possessed an attraction that made her mouth dry, her pulse racing even faster as he stepped forward.

"Why do you suppose?" he said when he was only two feet from her.

Em wished she had the defense of a crinoline, but she avoided such frippery in her practical shopping dress. Instead, she held her wicker basket in front of her, between them.

"You could not survive another moment without my company," she said blandly.

"I came for a report," he corrected.

"Report of what?" She was taunting him, but she needed time to decide what to tell him. There was so little to say.

He did not rise to her bait. "What my mother has said since I left you at the zoological park."

She sidestepped him and set the basket on the table. "It has only been two days. It is very hard to get anything of substance from her," she temporized.

"Then it shall be a short report, shan't it?" His voice was just behind her.

Em turned, then automatically leaned backward, her palms pressed flat against the tabletop, in reaction to his nearness. He reached out and plucked the comb from her hair, lifting her veil off with it. The stern creases of his brows softened slightly, making her breath catch a little in her throat.

"You shouldn't look at me," she said, but she made no attempt to retrieve the veil as he dropped it onto the table. It was far too late now to make a difference.

"You still have not given a good reason why not," Varcourt said. He reached out and unfastened the lowest button on her bodice with a twist that was echoed by a tightening in her midsection.

"Nor do I intend to," she said softly. "Lord Varcourt, I hope that you have not come to attempt to terrorize me again. It did not work when you first tried it, and I assure you that it will not work any better now."

He moved to the next button, his eyes gleaming like two black coals. "You are a witch," he said.

Em took a shuddering breath. "Because I can resist?"

"No. Because I can't." Three buttons, then four flicked through their buttonholes at the touch of his fingers.

She gripped the edge of the table. "And if I told you that

you must? That I did not want your hands pawing at me, your mouth sucking at me anymore?"

His hands stilled, his head stooping as he stared down at them. "Then you would be lying."

"Would our deal be over?" she pressed, needing to know.

"Would you want it to be?" When he raised his head, his eyes burned.

"What I want is rarely of consequence," she said brusquely. She pulled away from him, moving toward her bedroom, and he let her go.

"It can be."

Those words, so simply spoken, stopped her in her tracks. She turned, her hand dropping away from the door-knob. "I don't understand you."

"If you did, you would be the only one of us who could." Varcourt stood in the center of the room, taking up far more space than he had any right to. His arms hung empty at his sides, his palms outward. "I did not come here for this," he said.

"Why did you come, then?" Em challenged.

He shrugged. "For more information. Like I said."

If he had merely wanted information, he could have found some other place to meet her. With the spies about, her flat was the worst choice. He knew that as well as she did. He wanted far more from her, but he couldn't admit it yet. Maybe not even to himself. And she—what did she want from him? In the days since their encounter, she had burned for his touch as she'd never burned before. Not just his touch, either, but the memory of his face, his pain, his words. These things should have no effect on her. He might not be her enemy, precisely, but he was close enough to it to be just as dangerous. Yet she could not help herself—any more, it seemed, than he could.

A welter of emotion went through her, and before she could couch the words in prevarication and euphemism, she blurted, "I don't have what you want yet. I swear it. I am still meeting with your mother—daily—but she is not in a position to be pushed. If I pursued her any harder, I fear for her sanity."

"Do you really?"

Em stared at him, confused. "I just said—"

"No." He cut her off. "I mean, do you truly *fear*? Would you care if she goes mad?"

"Of course I would," Em said. "That is a terrible question."

Varcourt's smile was humorless. "Not when it is addressed to a woman who preys upon the desperate and the weak-minded."

"That is not fair," said Em, even though she knew perfectly well that it was.

"Why not?" he demanded.

"Because for most of them, it's just a game, something fashionable to play at to pass the time," Em said, repeating the excuses that she had rehearsed so many times inside her own head. "As for the rest—well, I make them happy. I offer them reassurances and give minds peace. That's not a crime."

"You pervert their memories of their loved ones with lies that you concocted in your own mind," he shot back. "That might not be a crime, but it should be."

Em shook her head. "I tell them only what they tell me they want to hear. Most of us tell ourselves lies, anyhow, to get through the day—lies about our importance, our attractiveness, our goodness. All I do is discover the lies they have already decided they want to hear, and I wrap them up in pretty little packages."

"They are still lies," Varcourt insisted.

"What do you understand about them?" she said, her irritation mounting. "Your life was charted out for you from birth, its one deviation bringing you greater status rather than diminishment. Of course you would have no need for lies. Sometimes, though, a lie is just another name for hope—when your future is bleak and empty and all you have to sustain you are the dreams into which you spin your days, until, if you are lucky, you can no longer tell what is real. . . . Not everyone can weave such fictions on their own, not and dupe themselves. For some, the world is too terrible a place to be borne. I tell those the stories that they cannot make themselves believe without my help."

"You sound like you believe yourself to be some kind of ministering angel," Varcourt said.

Em sighed, deflating as quickly as she had bristled. "No. I am a charlatan." He had no right to know these things, but she needed to say them, and he was the only one to whom she could say them—the only one who had confronted her with her deception. "I am merely a very useful charlatan. Perhaps the idea that I am kind is itself a story that I need. You should not think that I do not lie awake at night, questioning the day's deceptions and wondering if I might be tarnishing my soul irredeemably."

"And well you should," he said, his words hollow rather than malicious. "Well we all should."

"Eat, drink, and be merry, then, because tomorrow we are damned?" she said. "That seems a pessimistic way to live."

"Perhaps not that," he granted her.

She closed the distance between them, stopping an arm's length away. He was still too large, too frightening, but the reaction he stirred in her had only a little to do with fear. "Right now, I can tell you nothing that you don't already know about your mother. If that is what you want of me, you might as well leave until I have more to give you."

He did not move. "You met with her again yesterday," he said.

"Yes," she agreed. "We spoke. She told me more stories of Harry. I gained no new information that might be of use to you." She also had pursued her own cause, telling Lady Hamilton of dire dreams she'd had concerning the necklace that she had put into the countess' hands. Lady Hamilton had been quite distressed since the necklace had been confiscated by her son. Em had no intention of telling Varcourt what she knew about that, even though the knowledge that it was under his control filled her with apprehension.

Varcourt's mouth was a hard line. "I want answers, Esmeralda."

"You always do," she said with some asperity. "I can lie to you, Varcourt. I can tell you that she watched a servant hit your brother over the head with a shovel. What I can't do is move any faster with Lady Hamilton and still have hope of success."

"I need answers," he said again, stubbornly.

Em just shook her head. "You need more than any mortal can give."

"I brought something . . . of yours," he said, swiftly changing the subject.

Em looked at him warily. Varcourt reached into an inner pocket. When he uncurled his hand in front of her, the necklace sat upon it.

"Where did this come from?" he asked.

She reached out, gently brushing the single huge pearl and bright enamel with a fingertip. She had always loved the piece, even though there were more fashionable and expensive ones in the family collection. Uncle William's wife— even now she thought of him as Uncle William—had worn the quaint piece with a natural grace that had made the young Em ache to be a society beauty. It had been hard to sacrifice the necklace to her plan—hard, but necessary, as the dramatic distinctiveness that made it so appealing to her also made it best suited for her purposes.

"I found it," she said. She discovered that lying was a skill that got easier with practice, despite the growing injury that her conscience felt. "It was in the room of the first boarding house I lived in when I arrived in the city, left by a former boarder, apparently, and hidden behind a loose brick in the chimney that passed through the room. It was that which caused my landlord to cry thief and seize my belongings, but it was not his, and he had no idea of where it had come from or where I had found it."

"That is worth far more than a young girl's virginity," Varcourt said drily. "Even yours."

"Even mine?" Em's lips twisted. "I will take that as a compliment. I assure you that if he'd considered for a moment that it might have been more than a trinket, he would not have sold it to me at such a cheap price." She sneered at the word *cheap*.

"And so upon finding yourself in control of a necklace worth several hundred pounds, you then decide that you will give it away to one of your clients?" Varcourt scoffed.

"No," Em said evenly. "I tried to sell it. None of the legitimate jewelers would look at it, certain it must be stolen, and the illegitimate ones would only give me a tenth of its value. I've got far more than that from your mother—far more than that as a direct result of giving it to your mother." That much was true, at least.

"I don't believe a word of it, Merry," he said, almost wearily.

Em shook her head. "If you know you aren't going to like the answers, then you shouldn't ask the questions."

"Perhaps not." He returned the necklace to his pocket and crossed his arms. "I know that the necklace came from Lord Olthwaite's house."

"Did it?" Em said, not even making a show of surprise. "Do you have any idea of how it ended up in a boarding house in London?"

"In your hands, Merry," he said with a grimace.

"Of course," she said acidly.

He ignored her. "I wonder who Olthwaite would see if he saw you without your veil."

He was getting dangerous. It was time to deflect him. Em dropped her shawl, gloves, and veiled hat on the table and closed the remaining distance between them. "Whom do you see?" she challenged.

"A stranger. An unknown entity," he said.

She slid her hands to the front of her bodice and loosened the next button. "Is that all?"

"A desperate woman," he said. "Do not fear, Merry. We have an arrangement, as you've said. I shall not unmask you—yet."

The threat could not be more explicit. "I will find what you seek," she swore. She must, if she were to keep him from destroying her, even if she was forced to invent it. Invention had its own dangers, for thin lies could easily be found out when others knew the truth. But she hoped that she could find real answers for him for reasons other than fear.

"Of course you will," he said humorlessly. He caught her hands as she moved to the next button and pushed them aside, replacing them with his own.

Em held herself perfectly still, crushing the reactions of her body even as some part of her reveled in them. When had she ever been permitted to simply be, to feel, and no more? But everything twisted up together—the compromises she had made, selling of pieces of herself, the terror of being alone and friendless, the humiliation of sexual coercion, the horror of the night when a knock on the nursery-room door had dispelled her innocence forever. . . .

There was no way to shed that, as if it were a too-tight skin. She could only put it all together and box it up, along with her encounters with Lord Varcourt, and set it aside. But she had the growing sense that soon enough, there would be no box in the world large enough to hold it all.

And so she stood stiffly as her heart accelerated. The strange yet too-familiar sensations tingled in warm, languid waves through her limbs, and Varcourt's hands worked methodically up the front of her bodice.

"I hope that you have no intention of attempting to brain me this time," he said. "You have already sent a lamp, a board, and a candlestick flying at my head. I have been fortunate enough to survive this far, but such luck cannot continue."

"No plans at the moment," Em said, "but that can always change, depending upon the circumstances."

The last button was freed. The stiff taffeta rustled as he pushed the bodice from her shoulders. She gripped the tight sleeves and pulled them over her wrists.

"You offer yourself as a distraction," he said, and a note in his voice made her peer into the shadowed depths of his eyes.

"You say that as if it makes you sorry." She reached behind herself and pulled remorselessly at the fastenings that held up her skirts.

Varcourt stepped away from her, his expression growing chill with distance. "You are an astonishing woman," he said.

A bitter smile found its way to Em's lips. "Rarely has that been praise."

"You must know you are beautiful. You would have to be stupid to not realize it," he said.

The last of the tapes holding on her petticoats loosened. Em's fingers grew still, and she inclined her head. She *was* beautiful—she had known it since she was a girl and Nursie and the nursemaids had fussed over her curls, exclaiming what a shame it was that she wasn't a daughter of the family. Alice and Ann had long been jealous of her, in the cheerful, spiteless way particular to bosom friends. But it had all meant nothing in the end, as Ann's end had come so soon

and Alice had found her destiny successively in the ballroom, bridal chamber, and the grave.

Em's life had stalled at the threshold of the nursery, for
there was no place in the world for her. Beauty was a virtue
in a young woman from a good family, but it was a danger
in one who had no family willing to claim her. She had
learned too late what Nursie meant when she clicked her
tongue and said, *Such a pity!*

"No," she agreed finally. "I am not stupid."

"In my experience, most girls with even the slightest
amount of prettiness act as if their physical charms give
them greater-than-earthly status. Why, then, do you treat
yourself as if your body is no more than another bargaining
chip?" he pressed.

She shook her head. "They trade on their prettiness as
surely as I do. They merely have higher aspirations—a rich
husband and a healthy settlement. Those avenues are closed
to me."

"Were they ever open?" he asked swiftly, far too near the
mark for Em's comfort. His gaze swept over her, and her
bare arms prickled. "What happened? Did Olthwaite de-
spoil you and destroy your good name? Were you cast out
from your family and, in revenge, did you pilfer his family
jewels?"

Em recoiled involuntarily. "Lord Olthwaite never touched
me."

Varcourt's eyes lit with speculation as he stepped closer.
"What did he do to you?"

Em tried to say *Nothing,* but she choked on the word.
"Stop it," she said instead, her hands balling into fists of im-
potence, ignoring the sting of the cut on her palm. "Just
stop it."

Before she could react, he was holding her, kissing her,
his mouth silencing her protests. Her center tightened, her
skin shivering with awareness, the fabric of her corset,

her dress suddenly irritating its exquisite sensitivity. She clung to the collar of his coat, trying to keep her feet as his arms wrapped around her and trembling jolts passed through her limbs.

These are not arms to lean on, she warned herself. *They are not to be trusted.* But even as she thought the words, she felt her knees giving in.

Varcourt jerked the clasps that held her corset closed, unhooking her busk and shoving it from her shoulders with one hand while the other kept her steady.

"Shall we see what else you have in your box of tricks?" he asked.

Em shook her head almost convulsively. "No. I'll get the sheath."

"I prefer mine," he said. He slid his hands down her body, following the hard line of her corset and pushing the fabric of her skirts from her hips. "I want to see your naked body," he said.

"You have already seen it," she said as he freed her corset and set it aside.

"I want to see it again," he said. No longer constrained by her corset, Em's breath came no slower, nor did her dizziness ease. He was too much for her—too powerful, too strong. Why, then, did she want this so much? Was she looking for self-immolation?

She stepped out of the circle of his arms. "Undress yourself," she said, the words harsh.

His eyes narrowed, his smile dangerous. "Had you ever seen a naked man before me, Merry? Somehow I doubt it. I think your prior lovers tupped you with their trousers around their knees."

"I have seen enough," she said curtly. She yanked off her shoes and rolled down her stockings, tossing them away. Her pantaloons and chemise followed swiftly after until she stood, naked and shivering slightly. She wanted to fold her hands over her chest, to cover herself, but she did nothing, merely standing there, watching him as his eyes moved slowly, intimately across her body.

"I am sure you think you have," he said finally. "Just enough and no more." He shed his hat and overcoat, dropping them with great precision onto the center of the table. Next, he moved to his necktie. Em bit her lip as the silk hissed as he pulled it from his collar—she recognized it as a brother to the one that had held her immobile to his valet's bed only days before.

"Did you like that, Merry?" he asked, a challenge in his eyes as the necktie dangled from his fingers. "I suppose you would like me to tie you up again. I must regretfully decline, as I find myself insatiably curious about what you will do with your hands when you are not too terrified to touch me or bound to a bed."

"Drop it," she said, and he did, adding it to the pile.

His coat followed, then the waistcoat. His shoulders were in no way diminished by undressing. Instead, it just emphasized the hard angles of his body, narrowing down to his hips. Neither did it hide the hard erection that pushed against the front of his trousers.

"Why do you want this?" she asked softly. "Is it to torture me? To punish yourself?"

His face lost its hard, mocking edge, and for an instant, it shone with pure yearning. Varcourt hid the expression as he pulled out his shirttails, loosening his cuffs and unbuttoning the front with swift efficiency. "If I knew that, Merry, I might not be here at all."

"That makes no sense."

"Nothing between us makes any sense to me." His shirt came off, followed by his undershirt. Em's mouth went dry. Even though she had seen it before, the strength of his figure disturbed her. She did not know whether she wanted to run from him or put her hands against the flat planes of his chest.

"I cannot offer you absolution," she said. "It's not within my power."

"Maybe all I want is a quick fuck." The words wrenched out of him.

"If that were true, you would not be here," Em said steadily.

He bent to remove his footwear, and her eyes ran along the lines of the muscles of his back, lean and hard and merciless. He straightened and met her eyes. "Do you want me to go?"

She opened her mouth to say yes, but she could not make the word come out. She did not want him to go, but she did not want him to stay, either. She could not tell, from the emotions that battered her, what she wanted at all. She shook her head numbly, not an answer but a rejection of answering.

"That is what I feel, too, then," Varcourt said with satisfaction.

Em swallowed hard, trying to still the buzzing in her limbs. "Either finish undressing or leave. I have other plans for today." How blasé she had meant to sound—and how it was ruined when her voice shook. She cursed herself silently as his lips twisted briefly.

"Well enough," he said. Varcourt unbuckled his belt, and Em found her eyes riveted to his hands. He loosened the button, and then trousers and drawers came down together. He kicked them off, but Em scarcely noticed, for all her attention was focused upon the erection that jutted out from between the trunks of his legs.

"Terror or awe?" he asked her, but the mockery in his tone was reserved for himself. He walked around the table, moving toward her bedroom.

"Where are you going?" she demanded, thinking in blind panic of the box that she had shoved far under her bed.

He stopped. "To the room with the bed, of course."

"Let us stay out here," Em said, trying to make her voice light.

"Why?" he asked.

"The bedroom is so dull," she said. "Don't you think this room has a better atmosphere?"

He was not fooled. "This room is a part of your act. Your bedroom is not. This is no act, Merry."

She shook her head—too hard, she knew, but she couldn't help herself. "It has to be. It can be nothing else."

"Come. Now," he said.

She shook her head again.

He strode over to her. She wondered for an instant if he meant to pull her by force, but he bent and lifted her so that she had to wrap her arms around his neck to keep from falling as he held her against his impossibly hot chest.

"It was not a question," he said.

He carried her into the bedroom, kicking the door shut behind him. He jerked back the curtains to let in the light. Then, so gently that it could be taken for tenderness, he set her down.

Her body slid against his, touching her skin with his all the way down, until her feet reached the floor. Her nipples tightened against his chest, and she was excruciatingly aware of the damp tip of his erection pressing against her belly. She gasped a little at the shock the contact sent through her, grasping his arms to steady herself in a room that suddenly seemed to move. Reaction tightened in her center, sending little jolts through her limbs and dimming her vision as everything was given over to touch.

"God, Merry," Varcourt swore. "I can see your skin flush with wanting me."

"I don't want you," she said. "I just want . . . this. Be-

cause I am stupid and foolish and lost and confused. If you
were a gentleman, you would leave now, Varcourt."

"I am no gentleman, Merry," he said. "I am a viscount."

He kissed her then, softly at first and then harder, taking
her mouth and moving down her neck to the hollow of her
collarbone. She shivered, her legs giving way, pressing her
harder into his arms, against his chest until she could feel
each individual muscle of his stomach. He pushed her back,
toward the bed, and she offered no resistance, allowing herself to be laid upon it and spread out like a sacrifice.

"What do you want out of this?" she asked him.

His laugh was bitter. "Whatever I can get. Satiation. Self-
destruction. It hardly matters."

And then he moved down, on top of her, kissing her belly
and the faint hollows under her hip bones, his tongue and
mouth working across her ribs, circling her breasts and taking a nipple hard into his mouth until she cried out with
wanting him, a thousand separate lances shooting through
her body until her fingers and toes tingled with it. She
whimpered at his touch, moving under him, against him,
drawn into the rhythm of his mouth and hands across her
body.

He pulled away from her, and it was a second before her
mind registered the loss and her eyes refocused. He was
holding the rubber disk on his palm.

"Your turn, Merry," he said. "You know what to do now."

Acutely conscious that he was watching her, she sat up
and took it from him and filled the little well in the center
with saliva from her tongue.

"Now put in on me," he ordered.

Em quailed. "I can't."

"Come along, now. Haven't you been playing at courtesan for months?" he said. "You might as well do something
that any real courtesan would know. Hold me."

Em took a deep breath and wrapped her hand around his

erection, her fingers scarcely touching. It was both harder and
softer than she had expected, like a steel rod covered with the
finest velvet. It was hot, too, sending an answering wave of
heat through her own body. She licked her lips nervously.

"Now roll the sheath over it," Varcourt ordered, his eyes
burning like coals.

She did. It was awkward to start, hard to keep it from
slickly slipping off the tip. But once it started, it was easier,
sliding tightly down. She used both hands to bring it down
to the base, where his erection joined his body. He swallowed visibly, and she wondered if the tight sheath hurt. She
didn't dare to ask.

"Where did you put the box?" he asked when she had
finished.

Em opened her mouth to protest, then, thinking better of
it, reached under her bed and withdrew the box. He opened
it and took the bottle of oil again. To Em's infinite relief, he
flipped the box shut again and set it on the floor.

"Now," he said, "I will show you exactly how much pleasure this can give. Lie down."

She obeyed, every nerve in her body alive with expectation. She was acutely aware of the fold in the counterpane
under her shoulder blades, of the difference in the way the
air touched the parts of her that were damp from his mouth.
He looked at her steadily, then poured a measure of the oil
into his palm. His tongue darted out to lick it, and he smiled.

"Good," he said.

He tilted his palm over her belly so that the oil drizzled
out in a fine line, the shock of the liquid against her naked
skin sending a shudder through her. He tipped the bottle
then, pouring lines and loops across her body, from her neck
down into the curls between her legs as she lay frozen upon
the bed.

Then he stoppered the bottle and laid it aside, smoothing
the oil across her with his hands. They moved methodically,

slickly across her skin, almost impersonally across breasts, ribs, and belly alike. Tension wrapped inside her with each pass of his hands, so unlike the teasing torture of his mouth moments before, claiming her, taking possession of every inch of her.

Then he bent over her again, and his mouth took control where his hands had stopped, moving across the same places he had before. But the oil brought a different quality to his movements, making the touch of his tongue smoother, his teeth sharper, and soon she was shaking with the reactions inside her body.

He opened the bottle again, measuring more into his hand, and she prepared herself for him to pour more on her, but instead, he tipped it so that it ran down from his palm across two of his fingers. Before Em realized what he meant to do with them, he pressed her legs apart and pushed his fingers deep inside of her with a single smooth movement. The tension in her center jerked tighter, pulling a gasp from her. She could feel the oil sliding across his fingers deep into her, the strange sensation setting her nerves to jangling. Before she could react, he withdrew and settled his hips between her legs, tilting her hips up as he slid his erection into her, her dampness and the oil smoothing his passage. She felt her body spasm around him with the first thrust, and he made a kind of groan, holding himself deep inside her as his entire body strained as if lifting a great weight.

"You burn for me," he said, and then he began to move, slow, long thrusts, each of which sent a buzzing wave of heat through her body, the slickness of them almost frightening her. He sped up gradually, and she knew that he was feeling her reactions, gauging them. But the harder she tried to remain still and silent, the more she betrayed herself, her body twisting out of her control. He found the rhythm that made her breath come in little sobbing gasps against the tight heat that was building in her center, and he drove her implacably onward, until the heat roared up and took her and all her self-restraint, immolating her within it. She crested on that wave of fire until a new sensation surged through her body as his oil-slick thumb found the nub above her opening and stroked it with his thrusts. The new sharpness insinuated itself in the places the fiercer heat could not go, tearing her apart until there was nothing left but sensation—sensation and his body, moving with hers, the intense awareness of him that she could not shut out or send away no matter how hard she tried.

Finally, slowly, she came back to herself. She lay gasping, unable to move, staring at the blank white plaster ceiling above her as Varcourt rolled away, standing and stripping off the sheath.

She stared at him dully as he went to the doorway leading to the parlor.

"I will leave on your table a list of the guests who were at the house party when Harry died. When I see you again, I must know what my mother saw," Varcourt said.

He stepped through and shut the door behind him. Em lay boneless, unmoving, until she heard the sound of the outer door closing several minutes later.

Varcourt was gone, but for how long? And what parts of her, asked a small voice deep inside her brain, had he taken with him?

Chapter Fifteen

Em sat next to Lady Hamilton on the long red sofa before the empty hearth. The countess was almost invariably cold, and the lack of a sparking fire was a greater indication of the level of her agitation than even the nervous twisting of the handkerchief in her hands or the redness of her eyes.

Em had not seen Lord Varcourt for two days now, and in that time, she had pressed Lady Hamilton as hard as she had dared, to the point where her atrophied sense of justice was rebelling and her own sleep had been disturbed by nightmares centered around the older woman. After sending an urgent request for Em that morning, the countess had merely had the spiritualist stay nearby all day, without speaking more than half a dozen words to her. Em needed answers to satisfy Varcourt, but she had begun to fear what would happen to Lady Hamilton when Esmeralda disappeared for good.

"I am having a ball in three days," Lady Hamilton said, so abruptly that Em jumped.

"I know," Em said.

"You must be there." The countess fixed her with her disconcerting blue gaze.

"Balls are no place for me," Em said automatically.

"I don't see why not," Lady Hamilton said with the echo of imperiousness that she once must have summoned at will. More softly she added, "I need you, Esmeralda. I don't think I can face it alone."

"Perhaps," Em said. She should leap at both the chance and the indication of her importance to Lady Hamilton; the precedent of appearing at one social event of such standing should open doors for her that she would very much need when it came time to stage the finale of her charade. And yet her stomach knotted at the thought of attending a ball, even as Lady Hamilton's attendant.

But she had sacrificed so much else that memories, however painful, could be no barrier. She knew she would accept Lady Hamilton's invitation. She had to.

"I cannot sleep." Lady Hamilton suddenly changed the subject.

"Something is out of balance." It was the automatic answer that Em always gave to such a statement—an answer as thoroughly meaningless as it was useful. Whether she declared the affliction an excess of cabbage or a spiritual assault, there was little that could not be bent to the word *balance*.

Lady Hamilton's laugh, usually a bright tinkle, rang hollow. "Something is indeed out of balance, Madame Esmeralda. How does it go? 'The voice of thy brother's blood crieth unto me from the ground . . .' Something like that."

"Lady Hamilton, you are not responsible for your son's death—" Em began earnestly, but the countess held up a hand.

"You cannot know that," she said. "And do not tell me that Harry sends his reassurances from beyond; spirits can lie, too, if they choose. You do not know what I do."

"What, then?" Em asked, despairing.

"You can't know what kind of mother I was." The old

woman gave the lace handkerchief in her hands another twist. "Or that I wasn't."

"Harry didn't die because of bad mothering," Em insisted.

"But good mothering might have saved him." She dropped the handkerchief in her lap. A half dozen small rents marred the delicate lace. "Lord Hamilton told me that I should do more with the boy. That I had my head in the sand, pretending that nothing was wrong. But I thought . . . I thought that if something *was* wrong, the best thing couldn't be to pay a great deal of heed to it. My nurse always said that most faults in children are encouraged by attention. I thought the best thing would be to pretend that it wasn't there. And in time, it wouldn't be."

"But it did not happen that way, did it?" Em said, feeling helplessly drawn into the woman's self-torture.

Again, that laugh. "Scarcely."

"What did you see the day that Harry died?" she asked, voicing the words she'd never dared say aloud until then. "I, too, have suffered in my sleep—because of the whispers of the spirits, telling me again and again that you know more than you will say. They shall not let me rest until you have confessed the truth."

Lady Hamilton's swollen hands spasmed around one another. "People say *truth* as if they mean a single, uncomplicated thing," she said. "It isn't so."

"What did you see?" Em pursued softly, mercilessly. She could not afford mercy.

"I didn't stay in the house when Thomas came back without Harry. How could I?" she said. "I may not be an eager rider, but I can sit a horse. After everyone else left in a rush, I had my gelding saddled and followed after. The fields were alive with men and women on horseback, gentlemen, ladies, and menservants alive, calling. Harry had never answered to a call, not with all the encouragement the nurses could muster, and so I knew that he certainly would not answer to one now, wet and tired as he would be. So I didn't call. I just rode to the stream, chose a direction, and began riding along it. Before long, I saw—" She broke off and jerked to her feet in agitation.

With steps belonging to a woman much older than she was, she tottered over to a spirits cabinet. There was one in almost every room in Hamilton House, some disguised as secretaries or hidden in the lower parts of curio cabinets, each a silent testament to its lady's weakness. This one, however, didn't even try to pretend to be what it was not— either because it came before the time when Lady Hamilton became conscious of how many she had or after the time that she cared whether others knew.

She poured out a measure of brandy and then, not even bothering to hide her motions, she took a smaller bottle from the corner and tipped it into the glass, sending pale, rippling clouds through the amber liquid before the laudanum dissolved into the alcohol. Shutting the cabinet with exaggerated care, Lady Hamilton cradled the tumbler in her other hand. She drank in quick, ladylike swallows, then set the heavy glass down with a dull clunk. She stood, poised as if for flight, for several long moments. Then she relaxed fractionally, and thus fortified, glided more steadily back to her place on the sofa.

"I know that you found something," Em said. "Something important."

"You are the only one," Lady Hamilton said. "I saw—" She stopped, and Em watched her visibly reformulate her thoughts, moving to a different point in her narrative. "I saw my son, lying by the water. He had a whip mark across his cheek and a great bruise on his forehead, and he was dead."

Em took that in. It seemed ominous, but all this was evidence that had been known at the inquest—and found insufficient to declare death by murder. Lady Hamilton would have found it out in any case. She had no need to confess her ride only to give no novel information.

"What did you see before?" she pressed. "As you were riding along the stream, you saw something, something of which you have never spoken. Tell me."

"I—it was someone, not something," Lady Hamilton said, and then, eyes going wide, she clamped her mouth shut.

"Who?" Em demanded.

"I don't know." That was a patent lie, but Em knew she would get no more.

Some*one*. Em allowed the conversation to lapse into silence as she digested this information. Someone other than the poor dead Harry, someone that Lady Hamilton believed to be a murderer. Em's thoughts slid inexorably back to Lord Varcourt, whom Lady Hamilton treated with such fear. Could it have been him? Lady Hamilton's story seemed to disallow the most likely scenario, that Varcourt had fought his brother at the streamside and left him for dead long before he had returned to the manor house. What other possibility could there be? He had ridden back to the manor house, discovered that his brother had not made it home, raised the alarm, gone out in search of him . . . and what, struck him down when he finally found him again, to be spied by Lady Hamilton as he left the scene?

That was ridiculous. Em closed her eyes, drawing in her mind the expression that Lady Hamilton wore when her surviving son was in the room. Fear, yes, that was obvious to anyone—but also, in the tight shifting of her eyes, guilt.

Guilt, Em realized suddenly, because of the weight of suspicion that Varcourt had so unjustly borne all those years, the suspicion that Lady Hamilton had known to be false but had kept silent about. But why? All Em could sense when she tested that question was more guilt and more fear.

"Thomas returned the necklace you had visions of," Lady

Hamilton said suddenly, her hand shaking slightly as she slipped it into a hidden pocket in her skirts. She drew it out, spreading it in her lap.

"Did he say why?" Em asked.

"He said that he had gotten from it everything he could. He said that you would know when it was right for me to wear it again." She gazed at the bright enamel and luminous pearls.

Em knew exactly what he meant. Varcourt was keeping his side of the bargain—if only she would keep hers. He would ask her next time what his mother had seen, and if she had no answers, their arrangement would be over.

Em looked at Lady Hamilton, so frail and yet so determined. She could break the woman, forcing answers from her out of sheer terror. Or she could lie. Lying about something that could be caught out was something she tried to avoid—it was far too dangerous a gamble to make statements that another had the certain knowledge to refute.

But all she had to do was to spin things out for a couple weeks more, to bring all the strings together, not merely to finish working upon Lady Hamilton, as important as her influence would be, but also to bring Lady James, Mrs. Weldon, Miss Hawthorne, and others to her side. For every hour she spent with Lady Hamilton, she spent four more among other women, persuading them of her connection to the beyond and her sure knowledge of some dire injustice that had brought her here. It was only the sessions with Lady Hamilton that left her feeling so drained, beaten, and soiled.

She could invent a story to hold Lord Varcourt off until it was too late. Already, her mind was weaving a tale from the fragments that Lady Hamilton had given her, filling in the pieces, smoothing over the rough places. And if the image of his face, fierce and aching, hurt her—well, then, it was no more than she deserved.

Lady Hamilton glided off half an hour later. It was a dismissal that Em had become accustomed to, but for a long moment after the countess had left, she simply sat, staring dully into the empty fireplace. There was a stirring noise in the doorway. Em looked up, then stood quickly as she took in the figure who stood there.

"Lord Hamilton," she said, trying not to squeak.

"Madame Esmeralda," he said.

Em simply stood there. Lord Hamilton had always been a shadow in the house, the unseen guiding force. She had heard his voice before, and certainly felt his power, as her visits would have been impossible with Varcourt's opposition except under his aegis. But never before had he acknowledged her presence so far as to appear before her.

"My son has come to see you," he said heavily.

Em inclined her head. The physical resemblance between the two was uncanny, except that Lord Hamilton was worn down, like a mountain face that was slowly disintegrating under the power of a great river. She had a sudden, stray flash of hope that Varcourt would never look so careworn. She quashed that thought before it was even fully formulated.

"I hope that he is not placing undue pressure upon you," the earl said coldly. "I have allowed you into my home because I have seen how the distress of the countess is eased in your presence."

"Yes, sir," Em said. The corollary was clear: If Lady Hamilton ceased to be eased, Em would cease to be welcome. "I understand, sir."

The earl looked her slowly up and down. "I hope for your sake that you do." He turned and walked away, his steps too shuffling for his broad shoulders and still-powerful legs.

Martha was waiting in Em's parlor when she returned to her rooms. She was the Greys' daughter and the most fortunate stroke of luck in the entire arrangement between Em and the Gypsies who owned the pub. Martha was very near Em's size and shape, and Em had crafted Esmeralda's accent to be as near to Martha's attempt at aristocratic tones as possible.

Em might be a non-Gypsy and therefore unclean, but her previous contact with the Roma had taught her enough about their ways that she had acquired not only the flat but also the landlord's permission to hire his daughter for her scheme. If she could depend upon anyone not to give her secrets away, it was the Roma—not because of any loyalty to her but because of an abhorrence of alien authority.

"Are dem dresses ready?" Martha asked, clearly trying not to look eager and just as clearly failing.

"I picked them up yesterday," Em said. She went into the dressing room, Martha trailing along behind, and nodded to the two brilliant scarlet dresses. They were identical in design except that Em's was only lightly basted together so that it could be removed hastily to reveal what was beneath.

Martha murmured something in Romany and touched one of them gently with her fingertips, her eyes glowing. "Dey're beautiful," she said.

"If it goes well, you may have it after your performance," Em said. "You may have all of the dresses."

Martha's experienced eye swept across her wardrobe. "They must be worth fifty quid," she said.

"Quite," Em agreed. They represented a healthy portion of what the society ladies had given her, but in her new life, they would be only a danger, tying her to the past.

"I could do a lot with 'em," Martha said, her expression calculating.

"Just so long as you don't play at being Esmeralda," Em warned.

Martha said, "I wonder if you look like me underneath dat veil."

"If I did, then I wouldn't have chosen you," Em said

coldly. "Did you turn the letter in to Scotland Yard like I told you to?"

"Yeah. I 'ad George do it. 'E looks more the part of the mudlark." The speculation in her gaze grew even sharper.

Em frowned even though she knew the girl could not see it. "You got someone to read it to you."

"Maybe I did," said the girl.

"It won't mean anything to anyone except the one for whom it is intended." Lord Olthwaite had seen the necklace— now she needed to make sure he did not come looking for her, so that Em could continue to hide as Esmeralda under his very nose. The mud-caked letter, sent to her from Alice during her second season, would see to that, along with the story that it had been recovered from a woman's body on the Thames. A body that would never be found, of course, but that hardly mattered.

Em changed the subject. "Now, do you have all your lines memorized?"

"Of course," the Rom girl said.

"Let's hear it, then," said Em.

Martha sighed and began to recite.

After she had satisfied Em, Martha went back down-stairs, leaving Em to sit on the bed and study the list of names of those who had been at the Hamilton manor the day that Harry died. She had read them one hundred times al-ready without enlightenment—this made the hundred and first, and still she was no closer to an answer even though she was now certain that someone had killed Harry. It read like the guest list of any popular party—predictably enough, since that's what it had been. Lord Olthwaite's name nagged at her from the score of others. It would be so easy to point the finger at him—and so wrong, wrong beyond anything she had done before. She couldn't do that, even if Lord Var-court wouldn't disbelieve her.

She closed her eyes as thoughts of Varcourt invaded her

mind. There could be nothing between them that mattered, and yet his presence now made her heart ache almost more than it scared her. His pain burned her, even though it had no reason to. Even if she had been a true daughter of her family, he would have been considered slightly beyond her grasp. As it was, nothing was possible, even setting aside their antagonism. With that taken into account, any sentiment took on the proportions of gross folly.

And that she could not afford.

"Then where did she go?" Thomas asked wearily.

"Then she 'ad me drive 'er back to dat Gypsy place," the cab driver said, kneading his hat in his hands. "You sure dis is all right to tell you, guv? She always was kind to me. Always asks for me special and pays me a little something extra, though she don't seem flush with chink 'erself, eh. You sure I'm not getting 'er in any kind of trouble?"

"Quite the reverse," Thomas said. "Thank you." He slid a pound note across the table.

The cab driver tugged his forelock and left, muttering uneasily under his breath.

"I don't have the taste for this, Edgington," Thomas said after the man had gone.

Edgington moved from the shadows by the fireplace in Thomas' parlor. "You are the one who wanted her followed. Are you sure there is a link between her and Olthwaite? Or are you sending me haring after your personal demons?"

Thomas poured himself a measure of brandy. He offered another tumbler to Edgington, but the baron shook his head. "I am as sure as I can be about anything in this business. Olthwaite recognized that necklace. You saw his expression."

"Yes," Edgington conceded.

Thomas took a quick swallow of the brandy. There was a

strange aftertaste, slightly bitter. "The necklace is one of Olthwaite's family pieces."

"Has it occurred to you that she might be telling the truth about finding it?" Edgington asked.

"I am certain she knows him. You did not see her reaction when I suggested that he had taken advantage of her. She was horrified." He took another swallow. Yes, there was definitely something wrong with the brandy. Thomas set his tumbler down, still half full.

Edgington looked unconvinced. "Any woman would be, when her honor is impugned."

"Madame Esmeralda plays the seductress. A week ago, I would have sworn that she would agree that she had been with almost any man I named." Thomas leaned forward. "We need to know what made Olthwaite so afraid. That's the heart of it."

"If you are right, then your Esmeralda might hold the key to it all."

Thomas blinked at Edgington, who seemed determined to slide out of focus. "Which is why we must have her every move followed."

Edgington shook his head. "I doubt she's reporting to anyone at this point, Varcourt."

"But she might do something, say something. . . ." Thomas trailed off, blinking again. The room was suddenly fuzzy. He looked at the half-empty brandy glass. Had he had any since Esmeralda had last been here? He thought back with difficulty. Port, yes—he'd had a glass of port just the other night. But he hadn't touched the brandy since he had poured Esmeralda a glass. He stepped toward the spirits cabinet, and the world shifted alarmingly.

"Varcourt?" Edgington said.

Thomas ignored him. He opened the door and groped in the back. He found the small bottle hidden behind the others and pulled it out. Empty. He laughed, the sound coming as if from far away, and turned toward the baron as the world slowly slid sideways. She was brilliant. Brilliant and dangerous, and the thought of her filled him with an irrational glow.

"Edgington, I'd appreciate it if you might do me a favor," he said, pronouncing each word with great care.

"Yes?" the other man said warily.

"Drag me to the bed after I pass out. Then pour out that damned brandy. I'm afraid I've been given a dose of my own medicine." And with that, he let the world go gently black, sliding down onto the blessedly thick carpet.

A vision of Esmeralda's face rose in front of his eyes before he lost consciousness, smiling at her trick. He smiled back and took her extended hand, and she led him into opium dreams.

Chapter Sixteen

The ballroom was already hot, glaring gaslight and elegant bodies filling the air with a miasma of smells. Breasts damp with a sheen of sweat were propped up by the wizardry of modern corsetry, displayed like the wilting flowers that cascaded from tress to dress. Swaying with every shift and step, skirts offered kaleidoscopes of petticoat and ankle, and between their overblown circumferences stalked the men, severe in black with bristling mustachios and oiled hair.

The scene was perfectly interchangeable with a hundred other balls, Em knew. But Em had not attended a hundred other balls—with the circumscribed life that had attended her putative status in Uncle William's house, she had been to only one, a momentous event that had seared itself upon her life as a pivotal moment without reference to which nothing else made sense.

And so memories from the other ballroom merged with this one in her mind's eye. Even that would not have been so bad except that her memory inevitably continued forward to the denouement, following her own path upward to the nursery with its too-small bed and its faded wallpaper of plump shepherdesses and plumper sheep.

In her mind, everything came together in a swirling riot. The blissful days when she had been tucked, pink and damp from scrubbing, into bed with the children of the house only to whisper and giggle with her bedmate until Nursie was roused to sternly call for silence. The peaceful evenings filled with books and candlelight after the other children had been promoted to rooms of their own, and she, who alone had no legitimate place in the world, had been left to an indefinitely extended childhood. And the last, the most terrible—the night she had left her first ball lightfooted and breathless with joy to tumble into her bed, only to be interrupted in her undressing by the knock of one of the baron's guests. On that night, the cheerful comfort of the room had revealed itself as a trap and a lie. . . .

Em stood next to one of the French windows, so close to the wall that the draperies pressed into her skirts, the heavy brocade folds whispering across the plum velvet of her dress whenever a shocky shiver overtook her. Panic thickened in her throat, churning up from her belly to choke her lungs, swirling in a sick counterrhythm to the music that pulsed in the air.

It had been a mistake to accept Lady Hamilton's invitation. She was no lady's companion, to attend upon a society matron's every move—not that the countess had kept her near once the guests had begun to arrive. Em had set herself up to be no more than a social entertainment, and a ball was no place for a performer. In such an atmosphere, she would not be asked to tell fortunes or contact the dead. She could only lose some part of her mystery by being seen too much to no purpose.

Yet here she was. Not only had she come, but she had allowed Lady Hamilton to send her own dressmaker to invalidate her demur that she owned nothing to wear, and the result was exquisite but frightening. Em had not dared to make more than the feeblest suggestions to the dressmaker, which were overridden by the assurance that Lady Hamilton had already chosen a design, and the result was a fashionably low bodice that made Em feel naked despite the gauzy layer of her veil and the yards of fabric below. The gown was glorious, and it was also grossly inappropriate to her station in life, past or present.

If she had even been able to take her place as Lady Hamilton's shadow, all might have been restored. But this had been one of the countess' good days, and after a heartfelt greeting and a warm embrace, Lady Hamilton had set Em adrift. She had gravitated toward the circumference of the room, but no corner offered her the shadows she so desperately sought.

"Care to dance with me, Madame Esmeralda?" Lord Gifford made the mocking request as he strolled by, a flute of champagne dangling negligently between two fingers.

"My dances are not suited for ballrooms." The cool reply came unbidden now—she scarcely had to think of making a response anymore for the words of Esmeralda to form on her lips. She wondered if the persona would be as easily shed or if her creation had somehow grafted itself to her. The idea was unnerving, and it sent another shudder through her.

Lord Gifford chuckled, a rich, dark sound, but he did not pause in his progress, which carried him to the side of Thomas' sisters, who fearlessly returned tease for tease until one stepped out onto the ballroom floor and into the steps of the mazurka that was just beginning.

Lord Olthwaite took the other girl's hand and bowed over it, but she pulled it back with a pretty little shake of her coppery curls. The heavyset man strolled off through the crowd, nodding to people on either side as roiling, angry queasiness curled in Em's belly. She tried to tear her eyes away from the figure. She was doing nothing from vindictiveness, she told herself. As much as she might hate the man, it was not his downfall that she schemed but her own salvation, his part being merely incidental to her restoration. If he suffered, then she would not deny that some part of her would rejoice. But she did not seek empty vengeance, not even though he filled her with a hatred that made her quake.

"I shall not ask you to dance with me."

Those words came from behind her, in the darkness of the garden beyond the French windows, without a trace of levity. She turned to see Lord Varcourt looming out of the shadows and into the halo of gaslight and torch as he approached the ballroom, his face thrown into sharp planes above the starched perfection of his black evening suit. She couldn't handle him here, now—could not handle the past that kept rushing up to assault her on top of this new confusion.

"Good. Because I do not know how," she said around lips that were suddenly stiff.

"I do not believe that," Varcourt said. He leaned against the doorjamb next to her, and it was all she could do not to jerk away. "Which is why I do not ask but order. Dance with me, Merry. Now."

"It would injure my reputation as a sphinx," she said, her heart stuttering as she balled her hands into fists in the luxuriant velvet.

Varcourt's dark eyes narrowed. "If you dance well enough, the guests will be reminded of your presence and titillated with questions."

"I do not dance well," she said bluntly. "They will suspect that we are in league."

"Our first rendezvous made them suspect. Our meeting in the park—perhaps that made them doubt, the way you rejected me. Let us stir them again with more guesses."

"Let us give them no more fodder for their speculations," Em countered.

"I did not ask." He grasped her shoulder with one hand and began to bear her toward the dance floor with a force that she could not resist without making a scene.

The whirling couples loomed up before her with all the horror of a nightmare. The ballroom looked nothing like her childhood home—it was too grand, too sternly elegant. But none of that made a difference. Em tightened her hand around his own, where it rested upon her shoulder.

"You will destroy my mystery," she hissed. "And then where shall you be?"

"People are beginning to take you for granted, Merry," he said, his gaze slicing through her defenses. "This shall be the scandal that renews society's interest."

Em's throat tightened. It was true, too true. Only Lady Hamilton was clinging to her with the same strength as before, and soon, if the countess did not shed her, she would become a laughingstock. Em's invitations had fallen away so that it was becoming increasingly difficult for her to fill up her days and nights, and ladies were growing bored with her talk of spirits. "If they were tired of me, you would have tossed me aside already," she said.

"But we still have a deal, don't we?" He stepped onto the ballroom floor, turning her into a dance hold with a hook of his arm.

"Everyone shall know about it now," she whispered.

"No. They shall suspect—not one thing but many." His right arm slid down to her waist as his left closed around her hand and he began the steps of the mazurka. Around the perimeter of the floor came a flurry of reaction, audible above the orchestra, ladies whispering behind fans as men gazed after them with varying degrees of consideration and envy.

Em's feet automatically moved in the patterns that she had learned dancing stiffly in the arms of the other children of the house under the governess' and dancing master's sharp eyes. Only once before had she danced in the arms of men, on the night that she had come to rue more sharply than any other time in her short life.

Varcourt was tall and strong, as those half-grown men had seemed to her that night, but there the similarities ended, for her partners of that evening had been laughing, boisterous, their hilarity infectious to a girl not often given a reason to smile. And she knew enough now to realize that they'd been drunk. Even on that night, she had not been oblivious to the half-suppressed sexuality of their glances. Far from it. She had felt herself blooming, unfolding under their admiring gazes, believing that this was what Alice had felt when she had been the toast of the season. Em had drunk the sensation until she had feared she would burst, and then she had slipped from the room to drift upstairs on a cloud of bliss, only to be thrust abruptly back into the harsh realities of the world by that knock on the nursery door.

Varcourt could scarcely be more different than those men. Except for the heat of his body that seared hers through their clothes, he might have been sculpted of ice. And yet he made her body flame more than the deft compliments and skillful ambuscades of all the men during that last night of her girlhood. If those smiling, charming men could have been dangerous, this chilly mountain of a man might be capable of anything.

He held her firmly to him as he moved through the steps, her corset pressing against his evening jacket. He danced with stern confidence, neither pushing nor crushing her but somehow moving himself so that she moved, too, without even meaning to, his silence giving her no distraction from the way their bodies moved together. Em found herself unnaturally aware of the texture of the clothing that separated them, her velvet and lace catching at the cassimere and causing his coat's slick lining to rub against his waistcoat. She tried to restrict her awareness to that, to forget the firmness of the man behind the cloth, the staring eyes, the memory of the other dances in other arms. . . .

Suddenly, he stopped, and she found that her feet had come to a standstill with him. She blinked and muzzily realized that the song had ended.

"Come for a walk with me," Lord Varcourt said, and before she could regain her composure, he had pulled her through the perimeter crowd and was moving out of a French window into the harlequin darkness of the terrace.

Em suppressed the urge to ask where they were going as he drew her along. He ignored the torch-lined brick steps leading down to the lower gardens and chose a shadowed stretch of slope. The well-rolled turf was damp and springy beneath her feet. As soon as she reached level ground, she stopped dead, bracing against the force on her arm that was surely to follow. But instead, Varcourt turned so that he was facing her, their arms still half-linked.

"What do you want?" she said when he did not break the silence. "Why are you hounding me?" She could not make out his expression in the shadows through her veil.

He said, "I am not hounding. I am probing. I want to learn more about you."

"Why?" she demanded in frustration. "What is it to you? Soon enough, you shall know what you want from your mother. I shall have fulfilled my purpose, and I will leave your world forever."

"Maybe I don't want you to," he said.

"And maybe you're a fool," she returned, pulling away. She started walking blindly into the dark gardens.

"Most likely," he said. "I certainly was made a fool of two nights ago." He kept pace with her.

"Oh?" Em chose a path at random and began walking down it.

"Indeed. I sat down to a nice brandy and did not wake up until the next morning."

Em hesitated slightly, breaking the rhythm of her stride, but recovered quickly and pressed on. "You deserved it."

"Perhaps. Would it make you feel any better if I told you that I had truly meant only to calm you?" he asked.

"I was already calm," she said. Great lavender bushes, grown up like trees, loomed on either side. "Do you keep laudanum on hand in case you have a need to drug uncooperative women?"

"The countess . . . left it. Of course you were calm. It is a normal thing for a calm person to slice her own hand open with a knife," Varcourt said.

"As normal as it is for her to offer her body as a mere distraction." She turned suddenly, and he almost careered into her, fetching up a mere foot away. She curled her fingers into a ball—she scarcely noticed the twinge of the shallow gash unless she paid special attention to it. "I was fine."

"You haven't been fine since I met you," Varcourt said. He was little more than a dark mass in the starlight, a deeper shadow among the patterns that the branches made of the distant torchlight along other paths.

"What did you learn of me just now, on the ballroom floor?" she asked despite herself.

"That you were taught to dance properly but that you are unlikely to be used to being in the arms of a man."

His swift reply came too near the mark. "Perhaps I studied it from a book. Or I practiced in the scullery between the dishes from the soup and the first entrée."

"And perhaps I am a charwoman's son, smuggled into my mother's birthing chamber in a warming pan." She could feel his eyes in the darkness. "I shall discover who you are. It is just a matter of time."

"Why does it matter?" Em demanded.

"I want to know how you tick. How you are put together."

"How you can take me apart," she supplied, ignoring the seductive shiver that his words sent over her.

"If need be," he said.

She turned away from him. "Trust me. There is nothing in my past that is of interest to a man such as you."

Varcourt snorted. "I think that I am a better judge of that than you are."

"We have a deal. That's all you need to know about me." She made the words as flat and ugly as she could, stepping away from him.

He caught her arm and pulled her against him, sending her skirts swaying out behind him. "Maybe that's not enough. You were gently bred, gently reared, gently trained. Who were you? Not a petted tradesman's brat. A gentleman farmer's daughter? A vicar's get? You have fallen a long way."

"Or been pushed," she retorted heedlessly, and instantly regretted it.

"What was stolen from you?" he insisted. "Your inheritance? Your virtue?"

The multitude of secrets in her life crowded around her in the darkness, clamoring in her ears, forcing her tongue to speak. "Everything, twice over."

"Tell me." The intensity of the words shivered in the air.

Almost without meaning to, Em found herself speaking— not the words she longed to say, not the story that had scored itself in injustice and betrayal upon her heart, but at least some echo of it. "A woman's virtue is her shield, perhaps, but virtue is a condition of courtesy not extended to us all."

"Who hurt you, Merry?" he whispered.

She smiled bitterly. "Do you want to take notes, so that you can repeat what was done, if necessary?"

"I want—" He broke off, holding her harder against him. "I just *want*."

"Me?" She laughed unsteadily. "I have done my job too well, then. Exerting my wiles upon you."

"To control me." The words were bald.

"I never aspired so high. To distract you, since you seemed hell-bent upon destroying me." Truth, every word of it.

"And that is all you ever wanted of me?" he demanded.

"What do you wish me to say? That I dreamt that you would fall to your knees and confess your adoration, whisking me away from my squalid little life to become your viscountess?" She laughed, the sound tearing at her throat. "Do assign to me some measure of sense. I am not that stupid, Lord Varcourt."

"Do you feel something that would excite such fancies about me?" His hands tightened on her upper arms.

"I feel fear," she said simply. "And, of course, desire. They make a heady brew."

"What else?"

She stared at the shadow where his face was. "There can't be anything else that matters, not between the two of us. But I also feel pity and . . . a kind of pain, or regret, or something that has no name and does not deserve one."

His grip loosened. "Everything deserves a name, Merry," he said, his voice abruptly subdued. Em's heart was still beating too hard in her chest, and she swayed a little, uncertain as to whether she had given the right answer.

"You know so much about me," Varcourt continued, "while I only know what you became after—after you were hurt. What were you like as a child?"

"What does it matter?" she asked, but tiredly, not acerbically.

"It doesn't," he said. "It will betray none of your secrets. Answer for me, then, my meaningless questions. Did you laugh much?"

After a long silence, Em said, "Enough that I felt no great lack of laughter."

"That is no answer." She could imagine his skeptical, narrowed gaze.

Em hesitated again. Finally, she said, "I had . . . a sister."
That was both close enough to the truth and far enough from
it to be safe. "Of all the children, she was my favorite. We
would talk and laugh for hours."

"Did you have a falling-out with her?"

"She died. The German measles. I was twelve then—she
was nine, the youngest of us all. After that, there weren't as
many reasons to laugh, though I grew much closer to our
other sister. She married, but soon she was dead, too." Em
was saying too much, far too much, but once she began to
speak, she could hardly stop herself. There had never been
anyone to listen to her before, never anyone who had shown
the slightest interest in her secret history or private pain.

"I am sorry," Varcourt said.

The statement took her aback. "Are you? That would be
curious, considering what you've done to me."

"Man is a contradictory creature," he said aridly. "Can I
not be sorry?"

"You can be whatever you like." Em bit her tongue, but it
was too late—the accusation in the word *you* was too clear
for him to miss.

"But you couldn't," he filled in.

She had given away too much—his comments were
growing too insightful. She had to distract him. Pulling
back, she said, "Why don't you stick with the subject of
greater interest to you?"

She felt his skepticism. "Who is to say that you are not of
interest?"

"You told me the last time that we met that I had better
have answers for you today."

"And do you?" The tension in his body changed, becoming harder, rougher.

"Your mother is wearing the necklace I gave her again. If
I took your message to mean what you meant it to, I believe
that answers your question." Lying was so simple; once she

had begun, the words spilled out with an ease that made her sick at herself.

"What did she see?"

Em knew better than to toy with him any further—she needed one more thing from him, the last piece of information to remove all her doubts and to make certain that her story rang true. She would need all her experience at manipulation for this. "She went out to find your brother on her own mount after everyone else had left. She was the one who first found his body, not your father." She took a deep breath. "There was a whip lash on his cheek, and his forehead was battered. But that was not all that she saw. Tell me, now, did you strike your brother on the day he died?"

"I did not kill him."

The distinct agony of each word cut into Em. She closed her eyes, sending a silent plea of forgiveness to Varcourt even as she knew that she was about to commit an unforgivable act. "I was not asking you that. I ask only, Did you hit him?"

There was a long silence. Em could hear Varcourt's agitated breath. "He was supposed to be my big brother. He was supposed to have been the one to teach me how to ride, not the one sniveling by a streamside because he'd gotten a little damp. He was supposed to be the next heir, dammit."

"So you struck him," she said. Her stomach dropped. It couldn't be. She realized how thoroughly she had convinced herself that he could not have killed his brother, even as she pretended to herself that she had doubt. There had to be another explanation.

"Once, across the face with the whip," he agreed, the words barely audible. "He just howled louder. I turned and rode away, before I hurt him more. He was standing beside the stream when I left and screaming his lungs out. The next time I saw him, he was dead."

She was grateful, pathetically grateful to be able to believe that, but she kept every trace of it from her voice. "Someone killed him," she said. "Your mother saw him, walking away from the place where your brother lay." That was the first lie. His mother had seem someone, but Em knew nothing more than that. Still, she had not spoken the great lie, the irredeemable one.

"Who?"

She stood for a moment, swaying. Varcourt had every right to know the truth, but did he have the right to destroy his mother in getting it? He would not settle for half answers—he wanted something complete, and somehow, Em was certain that whatever secret was so terrible that his mother had kept it for all these years was not an answer that Varcourt would accept from her.

Em made her choice.

Chapter Seventeen

"Your mother did not recognize him," Em said. "She was too far away. She saw someone dismount from his horse next to a standing figure. Then they both began to gesture excitedly. One figure turned away, and the other reached out and struck him, sending him sprawling into the stream. The remaining one mounted his horse again and rode away. When she reached the fallen figure, she discovered that it was your brother." Every word a fabrication.

"And she did not call for help?" Varcourt demanded.

"He was already dead, his skull broken," Em said, ignoring the clenching of her guts and the pounding of her heart. It was too late now. The lie had been said, and she was committed to it. "She was frightened that if she called out, the murderer would be the first to come. And so she rode back home again, leaving him there, and was back before anyone but the grooms knew she had left. She has felt guilty for years on your account because she never confessed to what she saw, didn't exonerate you when your innocence was in doubt. At first she was frightened, and then she was afraid that you would hate her."

"But who killed him?" Those words were soft, not meant for Em's ears.

She answered anyway. "Who was searching?"

"Half a dozen servants and many of the guests," Varcourt said. His voice sounded a thousand miles away. "I was out, of course, along with my father. Lord and Lady James. The Duke of Rushworth and his son Gifford and daughter Lady Victoria. Lord Edgington and his son, the present baron. Old Lord Olthwaite and his son and daughter, both. Grimsthorpe, de Lint, Morel, and their elders. Near half the older generation are dead now. The truth may have died with them."

"Yes, it may have," Em agreed. Olthwaite. Yes, that was one lie she'd left unsaid, even if by using it she could have brought Varcourt permanently and forcefully to her side. But no—the deception was grave enough when she accused no one. She could not tell Varcourt that the young Lord Olthwaite killed his brother, no matter how much it might help her.

"I must be getting back to the party before the dew ruins my dress," she said instead. "Many saw me leave with you, and I shall be missed."

"Go, then," Varcourt said roughly.

A note in his voice cut her. She raised a gloved hand to caress his cheek, then impulsively lifted her veil to kiss him, gently, on his unresponsive lips.

"I am so sorry," she whispered, knowing that he could not understand all that she meant. She lowered her veil and walked away, leaving him standing like a black granite statue in the shadows of the garden.

Em strode swiftly back up the path toward the house. The veil and the darkness formed a nearly impenetrable screen, so she was grateful for the well-groomed paths and neatly trimmed hedges. Her mind buzzed with the stories she could invent, the new details she could drop like pearls in Varcourt's hand to string him onward.

Those automatic fabrications sickened her, and she closed her mind to them. She had done what she had to, and she would do no more. This was not like the riddles from anonymous spirits from beyond, nor was it even like the vague reassurances that she dispensed to most people seeking a message from a particular loved one. It wasn't a lie about her own past or her motivations. It was a fabrication that deeply affected the living, in a tangible way. There was nothing harmless or playacting about it.

The worst part was, she had wanted to give him the truth. God knew he deserved it. But he would not take a partial answer, and Em could not destroy his mother to get the whole of it. Lady Hamilton did not merit that, no matter what secret she hid in her heart. So Em had damned herself. It was, a nasty little voice whispered in her mind, no better than she deserved, after all.

In her hurry, Em nearly rebounded off the three figures coming up the path. She dug her heels into the white gravel of the walk, her skirts swinging chaotically forward against her weight.

"I told you she'd come this way," said one voice jovially to the others.

Em squeezed her eyes shut against sudden pain and panic. She would know that voice anywhere. Lord Olthwaite.

"Madame Esmeralda, you severely injured me by refusing a dance and then floating off in the arms of another." That bored, aristocratic drawl could only be Lord Gifford's.

She got control of her breathing and opened her eyes again. The figures were clear against the distant torchlight, but she could not make out their features or expressions. Her veil served only to blind her here.

"Perhaps you weren't forceful enough," the third man offered. "It didn't look like Varcourt gave her much of a choice. Maybe she's one of those chits from whom you have to take what you want."

"Do not be vulgar, Algy," Gifford said. "At least, not in front of a . . . lady. As our Esmeralda is already returning, your suspicion of an assignation was incorrect, Olthwaite. I believe that you owe me five pounds?"

"She's returning alone," Olthwaite pointed out. "Perhaps it isn't that there was no assignation so much as it was that Varcourt is as ham-fisted about that as he is about parliamentary matters. Let me give her a try."

He barged forward, straight into Em, almost toppling over. He caught her awkwardly in both hands. His breath smelled of a rank mixture of whiskey and cigars.

"I have no interest in dallying with you," she said in the chilly, accented tones of Esmeralda.

"Don't be such a cold bitch," Olthwaite said, holding her harder.

Em forced herself not to strike him. He was stronger than she was, and the two men looking on might very well decide to help one of their own. At the least, her dress would be torn, and then she would have to find some way to flee unseen, so that her appearance would not thrust the appearance of impropriety into the faces of the matrons of society. Society could overlook any indiscretion provided the forms were kept—and none if they were not.

Instead, on a sudden inspiration, she leaned forward, avoiding his clumsy attempt to kiss her, and murmured in her own voice, "You know whose spirit this is, Edgar. Let her go, or I swear that the poltergeists of Hades shall never leave you."

"Emmeline!" He said her name like an oath and threw her from him. Em barely managed to keep herself from sprawling on the path.

"What happened?" Gifford said tensely, stepping up to steady the drunk stagger of the other man.

"That woman—she's a witch!" Olthwaite said. "Get her away from me."

Em turned, only to rebound against another male chest. *Trapped.*

Thomas stood in the darkness at the intersection of two paths, trying to assimilate what Esmeralda had told him. Was it the truth? Had someone killed Harry in the sight of his mother? He didn't dare believe—not yet—but it could explain so much.

If it was true, who had killed his brother? His body burned with the possibility that there had been a murderer out there all along. After twelve years of guilt, twelve years of self-recrimination because he had left his brother by the side of the stream to slip upon the bank and break his head on a stone, he was almost dizzy with the possibility that it was not an accident—and enraged at the thought that someone had killed his brother in cold blood all those years ago and had never been held accountable.

He wanted to believe as a drowning man clutches at sticks and weeds, and that was precisely why he held himself back. He took a long, steadying breath and packed away those riotous feelings. He would hope everything, but he needed confirmation for more than that. He must speak to his mother himself. Only then would he believe.

He started down the path, tracing Esmeralda's steps back toward the house. A scuffling sound ahead made him quicken his steps. Then he heard a voice: "Emmeline!"

His jaw tightened. He'd listened to that voice in Parliament for months. Olthwaite. He turned the corner as more voices erupted in consternation, and a slender figure spun and reeled into him in a swirl of skirts. He caught her reflexively.

"Madame Esmeralda," he said, looking at the three men who stood before her. Gifford, Olthwaite, and Morel. None of them was good news for a woman of a certain reputation to meet on a dark night. "Is there a problem?"

"No, no problem, Lord Varcourt, though I would enjoy

your company if you might choose to escort me back to the ballroom," Esmeralda said swiftly, taking his arm.

"It would be my pleasure," he said. He stepped forward, and the three other men moved off the path. Esmeralda tightened her grip on his arm and swallowed as they passed Olthwaite.

"So. Emmeline," he said, after they were some distance away.

"That was the name of a girl he once knew. I told him that I knew her spirit," she said lightly—too lightly.

Thomas didn't buy it for a moment. "I am sure that is precisely what you said."

"What do you mean by that?" she demanded.

"I mean that Olthwaite wouldn't have been scared off with a few spooky declarations. Not like that." He looked narrowly at her. "First the necklace and now this. You are Emmeline, aren't you?"

"Perhaps I work for her," she said swiftly.

"I have given up on the idea that you work for anyone," he said.

"I knew her," she amended. "We were in the same lodging house. She disappeared, leaving a note saying that all her affects were to be mine. I took over her room, and that is how I knew to look behind the loose brick for the necklace."

There was a tremble in her voice that she could not quite seem to control. No, he would not fall for that one, either. Her relentless fabrications stung him because they made him distrust the story she had told him about his mother, he told himself, even though he knew that wasn't all.

"Stop it. You are Emmeline," Thomas said. She was silent. "The name suits you much better than Esmeralda." They had moved out of the half-hidden paths of the garden and onto the greensward of the lawn that rose up to a terrace above.

"More English?" Em offered.

"More . . . everything. Emmeline." The name nagged at him. "The name is far too familiar."

"It is a very common name," she said.

"I mean that it is familiar in reference to Olthwaite's family," he corrected. That was it. He spoke his thoughts aloud. "I went to their old pile a few times as a child. I seem to remember an Emmeline. A pale girl in a pale dress . . . Not one of young Edgar's sisters, as I recall—I knew those, Ann and Alice. Ann died in childhood. I remember the year Alice came out. She married one of the Radcliffe sons and died within the year. But you wouldn't know anything about that, would you?"

"Lord Varcourt—" she began, then broke off. He felt the tension pulling her body tight. "What are you going to do?" she asked instead.

Thomas stopped, looking at the woman before him. Her features were completely obscured by her veil, her voice unreadable. "We had a bargain," he said.

"I delivered." The words were brittle, distinct.

"You did," he agreed. That was its own hell, one he'd deal with later. Here and now, though, was the matter of Esmeralda—or rather Emmeline. He tried to remember something of her as a child, but there was nothing but that single image of a tall, quiet girl in long curls, standing apart from the other children. Thomas wasn't even certain how old he had been the last time his family had stayed at Forsham. Before Harry's death, certainly, and after Ann's. He had been just of an age to start paying attention to girls, and Alice had taken full advantage of that, tormenting him with the attention that she lavished on the Radcliffe brothers.

Emmeline had been a nonentity, a mere shadow in the background of those sunlit days, slightly older than Alice and far graver. Every great house had its poor relations, of no more note or consequence than the servants.

"This confirms what I have suspected for several days now, that whatever convoluted plan you may have, your intentions are personal, not political," Thomas said. There were too many people about for this conversation. He began leading her across the damp grass toward the seclusion of the summerhouse.

"As I told you," Emmeline said, offering no resistance, "I have nothing against your family."

"What about yours?" Thomas asked. "You called Ann and Alice your sisters. Was that another lie?"

"Half sisters," she said. "We did not know that we had blood ties then, nor what they were, but we loved each other like true siblings. I carry no bitterness toward them."

"Then your father . . ." Thomas let the word hang.

"Yes, he was the old baron. Edgar is three years my senior, Alice was one younger, and Ann was three. Uncle William, I was allowed to call him, but his wife I always called Lady Olthwaite." There was no feeling in her voice, but in its sheer chilliness, Thomas sensed an old, silent pain. "Upon his deathbed, he confessed our true relation."

Their shoes crunched on the gravel as he guided them onto the walk. Thomas tried to incorporate this information into the image that he had formed of her background. She was no petted daughter of an impoverished gentleman, nor was she the youngest daughter of a dozen offspring of a country squire. Instead, she was a member of the group of obligations that every upper-class family gathers by fair means or foul, one of the sorts that Thomas had always thought of contemptuously as a kind of human flotsam.

Children arrived as bastards, orphans, and from improvidently fecund branches of the family that found themselves with more mouths than bread. Every family had its share, too, of old maids and poor widows, as well as those relatives who came as guests and contrived, one way or another, to never leave, making instead a slow rotation of the houses of anyone that they could make a claim upon. Most of them eventually made themselves useful in one way or another, the male children being set up in service to the family as private secretaries, stewards, or barristers, the women variously serving as housekeepers, governesses, chaperones, companions, and nurses.

Thomas thought of how he had chafed against his future as the substitute for his brother's deficiencies and for the first time wondered how much bleaker the future would seem when one's destiny was to be an appurtenance for the family that took one in, in a state of debt that was not reckoned in mere numbers and could not be discharged.

How had Emmeline escaped that future? Or perhaps it was better to ask, How had she been cast from it?

He said, "You once had a comfortable life at Forsham. How did you come to be here? And why are you trying to terrorize your half brother?"

But Emmeline was already shaking her head. "I have told you what you might have found out by asking Edgar or anyone who knew me. What I am about or why I am doing it truly does not concern you. I was once a member of Lord Olthwaite's household. Now I must make my own way in the world. In order to do this, I have chosen to take on a mysterious foreign persona, and so I have hidden my identity from those who might know while using the information that my close association with this segment of society brought me. That must suffice for you."

This he believed. Perhaps it was because it made so much sense, perhaps because it was so damning. If she had stolen the items that Olthwaite was searching for, she could hang for it.

The summerhouse loomed before them, its pale pillars skeletally white in the faint moonlight. Thomas pushed its glass door open, standing aside in invitation, but Emmeline pulled away and planted herself in front of it, making no move to enter.

"Did he rape you?" Thomas demanded.

Emmeline stepped backward. "Edgar? If he had, what would you do about it? Call him out, call a constable, or thrash him yourself?"

"At least tell me that much," he insisted. "I deserve that much." He shut his mouth hard after the last statement, wondering where the hell such a nonsensical declaration had come from. What was between them could have no meaning beyond their agreement. He was a viscount; she was a charlatan and, it now appeared, a bastard as well as a danger to everything for which he had worked so hard.

Emmeline hesitated, her weight rocked forward on the balls of her feet as if prepared for flight. She should reject his claim to his deserving anything from her out of hand. But instead, she said, "My brother did not rape me. The tale of the trade of my virginity for my possessions was true."

"Possessions that included some of the Olthwaite family jewels. I would have thought that worth my own virtue, in your place," Thomas said drily. "Why did you steal them when you left? You can't pretend now that you found the necklace in a boardinghouse."

He could sense her stiffening. "I did not steal it. It was left for me by my father." The last word had a hint of a sneer in it.

"If it weren't stolen, you would have sold some of it," Thomas said flatly.

"How do you know what I've sold and what I haven't?" Emmeline demanded.

Thomas narrowed his eyes. "Let us just say that I have a political interest in what your brother does, and he has been searching for a list of items in every pawn and jewelry shop in London for some months now."

Her voice was subdued. "No one would believe that they

were mine. Most shopkeepers refused outright to buy any of the pieces, and the rest offered me the price they'd give to stolen goods. It seemed better to keep them."

"That was true, too, then," Thomas murmured, even though it couldn't be. She did not know that he knew about the rest of the family jewels being missing—never would a baron leave such a collection to a by-blow.

"I will not give you more, Lord Varcourt," she said gravely. "You are far too adept at putting pieces together to get a much fuller idea than that which I intended."

"And what do you intend?" Thomas asked. "This show, your investment in my mother, is no end in itself."

The unfamiliar sound of Emmeline's laughter as bitter as it was, startled him. "That is exactly what I mean. No, Varcourt, no more."

"You might be Olthwaite's tool," he said, "thrust into my family in order to enervate us politically."

Even in the darkness, her scorn was palpable. "You would have to be a greater fool than I take you for to believe that."

She was right. There was no way that Olthwaite's astonishment at seeing the necklace fall from Lady Hamilton's hand had been faked—and even if it had, to what purpose? Still less likely was the engineering of the exchange he had just witnessed. Olthwaite was a clever man, with a keen intelligence behind his bloodshot eyes and drunken slur, but he was also sincerely superstitious and had been since their youth. Emmeline's masquerade as a spiritualist was perfectly targeted for Olthwaite, not his mother.

"Where did you learn your trade?" He tried a different tack. "I doubt that contacting the spirits is part of a normal education in a baron's household."

She paused, as if considering what to answer. "There was a Gypsy campground near the manor house. Edgar was fascinated by the fortune-tellers, dragging all three of us girls down to the camp every opportunity that he got to squander his pocket money on the latest news from the spirit world. I was fascinated by how they worked. After a time, I figured out a few things for myself, and when the Gypsies saw what I could do, a few would sometimes give me hints. Edgar didn't know. He never paid any attention to what I did."

"A peculiar hobby," he noted.

"I was a peculiar girl," she retorted. "But enough of that. It is your turn to answer a question for me. Have you decided whether you are going to unmask me?"

Thomas paused. "I see no need at this point. After all, you did keep your bargain, and it seems more and more likely that you weren't lying when you assured me that you had no ill intentions toward my family."

"Thank you." Emmeline's answer was a bare whisper in the night breeze. Her form trembled suddenly as a shiver passed over it. "The air has the bite of autumn in it. I must go." She began to turn away.

"I shall escort you." When Emmeline froze and looked at him without responding, he said, "I will bring you as far as the terrace. You would not want a repetition of what happened with Olthwaite, Morel, and Gifford, now, would you?"

"Of course not," Emmeline said, and she stepped forward to take his extended arm.

They walked back in silence, Thomas attempting to control the turmoil in his guts. Even with all that had happened to him, he still found himself distracted by Emmeline's presence, the faint scent of the perfumed soap she took to the mean bathhouse teasing him, both with its fragrance and with the images of her body, nude and slick in that dim, steam-clouded room.

She had given him what she had promised, or at least appeared to. Their association, except so far as it touched his mother, was at an end. These new revelations about her past did a good deal toward easing his mind about her intentions toward his family, even though he now had more questions than before.

Thomas knew he couldn't trust her—knew that on some level, she dared not be trustworthy—but he could not seem to keep at bay his growing sense of association with her. Whether their bargain or, to put it crudely, their fornication had created this false kinship, he didn't know, but despite the jangling warning that the more sensible portions of his brain sent, he couldn't simply ignore the growing effect that she was having on him. Her voice, her body, the sheer breathtaking power of her will—it all got under his skin, into his head. When he told himself that he was just trying to figure her out in order to counteract whatever dastardly plan she hid, it rang false even in the privacy of his own mind.

At the edge of the grassy area that stretched up to the terrace, Emmeline stopped abruptly.

"You are likely wondering why I did not tell you who I was from the beginning," she said.

"The thought crossed my mind," Thomas said.

"If you had known, you could have destroyed everything I'd worked for—my life, my future. Not because I wished you ill but because discrediting me would have been the swiftest way to distance me from your mother. I hope that . . ." She trailed off. "I believe that you would not do that now. I must believe that. Because if you do it, you might as well put your hands around my throat and throttle the life out of me right here." Her voice shook slightly, echoing the tremor that ran through her body, sending an answering tension through him.

She stepped forward abruptly, her free hand shooting out to encircle his neck and bring his lips, briefly and roughly, against hers through the fabric of her veil. It was no accomplished seduction, no invitation to further delights, just a plea, pure and simple, expressed through every fiber of her body. Breathing roughly, she stumbled back.

"Upon my life, I shall not hurt your family," she whispered, and then she turned and was gone, fleeing up the hill toward the torch-lit terrace and the glowing doors of the ballroom beyond.

Thomas watched her go, his body still rocking from her short, fervent kiss, wanting to believe her but knowing that she would say whatever she felt that she must. He held all the cards now. The power that he had fought her for was now entirely in his hands. Yet the sense of victory eluded him, leaving a cold, dead weight in his belly.

Em balled her hands into fists to stop their shaking, forcing all the muscles in her body rigid even as her mind spun in terror. She had erred, erred badly, been lulled by Lord Varcourt—Lord Varcourt, who wanted nothing but her downfall!—into confessions that had seemed safe enough at the time.

Idiocy. It didn't matter what a relief it was to say something of her real past to someone. It was a self-indulgence she very well knew she couldn't afford. And now he knew far, far too much, enough to ruin her—to ruin everything. He had her head in a noose. The Olthwaite jewels felt as heavy as millstones, even from the distance of the Camden Town boardinghouse where she had them hidden.

Her father had left them to her, just as she had told Varcourt, but the cowardice that had marked every choice of his life had also been present in his will, as it had read "the one to whom they should rightfully belong." And they did rightfully belong only to her, for not only had old Lord Olthwaite acknowledged his paternity of her upon his deathbed, he also confessed his first marriage—to Em's mother. Without proof, though, she could very well hang for theft. Mary Catherine Dunn had been a Catholic from a middle-class barrister's family, not the sort of girl he could ever hope to be accepted by his family. So William Wythe had wed her in secret, promising to recognize her upon his father's death.

But he had not only lacked the nerve to confront his father with an undesirable wife; he had also succumbed to the pressure to make a match of his parent's choosing. He had kept his first wife in ignorance far away from his family seat, and when she had died of scarlet fever five years after their marriage, he had felt little more than relief. He had taken their infant daughter into his family's house to be raised with his other children, and soon after had inherited the barony. Not even then did he recognize Em, for that would have disinherited his only male child and humiliated his putative baroness.

And so Em had been the old baron's sacrifice.

Em took a steadying gulp of air before pushing back into the ballroom. She had to keep going and pretend that nothing had happened. If Varcourt wanted to end her game, there was nothing she could do to stop it.

As soon as she stepped inside, Lord Gifford approached to her.

"The little bird has returned home," he said. "I shall not take no for an answer this time, Madame Esmeralda. It is the height of bad manners to reject one man only to accept another for the same dance, and I do not like to be made a fool of."

"Trust me, Lord Gifford, you are the last man whom I wish to make into a fool," Em said, summoning steadiness from somewhere. With a sense of helplessness, she accepted his extended hand and allowed him to pull her onto the floor and into his arms for a waltz.

As they danced, she responded to his falsely amiable chatter with monosyllables. His arms were strong, his step certain—if anything, he was a rather better dancer than Varcourt had been and, admittedly, an extremely handsome

man. But Em felt no more than the slightest trickle of awareness even though his hand cradled her waist, his legs moving against her skirts as they turned around and around. She
sensed something—half laugh, half sob—coming up her
throat, and she swallowed it down. The sudden temperance
of her body almost seemed like another betrayal. If she
could be so strong now, why did Varcourt make her so
weak? Weak and unforgivably, irrecoverably stupid . . .

The song ended, and Lord Gifford deposited her back at
the edge of the dance floor. As he murmured his leave, she
found herself gazing past his shoulder at Lady Hamilton,
who was buttressed by the presence of her friends into
something approximating normality.

As she watched, Lord Hamilton, lured from his seclusion
by the social necessity of hosting the ball, passed by, and
Lady Hamilton . . . faded, shrinking into herself. He nodded
to his wife, the movement imbued with infinite dignity and
sadness, but did not pause.

If Em had not spent dozens of hours a week reading that
softly aged face, she would have missed the flash deep in
Lady Hamilton's eyes. But she saw it—and recognized it.
Behind the fear that anyone could see was something else:
fury, and a festering, despairing mixture of hatred and love
that made Em gasp, putting a hand over her suddenly lurching stomach.

That sight clicked into place with the story that Lady
Hamilton had told her the day before, forming a new and terrible picture. The countess had ridden out the day that her
son had gone missing, and in the distance, she had seen
someone—her own husband—doing something sinister near
or to Harry. She had pressed onward and discovered her
son's body. And she had panicked, fleeing back to the manor
house, where she had hidden what she had seen from both
her guilty husband and innocent second son, leaving Var-

court to face the indignity of being suspected, though never named, first in the inquest and then by the society gossips.

Em rocked on her feet. Varcourt—he deserved to know this. But she couldn't tell him, could not have told him even before she had committed herself to her lie, for she knew that she would never have been believed. The irony of it was bitter in her mouth. His own father. And she had lied to Varcourt. She had betrayed far more than she had ever imagined. . . .

"Madame Esmeralda, may I have this dance?" A sable-clad man stood before her, extending a gloved hand.

Em nodded numbly, her mind still whirling, and let herself be guided onto the floor and into the steps of a schottische. The night faded into a dizzying succession of men and dances, her feet hardly pausing at the edge of the floor before another man would come up to claim her.

She blinked as a glass of wine was thrust into her unresisting hands.

"Drink, but with care," a familiar voice said.

Em looked up into Varcourt's stony face, only the tension in his eyes betraying any emotion. Obediently, she raised the glass to her lips under her veil, taking two swallows before she had the presence of mind to stop. "Drugged—?" she managed.

A shadow of a smile flitted over his face. "No, Merry, not drugged. I have watched you dance for the past two hours, and nothing has passed your lips."

"Has it been so long?" She tried to count the dances, the dance partners.

"You have created quite a sensation tonight—and put the noses of not a few mammas out of joint, distracting the eligible gentlemen as you have been."

"Oh, dear," she said unthinkingly, the most un-Esmeralda-like response she could have made.

"Go now," he urged. "I've called your cab to the door.

Leave the ball while it is at its height and the men are hungry for you. They will soon turn their attentions and competitions elsewhere, and all will be mended."

She gripped his arm in confusion. "Why are you helping me?"

She felt his wry self-amusement, though it was only allowed to flicker across his face for an instant. "Call it weakness. Call it stupidity. This is how I mean to say that yes, we have a bargain, and at least for the moment, I plan to keep my part of it."

Em shook her head. "Thank you," she said. When he stepped back, pulling his arm away, she bent her head in acknowledgment and left, cradling her guilt like a fresh wound.

Chapter Eighteen

From the shadows beneath the staircase, Thomas watched the last of the guests leave, taking Lord and Lady Hamilton's hands in turn and murmuring their thanks for the evening. Even Mary and Elizabeth had flitted upstairs half an hour before, when the last dance was played and the remaining guests retired to the east parlor for conversation and Lord Hamilton's finer wines.

As soon as the footmen shut the door behind the last swirling mantle and long black overcoat, Thomas' father turned and, without a word, mounted the limestone stairs, his steps slow and heavy. With every passing year, the house that had been built as a testament to his ego seemed less like a castle and more like his mausoleum.

Thomas' mother stood still for a moment, facing the great carven door. She had been a devastatingly beautiful woman in her youth, with brilliant red-blond hair that had been far out of fashion but had only made her all the more unique in her attractions. The first white threads had appeared in the weeks after Harry's death, and now only streaks of copper and gold remained. One still felt that she was beautiful, despite the lines that fear and worry had carved into her face, whenever her brilliant blue eyes focused upon him, but with her growing affection for her bottles of laudanum, that was becoming less and less frequent.

Finally, Lady Hamilton turned toward the stairs with a sigh. Thomas stepped out of the shadows, and her hand flew to her throat, where the Olthwaite family necklace rested.

"My goodness, Thomas. You frightened me," she said.

Thomas watched in displeasure as tension rippled through her body, making her movements turn suddenly jerky. There had once been a time that his presence had not caused such a reaction in her—before Harry's death.

And perhaps again, after.

"I, too, want to forgive you," he said, pushing the words out before he could change his mind.

Her expression froze, then moved through shock before dissolving completely. "Oh, Thomas," she said softly. "Thomas."

He looked at the footmen who stood, in perfectly trained stillness, on either side of the door. "Come upstairs, madam. We will talk in your drawing room."

"Of course," she said, and she stepped forward tremulously to take the arm that he offered.

He did not speak until she had sent her lady's maid, Valette, from the room. The maid gave Thomas an anxious, distrustful glance, but disappeared without a murmur.

"Thomas," Lady Hamilton said softly, then stopped, her eyes full of pain. She stood and started to totter with none of her usual grace, crossing to the spirits cabinet disguised as a secretary in the corner of the room, but Thomas moved more swiftly and interposed himself between her and her goal.

"No, Mother. No laudanum. Talk to me," he said.

For a long moment, she just looked lost, a wavering old woman in the middle of a room so crowded with feminine curios and queer bits of furniture that there was scarcely room for them to both stand. Then she sighed and sank onto the nearest chair, pushing pillows from the seat almost absently to make room for her voluminous skirts.

"Thomas, I know that we have not often . . . spoken," she said.

An acrimonious reply sprang to his tongue, but he swallowed it with difficulty. "No, Mother, we have not."

"I fear that you think me cold," she said, her eyes flickering to his face and away, as if she were afraid of reading his reaction there.

"You were never cold to Harry," he said. "Or to Mary or Elizabeth." Perhaps that was why he still could not let go of Emmeline—she, too, was the second child of four, with an elder brother and two younger sisters. He had been born into a position that required him to make up for the faults of his brother; she'd had no position at all. These were fatuous comparisons, of course, and answered nothing, but he could draw some pretense of logic from them, which was far safer than what he feared the real reasons might be.

"Harry was . . ." Lady Hamilton struggled. "Harry was special. I thought if I loved him enough, gave him enough, everything would be fine. Perhaps I made a mistake. Perhaps if I'd ordered the nurses to be stricter with him—"

"The nurses were fine," Thomas assured her. Harry had gone through half a dozen before old Cate Bain had come to the nursery, and her sure hand and steady eye had righted Harry's increasingly unpredictable behavior, bringing a peace to the nursery that the four children had never before enjoyed.

"I still can't help but think that if I had done things just a little differently—" His mother broke off. "Harry was an exceptionally intelligent boy."

"Yes, madam, he was," Thomas said wearily. "But he could not be other than what he was. We all tried to make him normal, and though he made great strides, there would always be more strides before him, more than he could take in a lifetime."

"And your sisters . . ." She smiled. "What are daughters for, if not spoiling? French and music, drawing and dancing, a little arithmetic and geography and elegant needlework. Beyond that, all a man wants is a pretty thing to give him delightful conversation, brilliant parties, and fat babies. A little indulgence teaches a girl the importance of setting her sights high enough."

"But how many years have they been out now, madam?" Thomas asked, suppressing the comment that his sister had gotten far more than a little arithmetic from Harry's tutors and that their Greek was considerably better than their embroidery.

His mother waved a dismissal. "Three, four—what's another year in this age? Girls are waiting until they are twenty-two or twenty-three to settle on a choice all the time now. Look at the Duchess of Raeburn—she was thirty, if she was a day, when she wed. It isn't like in my time, where you were an old maid at twenty if you hadn't at least reached an understanding."

"What about me, madam?" he asked flatly.

She frowned. "Lord Hamilton has certain ideas about how a son ought to be raised. When it became apparent that Harry wasn't . . . wasn't everything he had wanted him to be, he let me have my way with him, in hopes that my mother's intuition might prove a better cure than his methods had. And I saw how your father looked at you, how he held you on his knee and took you riding and taught you to shoot a bow and arrow, and I thought that it was up to me to love Harry twice as hard. He was the eldest son, you see, and it should have been him that Lord Hamilton watched take his pony over his first jumps. Not you."

Thomas lowered his head in acknowledgment of that truth.

"Oh, Thomas!" his mother burst out. "You didn't need me like Harry did. Not until Harry was dead and it was far too late, and I realized that I didn't know my other son at all."

"I left him by the streamside, Mother," he said flatly. "Your favorite son, whom you loved with all your heart. I left him, and you wanted to, what, make those years up to me somehow?"

Lady Hamilton shook her head vehemently, seeming to be swept away in the moment. "But you didn't kill him. You did not even leave him to have an accident. Someone else killed our Harry, stole him from us forever."

Thomas closed his eyes. Emmeline had told him the truth. *Our Harry.* He summoned up all the conflicted emotions he felt for his elder brother and stripped away the outer layers of resentment, frustration, and entrapment, and let himself look, for the first time, at the core of it all—his desperate, helpless love for the brother who never could be the earl he had been born to be. If only Harry had been born to some other father, an engineer or inventor or horse breeder.

If only Harry had been the second son, to be packaged up and shipped off to Oxford, where he could have spent a happy if odd life among the numbers he loved so much. Instead, he had been thrust into a position in which all his failings were made painfully clear, day after day, in which his prodigious, astonishing gifts hardly mattered at all. If Thomas had been trapped, so had Harry, damned by primogeniture to a life he was no more capable of leading than a fish was of breathing air.

With that discovery, Thomas made peace with the ghost of his dead brother—realized for the first time that he had been at war. His mother's choices would take longer for him to forgive, even if he could now begin to understand them, but that, too, would come in time.

"We must find out who killed Harry," he said. "The murderer must have no mercy."

He stooped and kissed his mother's papery cheek. She raised her hand to the spot and looked at him with terrified eyes.

"The time for being afraid is over, Mother," he said from the doorway. "What we need now is the truth."

Em walked slowly up the stairs and along the galleries that circled the inside of the great globe, watching the countries spiral away—first the exotic latitudes of South America and Australia, then moving up Africa and the Americas until she was at the fat middle of the earth.

She had been fascinated by Alice's description in her letters of the Wyld's Monster Globe—fascinated by all of London but by that one attraction above everything else, even the dinosaur models in Hyde Park, the aging Crystal Palace, and the various great and royal residences.

The Monster Globe had never been more than a sideshow to the first Great Exhibition, and now, nearly fifteen years after its construction, a dated one at that. But something about the idea of a globe of the world that one could climb from the inside had captured Em's imagination, and it was that, as much as anything, that had led her wandering steps to London when she had turned away from the little town where she had hoped to find proof of her origins after fleeing Forsham. She had found the tiny Catholic church too late, for Edgar had been before her and had destroyed the marriage register so that all that was left was the testimony of one elderly priest.

Her hopes had died with that discovery, and she decided that if she was to have no future, to die penniless among strangers, then at least she would do it after having seen the greatest city in the world. It had been only later, when she had teetered at the brink and had chosen life, that she had developed her plan to take back her future.

The globe's painted nations were now like old friends to her; the stooped man who took her half-bob at the entrance had nodded to her familiarly. The names of exotic places teased her with their individual flavors, somehow far more real here than in the maps of her schoolbooks. They represented the millions of lives she would never know, the thousands of places she would never be but that seduced her imagination with possibilities.

Em heard the steward speaking below, out of sight in the entrance vestibule—someone else was entering, and she had only made it as far as Peking. Em sighed and made to leave; she disliked sharing the globe with anyone. But the voice that rumbled in reply to the old man's shaky greeting froze her in her tracks. Lord Varcourt.

"A guinea for you if you lock the door and go for a long luncheon across the street," the viscount was saying. "You may return when I leave."

What was he doing here? *Stupid question,* she chided herself at once. He could be here for only one reason: her. Her pulse accelerated despite willing herself to stay calm.

"There be a lady above already, sir," the steward was saying.

"I know."

"I hadn't thought she'd be—" The old man broke off. "Of course, sir. Thank ye kindly."

Em had a momentary urge to call out to the steward to stay. He would, surely; he'd always seemed to look on her kindly. But there was the sound of the door below opening and closing, and the moment was gone.

She stood, frozen to the spot, as Lord Varcourt emerged from the vestibule onto the small, flat, circular area that formed a floor at the level of the Antarctic Circle. He gazed up, but she stood just behind his head, and so he did not see her. She waited silently as he began to walk up the first flight of stairs. When he reached a point across from her, his scanning gaze paused on her figure, and he sped up. She held her ground, her back to the Sea of Japan, until he reached her side.

"I did not expect you here, Lord Varcourt," she said. "Why do you persist on having me followed?"

"My mother is still dependent upon you," he said simply.

She accepted the pain that statement caused as her due. "Did I not fulfill my part of the bargain?" she asked, grateful that he could not hear the beating of her heart. She had not fulfilled it, not at all, but there should be no way for him to know that.

"I need more of you," he said abruptly. He took a breath. "I want more," he amended. He was disheveled, his eyes too bright, their intensity burning her.

"Have you slept?" she asked, and foolishly, she found that she cared about the answer.

"I've shaven. Does that count?" he countered.

Em had slept—slept like the dead for the first time in two weeks. Nothing had been improved by her conversation with Lord Varcourt during the Hamilton ball; in fact, if anything, her position was even more precarious. But exhaustion had won out over terror, no doubt aided by the glass of wine on an empty stomach, and she had fallen asleep without even eating the dinner that Mrs. Grey had left out for her, and had woken ravenous.

"What do you want of me?" she asked.

His eyes were intent in a way that was almost as frightening as when he was angry. "I need you to find out more."

"About what? Your mother has told me all she can; I'll not have you making me torment her," Em said. "You may think that you want answers that badly, but you don't. Or if you don't care about your mother, I do."

He made an impatient gesture. "Not her."

Em was taken off guard. "Then who?"

His smile was macabre. "If I knew that, I wouldn't need you. I want you to find out who killed by brother. It must have been someone at that party—"

"A quarter of whom are now dead!" Em broke in, appalled. "You can't expect me to find answers now. There are no witnesses except your mother, and she doesn't know whom she saw."

"Doesn't she?" Varcourt said, his eyes narrowing dangerously. "I think she might be keeping it a secret from us all. But never mind that now. There was another witness—the perpetrator's conscience. I have seen you work your magic on people. They believe that you speak with a voice from the beyond. Find out who killed my brother, and I shall not be found ungrateful. I know you took all the Olthwaite jewels, not just a few baubles. I have not betrayed that knowledge. And I won't, not even if you fail. I need this."

Em stared at him. Damn it. He did not believe that the jewels were hers now. And neither would many judges or juries. She felt a sudden sense of vertigo. Everything seemed abruptly unreal—the globe, Lord Varcourt, his insane proposition. She could not tell him the truth. He would hate her, hate her forever even if he did believe her—and if he did, it would almost be worse, for that would be a rent between father and son that nothing could heal. Was the truth worth it?

She'd lived an ugly lie for most of her life, and she could confidently say that if that lie had hidden an even uglier truth, she would have preferred to never know it. Even as it was, all the truth had done was give her the courage to commit the biggest mistake in her life. It would have been better for her to always believe that she was the poor relation she had originally thought herself to be. No, there were some truths that were better off hidden.

"I don't believe I can find out anything for you at this late date," she told Varcourt.

He grimaced. "Try for me, Merry. Promise you'll try."

"I'm not Merry," she said softly. "She isn't real. You know that."

His smile was bitter. "You'll always be Merry to me. Help me."

He was giving her everything she wanted from him—a free hand, a pledge of silent support. She could not refuse that, even if she could turn her back on him for his own good. "I will try," she said.

"Do you swear on your life?" he asked.

Her throat tightened. "On my life, I swear that I will try to help you." And she meant every word, though she also knew that he could not see it that way.

"I came for another reason," he said abruptly. "I came because I need you. I could not go another hour without seeing you, tasting you, having you. You've stolen my sanity, or you've become my sanity. I don't know which. Kiss me, Emmeline," he whispered, his eyes burning into hers.

She lifted her veil, the world too bright for a moment as her eyes adjusted to the suddenly brighter flames of the lights. She rose onto her toes and kissed him. She did not do it out of fear or out of a hope that he would do what she wanted, though both of those would have been reason enough. No, she kissed him out of the desire, burning as pure and hot as the gaslights around them, to have his lips against hers. She kissed him because she needed him as much as he professed to needing her.

And then she knew that she was well and truly damned.

His lips lay hot and still under hers for a moment; then, if she had wakened him, they began to move with an insistence that made her head spin as he gathered her in his arms, taking from her, more and more. She found herself pushed backward under the onslaught, pressed against the curving wall of the globe. He stole her breath, stole her thought with the urgency of his mouth and hands, the heat of his body burning her.

Her skirts provided no barrier, for she was wearing her widow's weeds, and he pressed his knee between her legs, pushing hard up against her and sending a spike of desire through her as his mouth continued to take, take. She parted her lips, and his tongue slid between them, between her teeth, as if to draw her essence from her and drink it in. Finally, she grabbed hold of her dizzy brain long enough to break away.

"Not here," she said. "We can't."

"I've sent the keeper away," he said. "We can—and will."

Her hands balled into fists around the fine fabric of his overcoat. "I have already said that I cannot offer you absolution."

"I am not looking for absolution," he said. "I have no doubt that it is far too late for me to find that. I only aspire to a temporary oblivion."

Em put both hands flat against him and pushed hard enough that he retreated a step. "Find yourself a whore, then." She could not do this. She dared not, or she could lose herself.

"Merry—Emmeline," he said. He closed his eyes, furrows forming in the hard planes of his face. For an instant, Em had a vision of him as an older man—tired and broken. *No.* He would still be strong, fighting the fates with the same reckless determination to his grave. "You taunted me with your body the first time we exchanged two words. You welcomed my advances when you were tied to a bloody bed. What kind of game are you about, that you scorn me now?"

"I taunted you when it didn't mean anything," she replied, the harshness of her words tearing at her throat. "I couldn't imagine that it could mean anything. And now—it does. I can't be your palliative, even if it costs me everything I've worked for, because that would destroy me."

"What are you saying?" he demanded.

"I'm saying that this matters, you idiot," she said. "And I can't play at this anymore."

"Who said that I was playing? I have never been more serious about anything in my life." He closed the space between them before she could react, pulling her against him and lifting her, setting her on the railing with her back against a supporting strut as his mouth found hers and pushed her head back hard against the steel bar. She gripped his shoulders as he yanked up her skirts with impatient hands.

"Varcourt—" she began.

"Thomas. I want to hear you call me Thomas as you come," he said.

Bewildered, she gaped at him, momentarily losing track of her objections. But the touch of the warm leather of his glove against the pantaloon-clad skin of her inner thigh brought them bubbling up again. "Varcourt, Thomas, whatever you want me to call you—I can't."

"You can," he said. But instead of beginning to loosen the buttons of his fly, he dropped to his knees before her, so that his head was level with the froth of skirts in her lap.

"What are you doing?" she demanded.

"You may be my oblivion, but you are not my whore," he said, his black eyes burning. And then, with a hand on each knee, he urged her legs apart. "Open for me, Merry."

Swallowing her sudden panic, she did. He pressed her thighs apart, farther, farther, until the slit in her pantaloons gaped, offering her to him. With one last glittering look at her, he bent his head toward her exposed entrance. She knew what he was going to do—she had read of it in the pornographic novels she had hoarded in order to perfect her worldly guise, but she could hardly believe it.

She gasped as she felt his teeth rasping against the hard knot below her pubis, sending a shudder of need through her body, and a moment later, his hot tongue followed, pushing back her curls to leave it bare and trembling for his touch. His teeth came again, and she groaned, gripping the struts hard on either side of her as another pressed into her corseted back.

Her skin flamed even as a liquid chill ran through her bones. He drew at the nub with his lips, sucking against the flesh, pulling it into his mouth and making her nipples ache as waves of sensation ran up into them. She could feel herself heating, weeping wetness as the tension coiled tighter within her.

Then, suddenly, it broke, and just as she cried out and the first wave struck her, his mouth moved, his tongue slicing between her folds and deep into her cleft. She shook with it—with the surges of pleasure tearing through her, with the shattering knowledge of how intimate his awareness of her condition must be.

Then there was nothing but the blaze of a billion nerve endings—the heat of his mouth moving against her, the terrible glory that seared through every vein, crowding her vision with white heat. She arched hard against it, against the bite of her corset and the metal struts, pushing her own legs farther apart until the protest of ligaments added to the cacophony of sensations that screamed through her.

Finally, it receded, leaving her gasping and disoriented, her throat raw but with no memory of having cried out.

She pulled her head forward, away from the distant view of the Arctic far above. Varcourt stood there, with the searing gaze that seemed to cut her to her soul, rolling the sheath over the length of his erection.

"Now, Emmeline?" he said. And it was a real question.

Unable to speak, Em nodded, and he came to her, enfolding her in his arms as he pressed between her legs and deep into her center, penetrating her soul as he did her body, knocking down the barriers in her mind that she had spent years constructing. She took him, all of him, her body singing with it, with him and what he did to her.

He moved slowly, thrusting deep and slick into her, again and again, taking her mouth with his so that she tasted her own saltiness on his lips—and reveled in it. Gradually, anticipation built again, twisting tighter and tighter and sending little shivers of reaction across her skin, this time with less sharp urgency but with a marrow-deep power that she knew she could not withstand. He held her hard against him, as if against the world, and she let herself go, believing the lie, if only for a moment. She felt herself climbing, peaking—and he was there, falling with her at the center of the earth, as sensation swallowed all else.

"My name is Thomas." The words were panting, half-unintelligible, and she scarcely heard his voice above the roaring of the universe in her ears.

"Thomas," she said, the name choking in her throat. "Thomas, Thomas, Thomas . . ."

The deep waves took her, pulling her under and tossing her mind about in foreign surges and currents. It could not be called pleasure or pain, merely experience itself, intensely distilled so that it contained everything in one hot crucible of eternity. The darkness closed in, and she fought against it, but it sucked her into the void, where nothing remained.

Then the real world came back slowly, as if from very far away, and Em, the unclaimed child raised as a bastard in her father's house, lay with her head against the chest of the Viscount of Varcourt. She knew what that meant, just as she knew that he must, and she swallowed her instinctive protest as he stepped back.

Varcourt turned away as he rearranged his clothing. Em

pushed unsteadily to her feet, her skirts swishing back into place around her.

"It doesn't change anything." Em did not realize that she spoke aloud until her ears registered the words.

"It reminds me that I am human, which is everything," Varcourt said, turning back to her as he fastened the last button on his overcoat.

"If you need to turn to a woman you regarded as a dire enemy a mere week ago—" she began.

He cut her off. "I need to turn to you. It has nothing to do with what you were to me a week ago, or a month ago, or a lifetime ago."

"That makes no sense," she said softly.

He gave her a brief smile that looked out of place on his severe face. "It makes the only kind of sense that matters in the world."

He reached out, cupped her cheek briefly with one hand, studying her face as if memorizing it forever. *You can't trust me,* she wanted to say, but didn't. He knew it already, just as she still knew that she could not trust him.

Then he turned and walked away, climbing down the stairs and out the building without looking back.

Em stared after him for a long time, awash with a tumult of emotions and spinning thoughts that she did not have the courage to examine. Slowly, she lowered the veil back over her face, and with slightly unsteady steps, she continued her winding progress up to the top of the world.

She did not hear the steward return, but he was there as she was leaving, sitting behind his cramped little desk in the vestibule.

"He came back for ye after all, did he?" the wizened old man said with a broad wink.

"What?" Em asked blankly.

"Ye thought yer young man was lost in parts beyond," he

said, nodding encouragingly. "But he came back. Ye don't need to spend yer days mooning about the map anymore, eh?"

"Yes," Em said dully. "Yes, indeed. A great romance."

She left him grinning there and stepped out onto the pavement. She wished that she could weep, as she apparently had in the moment of her release, but she was afraid that she had forgotten how.

Chapter Nineteen

"My Lords, the State is a ship upon the sea, and its navigation is best left to proven men," Lord Olthwaite thundered, glaring across the chamber of the House of Lords. "Shall we then give the helm to the dockyard drunk, much less the footpads and murderers who lurk about the warehouses? That is sheer foolishness, gentlemen. You will enfranchise men who would like nothing more than to wreck us for the mere pleasure of anarchy."

Thomas watched the session from the gallery. Thomas was a Member of the House of Commons as the representative of the borough in which his family had its great estate, and he could remain a Member until he inherited and moved to the House of Lords. There, he had been subject to the almost identical speech only a few hours before, given by the Member from Olthwaite's borough. It was a variation on the theme that had split the Liberal party, causing the downfall of Cranborne as prime minister, and had ground the debate on the Reform Bill to a near standstill. It was a brilliant speech, perfectly tuned to prey on the fears of all upstanding citizens against the forces of lawlessness.

Something would have to give. The demands of the peo-

ple were too great to be ignored. Whatever the final shape of
the Reform Bill, Parliament did not dare do anything but
pass it. What the reforms should consist of—who should be
given suffrage and who still excluded from the vote—was
the issue of fierce contention. Thomas feared that his party
might emerge as shattered as Conservatives had been over
tariffs twenty years before.

Finally, Lord Olthwaite ended his speech and the session
was called to a close for the day. Thomas descended from
the gallery to catch Edgington as he exited.

"We need to put a cork in that man," Edgington muttered
as the two men walked down the echoing corridor, the other
MPs swirling around them in hotly debating groups.

"I fear that this year is already lost," Thomas murmured
back. "Parliament shall sit for less than two more weeks."

"Then there must be a Reform Act in 'sixty-seven. We
will have riots on our hands if there is not—and that would
drive the sides even farther apart, to the point of ineffectual-
ity." Edgington's expression was bleak.

Thomas frowned. "We cannot bend from our position of
total enfranchisement of adult male citizens. *Vox populi*, and
all that."

"If we value the state, we may not have a choice," Edgington said. "I meant to tell you—Olthwaite went to Scotland Yard several days before your mother's ball and came
out looking pale. Rob Kelly, one of the toughs working for
him, found out about a letter that was caked in mud that
some child had brought, saying he'd discovered it on a body
on the river, but I don't know what it said."

"Do you think it's important?" Thomas asked.

Edgington shrugged. "Who knows?"

"Varcourt!"

"Speak of the devil," Edgington muttered.

Thomas turned to see Olthwaite hurrying up behind

them. Edgington nodded a farewell and kept striding toward the exit.

"Looking for congratulations on your speech?" Thomas asked chillingly.

Olthwaite shook his jowly head. "Only if it changed your mind."

"You know better than that," Thomas said.

"I just wanted to find out where your mother got that remarkable necklace she had at the Rushworth dinner the other night. I know someone, a lady, who loves antiquities. . . ." He drifted off suggestively.

"I really can't say," Thomas said.

"It is very important. I think I tried to buy that very one from a woman, but I heard recently that she died," Olthwaite said.

Thomas watched him narrowly. "I believe I overheard my mother speaking to Lady James about it. It seems that some spiritualist had a vision about it from the beyond."

Olthwaite paled. "From the beyond, you say?"

"I think so."

"Hell," he swore. "She really is dead." Then he walked off, looking stunned, leaving Thomas in the middle of the corridor.

No sooner had that mystery appeared than it was neatly solved. Thomas smiled grimly. Emmeline was clever. He hoped she wasn't too clever for her own good. Or his. If she were, he didn't know what she might do.

"I have seen it in my dreams," Em said. "August the seventh is the very night."

"Are you certain?" Lady Hamilton said, fingering the enameled necklace at her throat.

The countess had been quite another woman during the three days since the ball, whether because of her confession to Em or from some other cause, Em did not know. She was

as nervous as she ever was, but instead of retreating into laudanum numbness, she was flitting about with uncharacteristic energy, ordering the servants hither and thither until their
heads spun as she had them turn out every room in the man-
sion. Even Harry's room, inviolate since his death, had received a thorough cleaning, all of his belongings crated and
sent up to the luggage room.

Em was not sure whether she should consider the changes
an improvement or a degradation of Lady Hamilton's condition, nor did she dare speculate what meaning might be behind it.

"Yes, I am quite certain," she said firmly. "The stars will
be in a most propitious alignment, with the barrier between
the living and the spirit worlds at their thinnest."

"Oh," said Lady Hamilton brightly. "I thought that was
supposed to be All Hallows' Eve."

Em struggled with the sensation that she was losing control of the conversation, which had been happening more
and more as Lady Hamilton's manic streak grew stronger.

"One might think that," she said, "but that is mere super-
stition. The propitious times change as the moon and plan-
ets move—so you see they cannot be at fixed points
throughout the year."

"Oh yes, I understand," said Lady Hamilton. "The spirits
of the dead, being above the stars, must be influenced by
them, yes?"

"Indeed," Em said, fighting the unsettled feeling that
Lady Hamilton was not entirely serious.

But the countess had already seemed to lose the thread of
the conversation, turning to order two maids about an
arrangement of a vase of flowers among a grotesque colony
of Wedgwood objects upon the great piano in the music
room.

When she finished, Em spoke again. "I believe that I can
even bring in that wandering spirit that I was speaking of."

"The sensitive who is near death from despair and persecution?" Lady Hamilton said, suddenly grave. "Oh, that poor thing. I shall be glad for it. She has suffered so terribly."

You haven't the first idea, Em thought, but she said, "She has, indeed. The more people we can have, the greater the force of our wills. We attempt something very difficult—and dramatic," she added, preying on Lady Hamilton's instinct for what might prove a party that would be discussed for weeks. "The more there are to help, the greater the effect."

"I do not believe there is to be any great ball or dinner on that night," Lady Hamilton said.

Em knew very well that there was not—she had been sure of it.

"I could host a kind of dinner séance," she continued. "And maybe a musical performance, too, in case the spirits are"—she paused delicately—"fickle."

"They shall not be," Em promised.

"They will, of course, need the aid of the proper atmosphere," Lady Hamilton continued. "Lights—maybe we could have them flicker, in case the spirits prove unobliging. Perhaps a little dais on which you can stand."

"That would be perfect, madam," Em blurted before she could stop herself.

Lady Hamilton looked at her, her eyes suddenly keen, and patted her on her arm. "You have done more for me than I can say, my dear," she said. "I would like your performance to be the best that it can be. After all, you must think for your future." Then her eyes grew bright and glazed again, and she gave Em a vague smile before fluttering away to change her orders about where the painting of her husband's great-great-aunt should be hung.

Two hours later, Em stepped out of the chinoiserie parlor and leaned, briefly, against the door after she closed it. She didn't know where she was with herself anymore. Memories of Lincroft beckoned to her—she longed for its golden peace with a fierceness that shook her. Yet she was afraid that it wouldn't be enough anymore, for she found herself yearning almost as powerfully for Varcourt's intoxicating embrace.

Intoxicating and deadly. He was no ally. She knew that in her heart, even if she did not want to face it.

Em sighed. She was already reaching for something that was out of her grasp. To demand more was sheer hubris and folly.

She had more immediate concerns—like her rash promise to help Lord Varcourt. How could she possibly aid him? She could not tell him what he sought. But she could not resign herself to making that promise a lie, either. She had told so many lies in her masquerade as Esmeralda that she feared they would choke her. Most of them had been harmless or about her and her own past, but those she had told to Varcourt had spiraled out of control. Not that it should matter what she told him, of course . . . and yet it did matter, it profoundly mattered, her lies heaping about her and cheapening everything she was striving for.

She shook her head. Time enough for those thoughts later. Today she had an appointment with Lady James in just two hours and another one with the Duchess of Rushworth after supper. Her star might be on the decline, but she could still fill her schedule. For now.

Her shoulders set, Em turned away from the door—and started as she came nearly face-to-face with Lord Hamilton.

"Your lordship," she murmured, bowing her head as her muscles clenched in sudden fear. She had nothing to be afraid of, she rationally understood that, but she could not quite control the trembling of her voice in the presence of Harry's murderer.

He frowned, his eyes narrow. "Madame Esmeralda, have

you anything to do with the sudden tumult of cleaning that has invaded my private rooms?"

"No, sir," she said. "It was Lady Hamilton's inspiration. She's been . . . energetic." That word was inadequate to describe her manic restlessness, but Em could not find the words to express exactly what she meant.

"I have seen that for myself," Lord Hamilton said. His frown deepened. "I hope that this does not indicate some degradation of her state of mind."

"I do not believe so, sir," Em said. "She has not felt the need for her medicine in several days. That can only be for the good." Meaning that Lady Hamilton had not drugged herself into a catatonic stupor.

"That may well be, but I dislike this frenetic activity, as well. It smacks of hysteria," he said.

"Yes, sir," Em said. Lord Hamilton looked far too like his son for her comfort. Though it was impossible that he could know what had passed between her and Varcourt, she could not escape the feeling that somehow their physical similarities mirrored some psychic bond. She shook herself mentally. Soon, she would start believing her own stories.

"I have allowed you into my house for the purpose of soothing her," the old earl said. "I fail to see how this agitation is in harmony with that goal. Did you speak of anything that might have brought this on?"

Em found herself answering before she could stop herself. "Her son's death."

He waved a hand dismissively. "She has talked about little else with you since you have arrived."

Em's heart beat so loudly that she feared it would betray her, but something pressed her onward, some recklessness or stupidity. "I mean the very moment of your son's death, sir." She drew a breath. "His murder."

Lord Hamilton's face darkened. "It was an accident. No one killed my son."

She pushed on. "Your lady wife—you must know what the countess believes."

"Lady Hamilton was mistaken. She has been mistaken for many years. I do not know how the obscene fancy entered her head, and even my utmost efforts have done nothing to eradicate it." His eyes, lighter than his son's black ones, were cold.

Em weighed the possibilities. Was Lady Hamilton at risk from this man? The lines etched on his face were of stern sorrow, not anger. She brought to mind the scene at the ball, when the countess had looked at him with such fear and anger. On his face had been only a distant pain and bitterness under the facade of stoicism. What could telling him the source of her conviction do? It was beyond hurting either one of them to a degree greater than they had already injured. Perhaps it might bring some kind of understanding, even if forgiveness was too far gone.

Em made her decision. "Lady Hamilton was out that day, sir. She saw someone in . . . in association with the streamside. When she followed his path, she found her son lying next to the stream, quite dead. She fled home in a terror and confessed to no one what she had seen."

"Someone," the earl said. "You mean that she saw me."

Em bowed her head, not daring to speak the words.

His face went gray and stony. "Of course she did. I was there." He gave her a keen look. "You are going to tell Varcourt about this, aren't you? I know he has made things difficult for you, and I have no doubt that he has found some lever to use against you in order that you might become his spy." He snorted, an expression so like his son's that it chilled her blood. "A spy. On his own mother. What monsters I have raised."

"I do not think Lord Varcourt is a monster," Em said softly. "Nor was his brother, from what I hear tell."

Lord Hamilton looked at her sharply. "You are a clever

one. A dangerously clever one. Well? Do you intend to go running to Varcourt with this report?"

"He has me in a difficult position, sir," she said, not certain what would be in her best interest to answer.

"Well, then, he should hear the truth—all of it," the earl said. "I have one under my roof who cannot bear to look at me. I shall not have another."

"And what is the truth, sir?" Em ventured.

His face went even harder, his eyes growing distant as he focused upon the past. "Lady Hamilton never told me that she saw me, but I am sure she gave you an honest report. I had seen Harry likely only minutes before—I spoke to him. He had climbed up the stream bank and was sitting on a stile a few dozen yards away, carrying on as if he were mortally wounded because of the red welt of a whip lash and, even more horrible in his mind, the dampness of his trousers.

"I saw him sitting there, with his child's tears on the thin, stooped body of a weak man, and I was filled with the wish that this—this sniveling creature were not my heir. We had coddled him, much to my eternal regret, and perhaps that had caused some of his weakness. The coddling, I determined, must come to an end—that day, that moment—or else he would bring the title to irretrievable shame. So I did not take him up behind me. Instead, from my horse, I ordered Harry to stand up, wipe off his tears, and walk home."

Lord Hamilton shook his head. "He stood, if unsteadily, and so I turned my horse back toward the manor house. I saw young Grimsthorpe as I was riding in, but I was too full of fury to tell him to call off the hunt. Lord Olthwaite's boy came pelting past me, riding hell-for-leather, but I never saw my wife. If I had, I would have spoken to her then and spared us both many difficulties. There was no one at the stables when I arrived, and I avoided the gossiping hens fluttering about and went upstairs to my study to await my errant son. When he did not appear after an hour, I retraced my steps and found him lying half in the stream, half out." Lord Hamilton's eyes were dead when they focused upon Em again. "And now, Madame Esmeralda, you may carry that report to my surviving son."

"Why did you not tell your wife?" Em whispered. "Why don't you now?"

Lord Hamilton's smile was humorless. "I did not choose my wife for the quality of our conversations. We had spoken little enough in our marriage. Upon hearing the news, she fled to her rooms, where she would admit no one, and I believed the reason to be her understandable grief at the loss of her son. By the time I realized that she carried some blame toward me, my words could do nothing to assuage it. Not when I half blamed myself for not taking Harry up on the back of my saddle. I did not realize that she thought I had lifted a hand against him until it was far too late to persuade her of anything."

"Did you not go to her in her sorrow?" Em asked, shocked. Uncle William and Lady Olthwaite had shared a cool kind of marriage, but she had seen how they had clung to each other upon Ann's death. It had, in fact, resulted in the pregnancy that led to Lady Olthwaite's own demise.

Lord Hamilton just looked at her. "There are times, Madame Esmeralda, that you play the eternal sage very well. Then you say something that reveals how little of men's hearts you truly understand." He gave her a short bow, which she returned automatically, and then walked away, his back unbent and head proud even though his steps carried him heavily, slowly into the depths of the house.

As soon as he was gone, Em shook herself and hurried away, out to the front wall and down the steps to the stone walk. "Home!" she called as she swung into the cab, shutting the door with a snap behind her. As the coach lurched into motion, she slumped forward, resting her head against the curtained window that was directly across from the single narrow bench.

She didn't want Lord Hamilton's confession. All it did was bring greater disquietude and confusion to a situation that was far too muddled at it was. She believed Lord Hamilton, too; he had betrayed not a single tell of a liar. But that only made it worse, because she might have been wrong about everything.

She should have at least told Lord Varcourt a different lie—stuck to the image of his mother witnessing a man riding away instead of giving him the neater story of a murder in progress. Then this could have been salvaged. She could have added Lord Hamilton's testimony and revised the murder back to an accident. It was far too late now, and she had given Varcourt a hobbyhorse for him to ride to hell. . . .

In her mind, two pictures warred with one another, one of Harry, with a face far too like his brother's, sitting on the stile several dozen yards from the water's edge. The other was that of Harry, lying the slope of the stream, with the water of the stream flowing over his lifeless legs. The pictures swirled and alternated grotesquely in her mind, and Em groaned, squeezing her eyes shut. Could she not even have peace in her own mind?

Harry, alive and squalling with the stream in the background, then limp with its current soaking through his clothes. The sound of the stream got louder and louder in her mind, obliterating the imaginary cries of Harry in the rush and burble of water.

"My God. That's it," said Em, sitting up suddenly and staring, wide-eyed, at the blank carriage wall before her. "The stream!"

She pushed the window of the cab open, biting back a curse as it jammed on the slides. She stuck out her head. "Not home, Stevenson. To Piccadilly."

She had to tell Lord Varcourt about this somehow. He deserved that much.

"Back so soon, Thomas?" Lady Hamilton said with a brittle smile. "Why, I have seen you more these past two weeks than I have in the past six months. I just left Madame Esmeralda below, you know. She may still be in the parlor."

Thomas raked his hand through his hair. They were in her drawing room and once again alone, though it had taken some persuasion to pull her away from her efforts at directing four laborers who were hanging new curtains in the morning room. "Her carriage was not out front. I came to see you. I need to know—I need to know what you saw on the day that my brother died. Everything, Mother; every detail from your own mouth."

Emmeline's story had haunted him the past three days, and her invariable reports, carried by the messengers that he sent to her, that she had discovered nothing new had goaded him to action, even if there was no purpose to it. Perhaps there was something more to it than she had told him—perhaps there was something that his mother had not said or that Emmeline had omitted in her retelling.

"Oh, Thomas, give it up," his mother said. "I cannot help you, not now. It has been too many years."

"I know that you saw something," he said.

Lady Hamilton's eyes were suddenly too perceptive. "Have you been troubling Esmeralda? She has done nothing to you—has shown me nothing but kindness." Her hand rose to the necklace that she wore. "She has been a great comfort to an old woman who has had very little consolation in her life."

"Please, Mother," he said tensely. "What did you see? Was it a man, a woman? Surely you could have made out that much."

"Whatever I saw, Thomas, it cannot be changed or remedied now," she said evenly.

"*Tell me!*" Thomas regained control of his temper with effort. "What happened? Was Harry pushed? Struck? Did he stumble? What *happened?*"

A puzzled expression crossed Lady Hamilton's face. "Pushed or struck? What makes you believe that I saw anyone hit your brother? All I saw was a lone man, riding away, and then your brother dead. . . ." Her gaze unfocused, fading into vagueness as the sense of false vigor faded from her. She fumbled in her skirts and, a moment later, drew out the hated, familiar bottle of laudanum.

But Thomas barely saw her, for her words had hit him with the force of a bullet. She had not seen Harry killed. Emmeline had lied. Lied, lied, lied . . .

Of course she lied, he told himself fiercely beneath that repeating litany. What else had she done since he met her but make a net of lies in which she could entangle him? She was a manipulator. It was her chosen profession, and the fact that he had unmasked her only made her more dangerous to him as she sought to find any way she could to protect herself.

He stood, upsetting the nearest dainty table and knocking half a dozen little conversational pieces to the ground. "Excuse me, madam," he said, his voice so strange and cold that it did not sound like his. "I must take my leave." With a mechanical bow, he strode jerkily from the room to the stables, where he swung upon his horse scarcely after the groom brought it to a stop. He leaned forward and gave his mount its head, and sensing the tension in his body, it threw itself into a headlong gallop up the drive, sending sprays of gravel into the air.

It was all lies. It could be nothing else. Every word, every look—God, every kiss and moan and cry that he had coerced from her. For it had been coercion, from the moment he had dragged her into the Duke of Rushworth's library. He had told her what form to take, and she had obligingly taken it. How he wanted to hate her, to despise her so that he would not have to despise himself. . . .

As the buildings began to grow thicker around the lane and rutted dirt gave way to smooth macadam, Thomas reined his horse to a more moderate trot. He was Lord Varcourt—and spies, as always, were everywhere. He would not let his political enemies know of his temporary weakness. For it was temporary; already he felt his heart congealing, the hot wound cooling as he hardened back into what he had been before—what he must be. Lord Varcourt was more stone than man, with a mind as dispassionate as clockwork. And so he would be again.

By the time he reached the livery stable, his mount was cool and he felt himself sliding back into his old, half-forgotten habits of thought and feeling. What a cold armor it was that he must wrap around himself again. Why had he not noticed before how it stole the heat and spirit from him? But armor it was, encasing, protecting, and he pulled it about himself as he passed through the vestibule of his building and mounted the stairs to his flat.

He put his key in automatically and turned it. He froze, for it met no resistance from the latch. He withdrew the key and tried the knob, and the door swung open to reveal his ordinary, familiar sitting room—and the most extraordinary woman who sat as still as a marble statue before the fire.

Chapter Twenty

Thomas swung the door closed, and Emmeline turned her face toward him. Her hat and mantle sat on the table, and her veil was lifted to cascade down her back. Why had he never noticed how cold her features were before, how her pale face and eyes made her look like she was carved of ice? And yet she was still so beautiful and heartbreaking that she stole his breath and knotted his midsection with desire.

"I did not expect to find you here," he said, stripping off his gloves, hat, and overcoat and tossing them onto the console beside the door.

"I can't imagine that you would," she said. "I haven't ever indulged in such folly before, to seek you out instead of waiting for you to find me."

Thomas nodded in recognition of that fact. No, she had very rarely shown herself to be foolish; he was the one guilty of that charge, not her. He wanted to seize her, to shake her, beat her, kiss her, make love to her. But he did none of those things. Instead, he turned to the looking glass and straightened his collar and the thin black band of his necktie.

"I have learned something," she said. She hesitated—

such uncertainty was unlike her, and Thomas feared that some of the maelstrom that he felt was betrayed in his expression. He smoothed it, checking carefully for any betraying tightness in the mirror before turning back to face her.

"Yes?" he asked.

She took a visible breath and repeated, "I have learned something. About who killed Harry."

"What would that be?" Damn—he sounded hostile. He was giving himself away. She was looking uncertain now. She stood, smoothing her smoky blue dress with the deliberation she had when she was covering nervousness.

"I am sorry, Emmeline," he made himself say. "I have had a very trying day." *Yes,* he added silently. *I found out how deeply you betrayed me.* But no, that wasn't fair, for he had forced her to agreements under duress. . . . The circle wound around again in another painful twist. *Oh, Emmeline, what have we done to ourselves?*

"I see," she said, swaying slightly, her uncertainty palpable. "I know . . . that is, I think I might know who it was who . . . did it."

The last words faded out, and Thomas reconsidered his initial assessment of her uncertainty. Perhaps she had reached a point where even her conscience balked, where she found her lies difficult to utter.

Good, he thought, despair turning to viciousness. *Let her suffer.* He clamped down on the anger that boiled through him, heating his skin and tightening his muscles with its violence.

"Who is that?" His voice sounded calm, even cool. With sudden bitter insight, he said, "No, let me guess. It was Edgar Wythe, the new Lord Olthwaite, was it not?"

She started. "How did—how could you know? I only just figured it out. No one else knows, not even your father—"

"What does my father have to do with it?" he demanded, losing his precarious control over his self-possession even as he hated himself for his weakness. "Or, hell, what does my mother even have to do with any of this, for that matter?"

She quailed, her eyes going wide and frightened. "I don't understand, Varcourt. What are you saying?"

"My mother never saw my brother murdered," he ground out, advancing on her. "Nor did she tell you that she did. You invented it—to shut me up, to keep me busy."

"No," she whispered, though what she was rejecting, he couldn't tell. Her denial only goaded him further.

"She never saw *anyone* kill my brother, Emmeline," he repeated. "Much less your too-convenient enemy. She may have seen something, something harmless she in her grief imbued with great meaning. She's half-mad, Emmeline— her interpretations, her conjectures and suspicions and superstitions cannot be trusted. You should know that. You must know that, having spent so many hours in her company. You promised me something real. If she had seen a man kill my brother, that would be something to believe. But a figure riding away? Half of us were out that afternoon. There were people everywhere, Emmeline. It means nothing."

"She is not mad," Emmeline said, with slightly more force.

Thomas knew his smile was more than a little crazed, but he was beyond caring. "She believes that you can contact the spirits of the dead. Isn't that proof of her insanity? She told you some half-baked story, and when you realized that was all she had to offer, you—you *fixed* it. You made it better, you made it into a lie, and then you gave it to me."

"I was trying to spare her!" she cried, her hands gripping her skirts.

"That's rich," he said, raking his eyes across her. "I doubt you've ever thought of anyone but yourself."

She rocked. "That's not true. It's not fair." She sounded lost now, like a child, but Thomas pushed away all pity.

"Life isn't fair, Emmeline. That's a lesson that both of us learned long ago. How can I fault you for looking after yourself? No one else ever has. You were born a bastard, and there is no room for bastards in this world."

"I am not a bastard!" As soon as she cried those words, her eyes flew wide, and she bit her lip so hard that Thomas feared she would draw blood.

He laughed harshly even as his gut clenched at the sight of her pain. (Was even that real? Or was that, too, a part of her performance? Doubt and guilt swirled through him. . . .) "I don't know whether this is a lie or whether you were lying to me before. God, Emmeline. I don't know whether I'm coming or going with you. What's the story now? Were you a neighbor's daughter? No, even better; you were full-blooded daughter of the baron, shunted aside because—because of what? You tell me, Emmeline—if even that is your name."

"It is my name," she said, regaining her composure and pulling a shell of dignity around herself.

"You lie to me and I catch you out, and then you have the nerve to tell me impossible things and expect me to believe you?" he said. "You lied about my brother to get me to stop pressing you. Blaming a murder on Olthwaite would kill two birds with one stone by pitting your two enemies against one another—to mutual annihilation, if you are lucky. If not, then at least one of the two of us would be removed."

She stood rigidly now, like a queen going to her own execution. "I am not lying. I'm not even certain that I'm right. If you will just hear me out! Your father said that he saw Edgar Wythe—"

Thomas' temper flared again. "Why the bloody hell were you talking to my father?"

"I wasn't," she said too quickly. "I mean, he spoke to me, sought me out, not the reverse. He wanted me to tell you—"

He raked his hand through his hair. "He doesn't need you to play messenger. If he wanted me to know something, he would tell me, not send some spiritualist with a story that she can twist however she wishes. What do you think you are going to get out of discrediting Olthwaite? Or is it just revenge that you are after?"

She looked at him for a long moment, her hands lying limp against her skirts. "You are right. I did lie about what your mother said. You said that I must have answers by the next time you saw me, but I didn't have the entire answer, only a part. So I made up the rest. I didn't dare do otherwise. I could tell you that I am sorry, but what did you expect me to do?"

He snorted. "Exactly what you did, if I had stopped for one moment and thought about it."

"Yes. And nothing can change that now. I realize that, even though I was sincerely trying—trying to tell you what I had just discovered."

She walked over to the table and pulled down her veil, wrapped her mantle around her shoulders, and tied on her hat. She seemed perfectly composed except for the shaking of her hands, which forced her to make two tries at the bow on her bonnet. Thomas' heart contracted hard at the sight, but he forced himself not to move. That reaction could be false, just like everything else about her. Or it could be genuine. It hardly mattered, for there was no way now that he could ever tell the two apart.

She stepped up to the door and lifted her veil again for a moment, folding it back across the brim of her hat. Her pale green eyes moved intently across his face, as if memorizing every feature. "When I swore on my life that I would help you, I was not lying," she said softly. "I know you can never believe me. But I was telling the truth."

She made to push past him, out the door, her hand rising to her veil. With a snarl, Thomas pulled her back, into his arms, taking her mouth one last time. She clung to him, and her kiss tasted of desperation. Her lips parted under his, her body melding to his so completely that his chest ached. She opened her lips and teeth, welcoming him, welcoming his invasion with her slick, hot mouth until he could bear it no longer.

He tore himself away with enough force to send her staggering slightly, her skirts swirling around her. When she regained her balance and looked at him, her eyes were dead.

"Good-bye, Thomas," she whispered.

"I am not Thomas to you," he said, the words twisting in his gut.

"Good-bye," she repeated.

"I can't let you do this," he said. "I will not let you turn my brother's death into your own vehicle for revenge."

Her eyes went even emptier. She ducked her head, whether in acknowledgment or simply to make it easier for her to lower her veil again, he didn't know. She opened the door and pushed out of the flat in a rustle of silk and a lingering scent of perfume.

Thomas slumped against the wall, feeling wrung out like an old rag as his mind raced uncontrollably, poring over every moment that they had spent together. He discarded her looks of softness, of vulnerability, of desire, and of ecstasy, stripping everything away but her words. The pattern that emerged was so damning that it made him want to vomit.

It had been she who had suggested that she find out what happened to his brother, who had teased him with promises of revelation until he had relented, giving her a halter to his private demon so that she might lead him about as she willed.

Had she planned it all even then? She might have had this laid out for months, just biding her time, waiting for him to take her bait. And he had—swallowed it down so that she hooked him in the guts, exploiting his alienation from his family to weave the perfect plot. Lord Varcourt, obsessed with his past, made a tool for her vengeance against her half brother—if Olthwaite even was that. It might have been far too late by the time Thomas had found out the truth.

And she—what would she gain from it all, aside from revenge? Revenge was a powerful enough motive, he knew, but it seemed a paltry thing when its fulfillment did nothing to ameliorate the prospects of an unstable and deprived future.

Was Emmeline that blind? That fixated? He had come near enough to that kind of single-mindedness himself in the past few days. But even though she was unquestionably driven, Thomas did not sense the festering obsession that would send her to the point of self-destruction.

Thomas did not know what she was planning now, but he was determined that his family and their past would have no part in it.

Em froze in the front hall of Hamilton House, her mantle, forgotten in her hand, extended toward the footman. The voice came again, floating down the stairs:

"I cannot but think that you are making a grave mistake. I do beg you to reconsider, especially as anything unseemly shall at this late date unfavorably impact next week's final vote on Amherst's bill."

Lord Varcourt. His voice was like a knife to her gut. Emmeline reanimated with effort, surrendering her mantle and following with her hat and gloves. Why must he be here, now?

The reply was inaudible, and his next words were lower, impossible to understand, but the tones of frustration were clear. Em reminded herself that this was not his household, not as long as the old earl still lived.

"Where is Lady Hamilton?" she asked the parlor maid who stood waiting to escort her, even though she was more than half-certain that she knew.

The girl's eyes flickered upward. "Above, m'm," she said, but she did not move at that subtle prompt.

"And is she receiving?" Em pushed further.

"She is at home to you always, m'm," the maid said, as if repeating instructions pronounced carefully at some time past.

Em relaxed. Varcourt had not gained too much ground with his mother.

"If you'll follow me, m'm," the maid said, and with palpable reluctance, she began to mount the stairs.

Em hid her own hesitation, keeping her head tall and back straight; she had even less desire than the maid to meet Lord Varcourt. All too soon, the maid brought her to the sitting room of Lady Hamilton's private suite, the voices of Varcourt and his mother growing louder as they approached. The door was already half-open; the maid made a polite knock before taking a visible breath and swinging the door wide.

"Madame Esmeralda, m'm," the girl squeaked with a curtsy so brief that it became a manic bob. With a single wide-eyed look at Lord Varcourt, she turned and fled past Em and down the corridor.

Even as she stepped into the room, Em wondered whether she, too, should not have beaten a retreat as soon as she heard Varcourt's voice. As she took in the room, her stomach sank.

The room had always been cluttered and somewhat claustrophobic, but now it was so full of tables and figurines, tatted doilies and pillow-crowded chairs that there was hardly any room to move. The curtains were pulled tight against the late-afternoon light, but the gaslights flared on the walls, and a fire leapt on the hearth with enough heat that Em regretted the necessity of her veil.

From the top shelf of an étagère, rows of china dogs looked down upon her as she entered, their glazed eyes glinting with the reflection of flames. Her skirts brushed against an accent table, upon which a mob of shepherdesses

and their sheep cavorted in their grotesquely bucolic poses
in such numbers that they clattered and rocked against each
other at the touch.

Lady Hamilton, dressed in a frothy gown of sea green, was
so ensconced in the muddle that it was almost possible to
overlook her. Lord Varcourt, however, could not have looked
more out of place, like a great black stone in the middle of the
filigreed room. He turned as she entered, and the accusation
in his eyes was clear. The entire room was an accusation—an
indication of her failure to bring peace to Lady Hamilton either with her presence or her fictions.

She froze, knowing that she could not communicate with
Lord Varcourt through her veil, but still struck with a word-
less guilt. He rose from a wide, square ottoman, the only
place other than the space that Lady Hamilton occupied that
was clear enough for a person to sit.

"You have company, madam," he said to his mother with
a bow so precise that Em feared it would cut her. "I shall
speak with you at a more propitious moment."

"Yes, Thomas," Lady Hamilton said.

Varcourt wove his way out of the room, pressing through
the narrow space between Em's skirts and the door. In the
doorway, he paused, looking at her with empty eyes that
made the breath hurt in her lungs.

"I will be waiting when you come out," he said to her,
and whether that was a promise or a threat, Em could not
tell.

Em let out her breath as he left, and maneuvered so that
she could shut the door behind him.

She looked at Lady Hamilton. The woman looked tired
and old far beyond her years. *I didn't mean to hurt you,* Em
thought. *I didn't mean to hurt anyone I didn't have to—and
then no further than their just deserts.*

It didn't matter what she had meant, she was coming to
believe. What mattered was what she had done. She

couldn't remember who it was who had written that good
intentions paved the path to hell, but she could feel those
flagstones beneath her feet, leading downward. *By their
fruits ye shall know them*—that quote was more familiar but
no less damning.

She had to let Lady Hamilton know the truth. Not her
growing conviction of her half brother's guilt—she was not
even sure that her own prejudices had not so polluted her
mind that her judgment in the matter had been perverted.
No, what Lady Hamilton had to know and believe was her
husband's innocence. That was Em's only hope of salvation,
of taking something from her life this past year that was
good and true.

And so she drew the persona of Madame Esmeralda
around her like an ill-fitting cloak. No longer did she fear
that she would lose herself in Esmeralda—suddenly, it was
Esmeralda who seemed lost, killed by the brutalities of the
real world and banished back into the shadows from whence
she had come.

Only a little longer, Em promised herself. Only a few
more days, and for good or for ill, Esmeralda could rest
forever.

"I have been hounded by visions since we last met," she
said solemnly as she took the ottoman that Varcourt had
vacated.

"Concerning the matter that brought you here?" Lady
Hamilton asked. Then, looking suddenly frail, she added,
"Or is it concerning Harry?"

Em dropped her voice. "It touches upon Harry—upon
him very directly, for he speaks to me with his own voice for
the first time."

Lady Hamilton paled. "There are not echoes that others
send to you, or mere pictures of him beyond?"

"No, it was his voice that I heard." She choked on the assurance that his eyes met hers directly and that he stood with

no tics or grimaces. Instead, she said, "He was as he was meant to be. He glories in the platonic purity and divine mathematics of the numbers of the beyond—they are not mere manifestations of an idea as they are here but are the thing itself."

Lady Hamilton's expression softened. "That's my Harry."

Em swallowed against the tightness in her throat. "I know. He knows that you will listen now."

"Of course," Lady Hamilton said, her eager eyes fixed upon Em.

"He knows whom you have believed for all these years to be his murderer. And he says that you are mistaken, terribly mistaken, and have wrongly hardened your heart against a man who should be closest to you," Em pressed on.

Lady Hamilton looked shocked. "He doesn't—he can't mean . . ."

Em shook her head. "He hesitates in telling me who he is speaking of. He does not want to further calumniate this man."

The countess looked around wildly. "Can you see him? Is he here?"

Em closed her eyes, shutting out the sight of the desperate woman. The lies that were the stock in trade of the spiritualist dissolved before Lady Hamilton's need to believe. "He is always with you," she said, "in your heart and your memory. You may not sense him or feel his presence as—as I have told you of the spirits beyond, but there is a bond formed by love that is indifferent to the sensitivities of the individual."

"Oh, Harry . . ." the countess quavered.

Em opened her eyes with effort. "Harry does not want to say the name, but I get a sense of it, anyway. He looks much like Lord Varcourt, only older, sterner. I believe it must be . . . your lord husband." She put astonishment into that pronouncement.

Lady Hamilton groaned and nodded.

"I see Harry now, on the last day of his life. He had balked at crossing the stream, turning back when the horse splashed water upon him. His brother, Thomas, was angry— very angry. They argued, and Thomas struck out with his whip, the end of it catching Harry on the cheek. Then he left, following the others, and Harry had bawled, letting his horse wander away and climbing upon a stile to sit away from the damp earth."

Em took a deep breath. "Now his lord father comes, riding a fine horse. He tries to speak to Harry, but Harry will not listen, and so the father turns away, ordering his son to walk home. Harry only cries harder and harder until someone else comes—someone who has malice in his heart. This man mocks Harry, and Harry strikes out. Soon they are fighting, down the slope and into the water. They are struggling, fighting—and then Harry's head hits a rock. It is over in a moment. The man is frightened, and he flees, disappearing in the other direction just before you come within sight of your son's form."

"Oh, no," Lady Hamilton whispered. "Is this true, Esmeralda?"

"I believe it to be so, yes," Em said. Truth carried on the back of a thousand lies—was it yet another evil, or had she finally done right?

"I love him, you know," the countess said.

"Yes," said Em, not knowing whether she meant her husband or son.

"I thought . . ." She broke off. "I saw the earl riding away, and then so soon after, I came upon Harry, dead in the water. I knew the earl must have just seen him, and I thought . . . I near drove myself mad thinking of what he'd stolen from me—what he'd done to his own son. But I still loved him. That has been the hardest thing of all, remembering Harry daily and sitting across from . . . from the man I thought had killed him every evening at supper."

"Lord Hamilton did not do it, madam," Em said.

"I think I understand that now," she said.

Even though it was not her concern, Em could not help but ask, "Why did you not say anything years ago, when Harry died? Why did you keep silent?"

Lady Hamilton's expression was intense. "I have never even had the courage to tell him that I love him. How could I bring an accusation against him as grave as that? Have you seen him angry? He is terrifying. He has lost his temper at times—never at me or the other children, and almost never at Harry—and it was a thing to see. I knew he wouldn't kill his own child on purpose. . . . But an accident, if Henry had provoked him and he had struck the boy so that he stumbled back, tripped, fell . . . Yes, that I could see. It could never be proven and could only stain the honor that Lord Hamilton holds dearer than his own life. But I could still see it."

Em let out a breath at the enormity of the situation: the pride and fear and stupidity that had all come together in a single travesty to destroy the attachment that Lord and Lady Hamilton shared—or, perhaps worse, not destroy it but to distort it into something ugly and inimical. For it had somehow survived twelve years of mistrust and silence. Lord Hamilton believed it now beyond help, for he had not even asked her to go to his wife with his story—only his son. Em prayed that he was wrong.

They sat in silence for a long moment, Em watching Lady Hamilton's distant eyes as the firelight played across her delicate, lined features. Finally, her expression firmed, an action so unfamiliar to Em that she almost did not recognize it for what it was: determination.

Lady Hamilton reached out for the bellpull. A moment later, the maid Valette appeared in the doorway.

"Yes, my lady?" she asked, her hands neatly folded over her black taffeta dress.

"Please go into my dressing rooms and pull out every dress that I have not worn in the past two years," Lady Hamilton ordered.

"Madam?" the maid said, her face slack with astonishment.

"Go, Valette," the countess said. "As soon as you are finished, send them with Jim to the secondhand clothes man. Move everything that remains back into my old dressing room. I intend to be sleeping in my old bedroom within two days."

"I do not think it shall all fit, madam," Valette said.

"Then I shall join you in a few hours and go through the things myself," Lady Hamilton said. "I have been living apart from the earl for too long."

Valette looked at her strangely. "For years, madam."

"All the more reason for haste, Valette!" Lady Hamilton said, a clear dismissal.

"Yes, madam," the maid said, straightening abruptly. She bobbed and left, shutting the door behind her.

"Now," said Lady Hamilton, "about the party you wanted . . ."

Chapter Twenty-one

Em left Lady Hamilton's sitting room feeling drained. She began to show herself out, as she always did, but a shadow in a doorway stopped her.

"Lord Varcourt," she said, making her voice cool even as her body tightened. "I suppose my farewell was premature."

"Emmeline," he returned. "As long as you continue to visit my mother, it is."

Em's heart leapt in fear at his use of her name, and she looked around reflexively to see if there were any servants within earshot. But the corridor was deserted. She regained control of herself. "Why are you here?" she asked.

"I have moved back into my old rooms for the moment," he said, nodding. Behind him, she could make out the shape of an ancient bedstead.

"To keep an eye on me," she supplied. "Aren't your spies doing a sufficient job of that?"

"They can watch you, but they cannot stop you," he said.

"If you want to stop me, then why have you not unmasked me?" Em asked. "It is within your power."

Varcourt regarded her without expression, his very flatness making her heart squeeze. "Yes, it is. But you stole the

Olthwaite family jewels. Such a theft is a hanging offense. You deserve many things, but not that."

Em started slightly as a housemaid pushed open the green baize door that led to the backstairs. The girl gave the two of them a long, curious stare before tearing her eyes away and hurrying into another room.

As soon as she was gone, Em said tightly, "If you wish to speak with me, at least let us go into a room."

Varcourt stepped back, inviting her into his bedchamber with a wave.

Em balked. "A lady would never accept."

His black eyes sparked. "But we both know you are no lady. My room—or we speak out here."

Reluctantly, Em stepped inside. He closed the door, then turned and leaned on it, crossing his arms over his chest in the familiar stance that made her ache. Despite herself, Em felt a small tremor of fear.

"Remove your veil," he said first.

Slowly, Em obeyed, loath to bare herself to him. He took in her face in one swift glance. She dared not speculate what her expression betrayed, but it caused his stoniness to soften fractionally. She ached for him and for herself. Self-consciously, Em smoothed back a stray wisp of hair.

"I sent men to investigate your story," he continued after the silence had stretched out for too long.

"Which one?" she countered. "As you have said, there are so many." She should not be antagonizing him—she couldn't afford to antagonize him now—but neither could she stop herself from lashing out like a wounded animal.

Varcourt's eyes went half-lidded for a moment in an expression that Em was too discomfited to analyze before it was gone, but he did not respond in kind. "The story of your origins. I have a last name to put with the first, as well—Emmeline Dunn."

Em bit her lip.

"Of your mother, I can discover nothing," he continued, "but you were indeed raised in old Lord Olthwaite's household, with his children. My agents spoke to your old nurse."

"You mean your spies," she corrected.

He shrugged. "Agents. Spies. It scarcely matters. You were particularly close to Ann, the youngest, as you said, but after she died, you became inseparable from Alice— until, of course, she had her seasons in London and made her match."

"Yes," she said, raising her chin.

"And then . . . and then everything goes murky," he said. "Your nurse had been retired to the village with a respectable legacy, courtesy of the old baron's will, and the tutors and governesses were long gone. You never got a lady's maid of your own."

"No. I did not merit a lady's maid," Em said. It had not been a wound back then, for she had been well schooled in gratefulness. But perspective changed everything, and now the memory of how she had been shunted aside, made to feel like an object of charity for every morsel that had been begrudged her, made her ache with old injustices.

"The old baron called you into his sickroom shortly before he died, but you cried on no one's shoulder; none can tell us what it was he said to you. But on the day of the funeral, all know that there was a violent row between you and the new baron, who swiftly left his estate." He paused. "This alone makes me curious—why he fled instead of merely casting you out. He seems unmoved by charity, and from what I saw myself at Eton, his natural contempt for those weaker than himself was only increased by his time away from home."

"He was always a bully," Em said with bitter memory. She looked at him. "You were at Eton when he was there?"

Varcourt's mouth creased in distaste. "For one year only—I am four years his senior. I cannot help but think that some of his political intransigence now is a result of the fact that most of the older boys who kept him in check at school were the sons of Whiggish families." He raised an eyebrow. "And before you ask, yes, I was one of those. But we are talking about you now, not me or my relationship to the young Lord Olthwaite."

"There is nothing more to tell of my life," Em said.

"On the contrary," said Varcourt, "the most important part remains. Thus far, we have an ordinary and rather tawdry story of the conflicts between a man's legitimate heir and his illegitimate offspring."

She bit off a retort.

"It is what comes after that is curious. A month after his inheritance, young Olthwaite returned to Forsham Manor, accompanied by a wide cross-section of the more wild branches of what is rather optimistically called good society. In an apparent attempt at rapprochement, Olthwaite had a fine gown made for you, and you more or less . . . came out. You danced, you laughed, a good time was had by all, but the next morning, you were gone, and Olthwaite would not emerge from his rooms for three days. The guests wandered off, none apparently missing you as the servants did, and you were never seen or heard from again."

"As you see, I am fine," Em said lightly, pushing back the swirl of memories and emotions that accompanied the bare narrative that Varcourt told so baldly. "Perhaps I tired of my half brother's charity and took my inheritance to London to find a new life out from under his thumb."

His brows lowered. "Still lying, Emmeline?"

She dropped her gaze. "No. No, I am not lying, even if I only give you a fragment of the truth."

"You are not going to tell me what happened that night, are you?" he asked.

"No, I am not." She looked up. "Some stories are better untold. And you could never confirm it, so you would not believe it, anyway. Know that I had reason enough to leave, to forget about Emmeline and put her behind me."

"But you have not," he said.

She sighed, rubbing her forehead in sudden weariness. "I tried to put her away, at least for a while."

"So you could work your revenge?" He asked that as if not even he believed it.

She shook her head. "So that I could create a new life, in which Em could live again."

"What I cannot understand is, when your intention was to deceive me, why you told me so much that was not a lie," he said heavily.

"I deceived no one out of pleasure," she said. "You must understand that." Why he must understand, why it was so important to her, she did not care to examine in detail. "I deceived you only as far as you forced me to, for my own self-preservation."

"That is why I cannot unmask you now." He frowned, and lines appeared around his mouth and eyes that made him look too much like his father. "I feel as if I know you, Emmeline. It may all be a lie, despite the truths I have uncovered, but I cannot help the sense that our very selves touched, if only for a moment."

Em smiled ruefully. "I believe I told you that you would find a paradise between my legs."

He snorted. "Amazing as that may have been, that is not it—or at least, not all of it."

"I know," she said softly. "And that, at least, was not a lie."

He nodded slowly. "I knew that you would say that. You had to say it."

"I don't expect you to believe me, Varcourt. I can only ask your forbearance for a short while longer. Then I will be gone forever, away from you, away from your family," she said.

His expression was bleak. "I do not know how much more of you my mother can take. I would unmask you for no other reason if the stakes were not so high and I did not fear that it would make her worse."

Em's breath caught, and her throat bubbled with angry accusations. But she swallowed them and said levelly, "I did no more to her than you asked me to, and far more than I wanted to. I believe—I hope—that she is somewhat better after today. I hope that it is enough to make up for the wrongs I have done her, however unintentionally."

Varcourt regarded her for a long moment, then finally nodded. "My forbearance does have limits. I know that you will stage some sort of grand demonstration in two days' time with my lady mother's help. I do not know what you plan, but I will not tolerate your turning my brother's death to your own purpose. If I find you doing that, then I will do everything in my power to bring your career to a sudden and ignominious end."

Her heart accelerated. She must tell him what she was about. She had hidden her plans out of fear and necessity, but new necessity now compelled her to make a fuller confession so that he would not misunderstood her intention. "Lord Olthwaite—" she began.

"No." He cut her off with a convulsive wave of his hand. "I will not hear you speak that name again."

She bowed her head, battling back pleas and excuses. He held her life in his hands, and she knew she could not press him on that point no matter how important it was for him to know. "I understand. You have—" She extended her hand, palm out, in a gesture of powerlessness. "You have my word that your brother has no part in this, however you may value it."

He nodded again and stepped away from the door. Em took the silent invitation, stepping past him to the doorway. Tentatively, she reached out, touching his cheek as if she could memorize his heat, his warmth and life. He wrapped his hand around hers and pulled it to his mouth as he held her eyes in his gaze, brushing his lips against the back of her hand. Em swayed for a moment as sensation shivered through her, closing her eyes against it, fighting the flood of memories that it caused in her, from their first encounter in Rushworth's library to everything that occurred between them since.

Wordlessly, he released her, and she pulled her veil back down and stepped from the room.

Everything about this party made Thomas' head throb a warning: the colored globes over the low gaslights, the Gypsy costumes and amulets that some of the guests had taken it upon themselves to wear, the series of lone fiddlers in each public room that his mother had playing Slavonic folk music. Even the food, laid out in a great buffet, was tilted toward the exotic, with pitas and couscous, figs and dates, served by swarthy men in embroidered waistcoats and pantaloons.

Worst of all, however, was the air of tense expectancy. The possibilities for this evening's entertainment dominated the conversation. Half the guests seemed to believe that Madame Esmeralda would produce a dancing bear and a circus troupe with a flare of flash powder, but the other half expected some real manifestation from the spirit world. Both groups seemed to be equally eager for the final revelation.

Emmeline moved through the middle of it all in a dress that was so brilliantly scarlet that it seemed to pulsate. Few tried to speak to her—most kept a fascinated kind of distance, some treating her with looks of awe for her purported powers, others looking at her as if she were a trick pony that might do something spectacularly clever at any moment.

She had opened the night standing on a dais in the ballroom with a declaration of the nearness of the spirit world and the approach of a propitious moment, all delivered with a tone and cadence that would make a governess attempting to teach an unruly girl recitation weep. Whether it was her voice alone or the shivering violin accompaniment, the guests were captivated, all eager for midnight, when she declared the revelation would occur.

Whatever she was going to do, whatever she had been scheming for all these months, it would happen then. And Thomas had no intention of letting her out of his sight until that moment. He caught her head turned toward him several times, and he nodded in acknowledgment, which she did not return. He ached for her, burned for her—she had haunted his dreams until he wondered if she truly did possess unearthly powers. But he made no move toward her, and somehow her slow circulation through the rooms never brought her near enough for speech.

"Good evening, Varcourt. Do you mind telling me what the hell this is about?"

Thomas turned to find Edgington glaring at him, jaw set and bearing the exquisite baroness on his arm. He gave them both a small, wary bow.

"Lady Edgington. Lord Edgington. I wouldn't think this was quite the language appropriate for the presence of ladies," he said.

Lady Edgington treated him to her unblinking, china-blue gaze. "Have no fear, Lord Varcourt. There are no ladies within earshot—only I."

Edgington shifted his grip on her arm slightly. A warning squeeze? It was gone too fast for Varcourt to read it, but Lady Edgington seemed to subside slightly, a small, unreadable smile on her face.

"You didn't answer my question," Edgington said.

"I would tell you if I knew, but I haven't any more idea than you do," Thomas said.

"You were the one who decided that she was dangerous,"

Edgington said tightly. "You said that you would handle her."

Thomas's gaze slipped over the baron's shoulder to the slender, veiled form who drifted silently by, her skirts a fantasy in scarlet. "I hope for all our sakes that I have."

Edgington raised an eyebrow. "I spent valuable resources in shipping someone all the way to Somerset to question the staff at Forsham. If Olthwaite doesn't know about it yet, he shall, and he will figure out who is behind it."

Thomas made a dismissive gesture. "He will know that the Whigs did it. Any more than that is idle speculation. If any of our conjectures about what might have happened to Emmeline Dunn are correct, knowing that someone is asking about her will have him wetting his trousers, not thinking up a counterattack."

"That is who Madame Esmeralda really is, isn't it?" Lady Edgington's brilliant eyes were narrow as she looked up at him. At Thomas' grim silence, she said tartly, "Don't take me for a child, Lord Varcourt. You sent our agents running around in circles after Esmeralda, nothing but Esmeralda, for weeks. Then all of a sudden you say that Esmeralda doesn't matter; it's this Emmeline whom we should be after."

Thomas looked at Edgington. "Do you tell her everything?"

Humor flickered across Edgington's golden features, then was gone. "It would be rather difficult not to."

"Do you have no idea at all what she is up to?" Lady Edgington broke in before he could devise a suitable reply. "After all those passionate embraces, those ecstatic nights, surely you must have learned something beyond what's between her legs."

This time, the warning squeeze was unmistakable—and so was Lady Edgington's tiny smile at Thomas' surprised reaction to her directness. He schooled his features to stillness.

"I have found out a great deal," Thomas said. "I just don't know whether to trust it."

"I hope she isn't planning some grand, stupid sacrifice," Edgington muttered.

"I think I can safely say that sacrifice is the last thing on her mind," Thomas said.

"Lord Olthwaite is coming," Lady Edgington murmured, her eyes disappearing behind a fringe of black lashes.

"We will speak more later," Edgington said, treating Thomas to a curt nod.

"Of course," he said. But Edgington was already moving off, his tiny wife floating delicately on his arm.

Lord Olthwaite lurched up. His portly face already shone with sweat, and Thomas was willing to bet that the wineglass clutched in his hand was far from his first drink. He remembered what Edgar Wythe had looked like at his first party after graduating from Eton—a powerful if stocky man, built like a bulldog. In the space of the last seven years, he'd lost that power to dissipation, his broad shoulders and thick neck swallowed by pads of fat. He used a cane now, not out of fashion but from necessity, as gout overcame him, and his eyes had a faint yellow tint. Given his determined pattern of self-destructive dissolution, Thomas would be willing to bet a hundred quid that he was syphilitic, too.

His political brilliance in such circumstances was little short of astonishing, and his reputation as a host of parties of a certain type was nearly as great. The Liberals had tried a hundred times to find some traction on him, some weakness to exploit, but they failed; seeming to be made of nothing but weaknesses, he possessed many places in which a lever might be used but no fixed fulcrum to push against.

Thomas had never seen him in such a state, despite the prodigious quantities of alcohol he often imbibed. He seemed so pissed that it was a small miracle he was still upright.

"If I had known that you were invited, I would have had my father lay on the whisky," Thomas said as Olthwaite came to a stop in front of him.

Olthwaite laughed. "Not the whisky, man. I have found a new vice—vodka!" He lifted his wineglass in a mimic of a toast. That, at least, contained the same claret Thomas was drinking. "Russia's greatest contribution to civilization. Do you know how many potatoes it takes to distill a bottle?"

"No, I am afraid I am not very conversant about the hard liquors of other nations," Thomas said.

Olthwaite sighed melodramatically. "You are denying yourself a world of experience."

Thomas raked his gaze across the man. "You look like you deny yourself nothing."

"Ha ha!" Olthwaite barked, swaying slightly. "Yes, very clever, Varcourt."

"Come on, now. You did not come here to trade insults with me. What is it that you want?" Thomas asked, not bothering to hide his impatience.

"I want to talk about . . . that woman," Olthwaite said, dropping his voice.

"Yes?" Thomas prompted.

"Madame Esmeralda. Or whoever the hell she is." He scowled. "She is dangerous. You shouldn't let her near your mother. I think she has been cavorting with a criminal element."

Thomas looked down at the man with dislike. "You mean like Emmeline Dunn?" he said. The man flinched. Maliciously, he continued, "Why would you consider your half sister criminal?"

"You *have* been poking about Forsham!" Olthwaite spat, going suddenly purple. "That is my home. You—you stay away from it. And—and anyway, she isn't my half sister."

The last rebuttal was tacked on, as if it only occurred to Olthwaite to reject a blood tie with Emmeline at the last moment. *Caught you,* Thomas thought. But the man's uncharacteristic clumsiness with words disturbed him. Was it only whisky? His eyes were too dilated, but he lacked the vagueness of opiate use.

"Don't worry, Olthwaite. I don't think you have to worry about her anymore," said Thomas.

"What do you mean?" Olthwaite demanded, his eyes full of distrust.

Thomas shrugged. "I strongly suspect that she is dead."

"Did Madame Esmeralda tell you that?" Olthwaite's expression was torn between fear and disbelief. "You need to be careful of her. She's dangerous."

"You would expect her to say something like that if she is in league with Miss Dunn," Thomas said coldly, ignoring the repetition of his earlier warning. There was something very wrong with the man. "Then again, that would only make sense if Miss Dunn really is a criminal and needs to disappear permanently. If Miss Dunn is innocent, then she had no reason to disappear, and Madame Esmeralda must be hearing her from the spirit world."

"Then they must be partners." Olthwaite's mouth spoke the words even as he paled, his eyes darting nervously toward the corner where Emmeline had temporarily come to rest. "She said something horrible to me when she gave me this drink." He waved it at Thomas. "It's gotten into my bones somehow, set my brain aswirl." He seemed to realize that he had said too much, and he clamped his jaw down on a slight whimper, then drank the rest of the wine in a single gulp.

More and more interesting. "I think you should find a spiritualist of your own," he suggested cruelly. "Ask her to contact the spirit of your dead half sister. If she can, then you have your answer."

Olthwaite grimaced. "There are so many charlatans today. You have to find the real thing."

"Go to a Gypsy," Thomas offered without expression. "Everyone knows they can really contact the dead."

Olthwaite's expression grew distant. "Yes. Yes, that's true enough. Madame Esmeralda told me I should talk to you about it, and she was right about that." He wandered off, moving with the extreme, drifting caution of the very drunk.

Looking up with alarm, Thomas scanned the parlor. At some point in his conversation with Olthwaite, Emmeline had vanished—undoubtedly, just as she had planned.

Damn.

He set off to find her.

Chapter Twenty-two

Thomas moved from room to room in search of Emmeline, but after he had reached the last of the public rooms, he still had not caught sight of her scarlet-clad form.

He found his mother in the ballroom and waited impatiently for the Duchess of Rushworth to move off. Despite himself, he found that he was drawn to watching Lady Hamilton speak—the animation in her eyes, the swiftness of her hands as she waved them to emphasize some point or another. This was not the frantic mania of the previous week but something that at least approximated normality. It had been years since he had seen her like this, particularly given the strain of hosting her second party in as many weeks.

Lady Hamilton had not been magically fixed by whatever Emmeline had said to her, but she was better than she had been in a very long time. Thomas still caught her reaching for her laudanum now and again, but she was in an opiate haze far less often and was self-conscious enough to try to hide it when she did turn to the clear little bottle. She was even speaking to her husband—and almost as astonishing, the earl was speaking back, developing a level of solicitousness that in another man Thomas might have called affection. However improbable and through whatever means, his mother seemed to be improving, adding yet another twist to his tumultuous feelings about the false spiritualist.

Finally, the duchess left, her new pinch-faced lady's companion following in her wake.

"Madam?" Thomas said to his mother.

Lady Hamilton turned. "Oh, Thomas, it's you," she said with a fragile smile.

"I was looking for Esmeralda," he said.

Her smile trembled. "Please do not hound the girl."

Thomas wondered what made her decide that Emmeline was a girl and not an old woman. "I have no plans to disturb her, mother. It is just that she is the centerpiece of this evening's entertainment. It is good to know where she is."

"You worry too much," said Lady Hamilton.

"Perhaps," he acknowledged. "But it is almost midnight." He nodded to the dais that occupied one end of the ballroom, where a great case clock had been set, its minute hand slowly sweeping up the clock face toward the peak. Already, the fiddlers were moving in from other rooms, ceasing their individual tunes and setting up toward the back of the dais as the guests began to gather in the ballroom for the climax of the entertainment.

Lady Hamilton looked around. "I have not seen her in some time. If she is not inside, why don't you try the terrace?" She nodded to the torch-lit darkness beyond the row of French windows.

"Thank you, madam," Thomas said, giving her a small bow and controlling his impatience.

He stepped out into the night and scanned the terrace. There was a bite in the air that had not been there the week before, a taste of the autumn to come. A small group of guests stood near the slope down to the gardens, but other than that, there was nothing.

Could Emmeline's grand plan be to socially embarrass his family? *Ridiculous,* he thought instantly. He was considering whether he should search the private rooms of the house or go down into the gardens when he saw a figure at the verge where hedged gardens met lawn. He had the disorienting sense that the shape was unfamiliar, but as the person approached, it resolved itself into scarlet skirts and a long veil.

He watched, arms folded, as Emmeline took the steps up to the terrace. She walked without looking to the right or the left, directly across the terrace toward the set of French windows at the end of the ballroom farthest from the dais. Thomas pursued her.

"Not even a greeting, Merry?" he asked.

She stopped, turning slowly to face him. For several seconds, she did nothing except stare at him. Then, across the night breeze came the sound of quiet laughter that contained a chilly note that raised the hairs on his arms and the back of his neck. He started, then realized that it must be coming from her.

"Merry?" he asked uncertainly. "Emmeline?"

The laughter cut off abruptly, and with a swish of scarlet silk, she turned away from him and passed into the ballroom, leaving him with a chill that had nothing to do with the breeze. He stared after her for a long moment. *What the hell does Emmeline think she is doing?*

Just then, the long case clock in the ballroom began to ring the hour, slowly, deliberately, one low toll for every slow swing of the pendulum. Thomas passed into the ballroom. It was crowded with people now and buzzing with anticipation. How many guests had his mother invited? One hundred? Two? Around him, they whispered and shifted, fans fluttering, feathers bobbing, a susurration of cultivated voices and expensive fabrics.

There was a movement in the crowd. He stared between the heads of the taller men. The guests were making a passage through the center of the room, parting before the figure of Emmeline in her brilliant dress. With every strike of the clock, she took a step, silence spreading out from her to lie over the room until Thomas swore he could hear the wind of the combined breaths of the company and each sound of Emmeline's heels against the floor between the strikes of the clock. He could not shake the sense of wrongness that seemed to hang over her, an indefinable difference in the way she stood and stepped.

The clock struck for the twelfth time and fell silent. In the emptiness came the inhalation of the guests—and then the faint strains of a Gypsy fiddle, then another, and another, strengthening as Emmeline advanced.

Thomas tore his eyes away from her and focused on the dais, realizing that the lights had been further dimmed as he was staring at her. An entire ensemble of fiddlers stood there, the gold embroidery of their costumes glinting in the colored lights, their parts swooping and twining around one another in a tune that was at once alien and familiar. Slowly, he realized where he had heard it before—on a concertina, in the Gypsy tavern the night that he had followed Emmeline home.

She mounted the two steps up to the platform, standing near the front edge. She began to speak, her voice trembling like the violins that sank to create a shivering counterpoint to her words.

"I was brought to these shores by grave injustice and dire need," she said. Her voice carried to the ends of the room, but the thinness of it disturbed Thomas, striking a warning note within him. "I have been searching for the truth since I arrived, through paths physical and spiritual, moving among the flocks of the happy dead and listening to the tale of woe. Tonight, I went into the darkness, and I found light!" she cried. "I found guilt, but also did I find truth."

Thomas' heart stuttered. She had promised that she would not bring his brother into this, promised that she could not use his death to persecute her enemies. Had she lied about this, then, too?

Up on the dais, her veiled face turned as if she were sweeping the assembly with her gaze, and she continued. "The truth must be known for the guilt to be washed from among us. There is one here who has done great wrong. One who is stained." She raised her voice. "Let him step forward before I call out one to accuse him. Let him come!" She extended her arm slowly, swaying as she moved it above the heads of the guests.

Thomas looked around him, his chest burning. Some faces were horrified, others avid, but all were watching the woman in rapt silence. *No.* He would not let this happen, his family made a farce of for Emmeline's petty revenge. He began pushing forward, elbowing his way to the cleared corridor up which Emmeline had passed. People began to shift and whisper, but he ignored them—just as Emmeline ignored him, her moving hand passing back and forth.

"Let the guilty come forward," she intoned. "Let the spirits speak and tell me his name. Speak! *Speak!*" Her voice rose, and the violins followed, hitting an unearthly note. "They come to me. I see them, thick as wishes, flying around us so that we breathe their essence, swirling, swirling above our heads until they find a man." Suddenly, her arm stopped moving, and she was pointing a trembling finger into the thick of the crowd.

Thomas bit back a curse as he broke into the cleared corridor. He knew he didn't have to look, but he did anyway, taking in the sweating, trembling man in a glance. More people were shifting and whispering, some staring at him, others at Emmeline, and the rest at the nerveless Olthwaite. Thomas' mind boiled with fury. He broke into a run, sprinting heedlessly at the figure on the dais so that he could catch her before she could cause any more harm.

"Tell me his name!" Emmeline shrieked as Thomas leapt

up the three stairs to the dais—then, in a voice he had never heard before, she cried out, "Edgar, called Wythe, false Lord Olthwaite, it is you I accuse!"

Thomas reached her just then and grabbed her around the waist, hauling her back against him. "I will not let you do this!" he hissed in her ear.

And the room exploded in confusion.

Em stood in the darkness next to the French windows, waiting for her cue. Her red dress lay in pieces, safely hidden away in a black bag in the hedge, and now she stood in the dress that she had worn the day her old life ended, the white gown of a debutante that had been made for the ball at Forsham.

All planning was over now. The foundations had been laid in a hundred minds; Edgar had been assaulted with every doubt she could conjure for him, and she had even been able to empty the small bottle of powdered hashish into a glass of his wine nearly half an hour before. Martha Grey, her false double, had practiced until she was word-perfect, and their exchange had gone off flawlessly. Every preparation she could think of had been undertaken. Now it was the moment of truth.

She listened to the chaos within and steeled herself to enter. Only a few more seconds.

"No!" One cry rang out above them all—that of Lord Olthwaite. "Liar—she's lying!" He was panicked, almost incoherent, and in the shadows next to the ballroom, Em wanted to weep in relief. The drugs had done their work. She would be saved.

"Silence!"

She rocked at that voice. It did not belong to Edgar or to Martha Grey but to Lord Varcourt. What was he doing? She had tried to warn him, tried to tell him, but he would not listen. Now he was going to destroy everything she had worked for— for which she had paid such a high price. Her heart beating wildly, she ran into the ballroom, shoving her way toward the clear space that Martha Grey had created with her passage.

The violins had cut off at Varcourt's shout, and a wave of stillness moved out from the dais. Emmeline caught a glimpse of him between two heads as she pushed desperately forward, heedless of her white gown, squeezing her hoops between the guests. He stood with his legs braced, holding Martha Grey hard against him, his face a terrible mask of grief and rage.

"You swore to leave your lies about my brother out of this," he ground out, his voice pitched low but carrying across the silent room.

Around Em, people gasped. Edgar's choking sound was clearly audible. He stumbled into the clear corridor just as Em reached it and went reeling toward the dais. Em nearly fell as her skirts came free, but no one was looking at her.

Edgar was babbling, the words coming out fast and incoherent, as disordered as Em could have hoped for when she tipped the drug into his drink. But it was going wrong, all wrong, and she had to stop it before her future was destroyed.

"Your brother? I didn't—What about your brother?" Edgar tried to climb the steps. His foot slipped, and he fell backward, sending another gasp around the room. He pushed onto all fours and scrambled, huffing and panting, up the steps. "I don't know anything about your brother," he repeated in a high, whining voice.

Varcourt looked down at him, his face a mask of contempt. "Get out of here, Olthwaite." He raised his voice. "This farce is over. Go home, all of you! It's over. This woman is a fraud." Coming to herself, Martha Grey began to struggle in his grip, clawing his arm and kicking ineffectually back against his shins. He held her hard with one arm and released the other long enough to take hold of her veil.

"Thomas—no!" Em shouted.

It was too late—Varcourt tore the delicate fabric from the

woman's face as she twisted around in his grip, revealing Martha's black hair curling around her dusky complexion.

"Let go of me," she hissed.

Nervelessly, he dropped her. She fell to the dais with a thud and a chaos of skirts, then scrambled to her feet and ran out the door behind the dais and into the depths of the house.

Another shocked silence fell over the room. Again, Em shouted, "No!"

Varcourt's gaze snapped up, following the empty corridor down to the other end of the ballroom until he met Em's gaze. She stood frozen, her arms outstretched, as his eyes widened, taking in her debutante's white chiffon and the cascade of her ash-brown hair.

His mouth formed the beginning of a question, but it was Edgar's voice that broke the silence, rising to a high, gibbering whine.

"I told you—I didn't kill him!" His eyes were fixed on Em with an expression of abject terror. "I didn't. I didn't! Now get that spiritualist back to send the ghost away!"

Em tore her gaze from Varcourt's face, moving it to rest on Edgar's cowering form.

"I shall not be banished with such ease," she said, all her strength going into her voice's icy mercilessness. "You must tell the truth." She stepped forward, slowly advancing on the dais.

Edgar began to cry, fat tears rolling down his flushed face. "You must believe me. It wasn't my fault. I didn't mean to hurt him."

Varcourt jerked and stared at the man at his feet, his expression filling with sudden revulsion.

"I do not care about what happened to Henry Hyde," Em said as she moved toward Edgar. "Tell everyone who I really am. What you did to me."

"*I* care about Harry," Varcourt ground out. "Tell me now. What did you do to him?"

The man was weeping openly now, shaking with sobs. "I didn't mean to do anything. I found him as he was walking home, and I thought I'd have some sport. I rode at him, hollering like a demon, but he just stared at me like the idiot he was, and when I pulled my horse up, he started screaming and throwing himself about because I'd got mud on him." His voice tightened. "The little tit pulled me from my horse. I thought I'd teach him a bit of a lesson, but when I came at him, he ran. I chased him across a field and down a riverbank. He stopped at the water's edge as if he'd been frozen. I was still going, couldn't stop. I ran into him, and he went forward, and there was the rock. . . ." He raised his voice. "It wasn't my fault! If he hadn't pulled me off my horse or stopped or been so bloody stupid, he never would have died."

Varcourt's expression turned so empty that it stole Em's breath. "Harry had ten times the mind you do. And, in spite of everything, ten times the heart."

"What about me, Edgar?" Em forced herself to say. Her heart thundered wildly in her chest—everything was slipping away, out of her control, and she had to get it back. If she lost now, she would be damned forever. Edgar's watering eyes focused on her again, and he whimpered.

"Tell them all who I was," she insisted. "Tell them who you were, you bastard!"

Two footmen fought their way through the crown to reach Em. They looked at Varcourt uncertainly, waiting for his command to drag her away. She sent every ounce of pleading that she had into her gaze, and he shook his head. The men fell back, and she advanced past them.

Edgar didn't seem to notice. "Father was out of his mind. He didn't know what he was saying."

She was implacable. "What about the church registry? Do you think he traveled fifty miles to forge that on his deathbed, too? Is that why you stole it?"

"Registry? What registry?" he squeaked, eyes darting from side to side as if he could escape.

"The truth, Edgar!" she demanded, her voice rising. She lifted her hand, curling her fingers. She was only a dozen feet from the dais now. She stopped. "Unless you want my cold fingers to squeeze your heart until it stops."

"It can't be true. It would make Father a bigamist!" Edgar spat.

"And you a bastard. You found it, didn't you, Edgar? The record of Mary Catharine Dunn's marriage to William Wythe, the future Lord Olthwaite—six months before he committed bigamy with your mother. And you stole it and destroyed it, so no one would ever find out that you were not your father's true heir. I was."

"It was a Catholic wedding!" he protested.

Em nearly swayed with relief. It was an admission—a direct admission of her legitimacy and his misdeeds before an assembly of some of the most influential and well-respected men and women in England. She had what she needed, but she wanted still more. "It was still a legal bond in England, one that cannot be superseded by a later Anglican marriage."

Edgar shook his head wildly as she stepped forward again, mounting the steps of the dais. He tried to stand up but fell back again and scrabbled away from her on all fours. "So what? You couldn't carry on the line. You were a female."

"And my mother dead a year after my birth," she agreed. "There are no legitimate male heirs. Only you, the bastard of a bigamous liaison." Now she was standing over him, looking down as he lay, panting and sweating, at her feet. She turned and looked out over the crowd. "Let everyone here bear witness: The so-called Lord Olthwaite has confessed to falsifying his own legitimacy, disinheriting his father's legitimate daughter, and to"—she paused, looking up at Varcourt, whose expression of empty horror had not changed—"to manslaughter," she finished.

She bent over Edgar. He stared at her slack-jawed, drooling in terror as he tried to make his drugged gaze focus upon her. "Boo," she said. She reached down as he tried to wriggle away, his feet not working on the slick wood of the dais, and placed a palm flat against his chest. His eyes grew wide with realization, his breath stilled, and then, suddenly, he rolled to his side and began to vomit.

"You bitch!" he spat between convulsions. "You're *alive*. What have you done to me?"

Em stared dispassionately at him as he curled at her feet. She did not hate him. Despite everything, she never had quite been able to rouse the pure loathing of hatred, spoiled as it was by the memory of the affection of his sisters for him and the small, thoughtless kindnesses he had shown her, once upon a time. She remembered the boy, the boy who shivered at ghost stories and drank in the Gypsies' lies, who played cruel pranks and stole her dolls, but she also remembered the boy who had given her rides upon his back and who had shown her how to bait a hook and throw a rock across a pond so that it skipped. No, she had no hatred for him, but disgust—yes, that she had much of.

"I've taken it all away, Edgar," she told him. "I've taken it all away."

She looked up at Varcourt, his face thawing into an open battleground of emotion, and shook her head even as she felt her heart rend.

"I didn't use your brother, Thomas. This had nothing to do with him—with any of you. I kept my promise. I wish you had believed me, even though I could give you no reason to do so."

Then she turned away and left, before he could see the tears in her eyes. She had, she found, remembered how to cry.

Chapter Twenty-three

Four weeks later . . .

"Is that it, then?" The Olthwaite barrister frowned at Thomas and his lawyer.

"We are satisfied," Thomas answered for them. "What about the Crown? And Miss Wythe?"

Pain flickered across Emmeline's face, stirring an echo in Thomas' stomach. He tried to suppress it, but even looking at her hurt him. He would have thought that the weeks of separation would have made it easier to bear, but instead, the tiniest detail that he had forgotten about her caused a gaping wound.

"Miss Dunn, please," she said. "If my father would not give me his name in life, I will not honor him by taking it after his death." She looked at her own barrister.

"Yes, we are satisfied," the man said.

They were gathered in the Lincoln Court office of Emmeline's barrister, the Crown prosecutor being disinclined to entertain such a bizarre deal in his own chambers. He still looked at all three parties with an expression of considerable doubt.

"This is highly irregular," said the Crown prosecutor. "Something of this magnitude—if others stir up trouble, it might take an act of Parliament."

"It shall pass," said Thomas flatly.

"I am not satisfied!" Lord Olthwaite objected. He looked half-terrified, but his mind was as sharp as it ever had been, the effects of the night of the confrontation leaving no lasting effect.

"It is the best you shall get, sir," said his barrister tensely, his face dark. "You are lucky that you aren't on trial for murder."

"That bitch poisoned me," he spat. "It was hashish. It had to be."

"Even if you could prove you were under the influence of a drug at the time of your confession, it would be well nigh impossible to prove that it wasn't self-administered, given your history, sir," his barrister muttered back in a tone that sounded like he'd said the same a thousand times before. "Be grateful you get to keep the title, your lands, and your life."

"Most of my lands," Olthwaite muttered. "And what good are they if I am in Australia or Canada or wherever?"

"India," Thomas said firmly. "You must go to India. Her Majesty will be grateful for your administrative talents, and you might live a long and honored life there."

"Or I might die of malaria the first year out!" Olthwaite said, his eyes bulging.

"Keep your peace," snapped the Crown prosecutor. "Is the deal acceptable to you, Lord Olthwaite, yes or no? Think very carefully before you answer."

Olthwaite lowered his head, staring at his thick fingers for a long minute. Finally, he looked up. "It is acceptable to me."

"Then the Crown finds no need to raise the question of manslaughter. Unless, of course, you return to England at any point," the prosecutor added pointedly. "And with the ninety-nine-year gift of Lincroft to Miss Dunn and her descendants, a settlement of ten thousand pounds upon her, and your agreement not to contest her ownership of the family jewels, your legitimacy shall not be legally challenged by her, at least."

"I understand," Olthwaite said.

"Then we are done here."

The contract was signed by all three parties, with the prosecutor and their barristers as witnesses. The Crown prosecutor took the document under his arm and shook hands all around.

"My secretary shall post you copies as soon as they are made," he said.

"Thank you," Emmeline said, her face as smooth as porcelain.

Olthwaite stumbled out first, accompanied by the family barrister. Thomas offered his arm to Emmeline, and after a small hesitation, she took it. They walked down the steps together and out into the court as his barrister took a different path through the building, toward his own rooms.

Thomas stopped and turned to Emmeline as lawyers' lackeys crisscrossed the cobbled court around them, bearing sheaves of paper. She was clad in a pale smoke green dress, its color almost perfectly matching her eyes. Her breath misted in the autumn air—the last month had evaporated in a whirlwind of legal moves and countermoves, but in the end, 167 witnesses had heard Olthwaite confess his guilt, and it was only a matter of time before the baron stopped fighting and accepted the inevitable. It would have been 168, but "Esmeralda" had disappeared as mysteriously as she had come. No one could give a coherent description of her, not even Thomas, who remembered only a flash of black hair and eyes, and so, after combing the Gypsy district and searching her abandoned rooms, the cause had been given up as lost.

Parliament had been prorogued, the Reform Bill surrendered for this year, and fashionable society had poured out into the countryside. Thomas had remained in Hamilton House. He had let his lease lapse on the Piccadilly flat—suddenly, it had seemed too claustrophobic, crowded with memories of Emmeline even though she had not spent twenty-four hours together in it.

"I understand that you have taken rooms in Camden Town," he said. It was the first time that he had spoken to her since the litigation began, on the strenuous advice of his barrister. He wondered if he could have kept away without that barrier.

She lifted one shoulder. "I always had rooms there, at least since I began being able to afford it." Since she had taken on her charade as a spiritualist, she meant. "I was merely—very reclusive."

"Practically invisible, I should imagine. Has anyone called upon you since you have become more available?" he asked.

"Lady Edgington did, before Parliament prorogued," she said. She raised her chin. "She was kind, but I told her that I would not need a patroness, as I was retiring to Lincroft at the soonest possible moment. The old Lord Olthwaite took the family there during grouse-hunting season every year, and it has always been my favorite place in the world. I never expected to be anything but a pariah, Lord Varcourt. I once dreamt about being a society debutante—but that was long ago, before many things happened to make that impossible. I don't think I have the constitution for it, anyway."

Some details had come out in the legal papers and sensational articles, others in the single brief letter she had sent him, demurely signed *Miss Dunn*. Both she and her brother had been witnesses to the old baron's confession of bigamy, and on the day before the funeral, Emmeline had pressed him for control of their smaller estate, Lincroft. Putting her off with promises, he had left to find and destroy the documentation of her mother's wedding to their father. One day after his return, she had confronted him again, and this confrontation had led to her decision to flee with the family jewels and her pocket money, which had sustained her as far as the church where her parents had wed, only to discover that her brother had beaten her there. With only the thin support of the testimony of a priest for her cause, she had given up on the usual legal avenues.

In the official version of the story, she had sought refuge in a respectable boardinghouse in London, where she had sought work as a lady's companion or governess until some spirit had taken possession of her, and she had woken to find herself lost and confused in Hamilton House at the end of the great scene. Only Thomas and, likely, the false Esmeralda knew any differently.

But there was one great piece still missing, and Thomas wanted it. He needed it, for reasons he did not care to examine too closely.

"Emmeline," he said. "What happened the night you ran away from your brother's house?"

Emmeline's smile was lopsided. "Do you trust me to tell the truth this time?"

"I think you've been honest about more than I ever suspected," he said.

"Now that I do not depend upon your faith, I may have it, yes? That should be funny. But . . . I thank you," she said, her smile fading. She took a deep breath, her gaze focusing somewhere in the distance. "Edgar gave a house party with a ball. He told me that he was going to take care of me as if I were Ann or Alice, and that it would be my coming-out. I even had a white dress. . . ." She trailed off.

"You wore it when you confronted Olthwaite," Thomas supplied.

She nodded. "It was, I think, a kind of joke of his. Two of his guests took the joke too far. They followed me up to my room, and when I opened at their knock, they started pawing at me and kissing me. I pushed them away, and they called me names, said my mother was a whore and that everybody knew that a whore's daughter was a whore, too." In those stark words was a world of pain.

"Emmeline—" he said, and broke off.

She shook her head. "Now I think of how stupid it was, all of it—how stupid I was to be so shocked and terrified. They were bullies, and they were angry and drunk, but they would not have actually raped me. Not then and not there, at any rate. I ran to my brother's room, weeping, begging him to throw them out . . . and he told me that I was an idiot not to take one of them to bed because that was the best I could ever hope for. Then he laughed. He said that no one would care what happened to me, not even if he bedded me against my will." Her eyes were bleak. "His own sister. It was a joke, a nasty, ugly joke, but I knew then that it might not stay a joke forever. So I ran."

"If I had known that—" Thomas began. He cut himself off with an oath. "India is too good for him."

"That is why I didn't tell you, even when it was over," Em said, her face once again as still and perfect as marble. "I didn't ever want revenge, Varcourt. Things are too mixed up for that. Edgar wasn't a bad brother—well, often—until he went to Eton. I loved his sisters—my sisters—and they loved him. It wouldn't be fair to their memories if I destroyed him. All I ever wanted was Lincroft, and peace."

"Is that all?" he asked, his gut clenching in a way it had no right to do.

She looked at him steadily, her eyes clear, and his heart tightened until he could not breathe. "No, not all. I have wanted a multitude of things that could never be mine. But it is all I have ever aspired to."

Thomas stepped away. "I understand," he said.

"I knew you would," she said, with a smile that drove straight through his heart. Then she pulled her mantle over her head, turned away, and disappeared into the mist.

Em dug into the rich earth, reveling in the clean feel of it against her skin. It was a living thing, giving strength, giving life—to her as much as to the two great oaks that grew on either side of the front door of Lincroft Cottage. There could be nothing more different from the filthy streets of London, with their small, circumscribed gardens where even rose petals grew dusky with soot before they faded.

"You shouldn't be out here, miss," said Mrs. Stevenson, the housekeeper. "The ground's half-frozen now, anyway. This is a job for the gardener."

"Yes, it is, isn't it?" Em said, turning the earth in preparation for the spring. She would have a bulb garden, she had decided, and a great lilac bush, and vegetables for the kitchen. Mrs. Stevenson just sighed and returned to the house. Em had a gardener now—and in addition to the housekeeper, a cook, two maids, a groom, and three tenant families. Emmeline Dunn, the poor relation, was now a minor member of county society, with a twelve-room cottage and her own light carriage.

The vicar, poor and hungry for a wife with money, had come to visit first, soon followed, at first tentatively, by the female representatives of other county families. Em took a backward pleasure in the irony of it and had, indeed, made several cautious friends. But except for the purity of the earth and sky, there was very little of the joy she had expected to feel at her victory.

Instead, she had found herself haunted by memories that would have best been forgotten. Thomas' spirit had germinated like a seed inside her mind, sending roots down into every part of her brain until nothing was safe from him. Every time she let her mind rest for an instant, it slipped back to him, pulled by the twining memories that choked out everything else. In Camden Town, she had begun to see him everywhere—in one man's broad back, in the way another held his shoulders. Even some faces, if she was not careful, had tried to reassemble themselves in her mind until they looked more like him.

But it was not him. He had never come.

She had thought such foolishness would be left behind in London, but here in Surrey, she had begun to imagine that she saw the flash of his coat in a shadow of the trees, and at times, when it was very quiet, his voice would come to her out of the silence of her own head. The memories of his caresses heated her when she was mending her stockings or trying to have a civil conversation with the farmwife whose land abutted hers. And Thomas ruled her dreams—making love to her, talking with her, fighting with her, blessing her and damning her, over and over until she began to wonder if some day she would not be able to tell the dreams and memories apart.

They were not soft, not the dreams or the memories. They had little of sweetness or light. But they were real, and they made her feel more alive than anything in her existence.

She had not fallen in love with Thomas Varcourt. That would be, she had decided, too foolish an act to contemplate. After all, when one was in love, wasn't it one's heart that was supposed to break? Em did not feel broken. She felt lost, scattered, fragmented, the ache settling deep in her bowels, her lungs, her bones. That was not love. It was insanity.

That was why, when she saw the figure coming down the lane, she did not react at once. The man looked like Thomas, sitting proud on a fine horse; he held himself like Thomas and moved like Thomas. But so had so many other phantasms over the past three months, and so Em turned her face away and stood, brushing the dirt from her skirt, and walked away, toward the bare-branched copse behind the stable.

"Emmeline!"

Em stood rooted to the ground as a shock of reaction shot through her. That was not the voice of a ghost, nor did it ring only inside her head. She turned, pivoting slowly on the spot, her heart squeezing and her lungs aching with fear and hope she could not name.

"Thomas," she whispered. It was him. He was larger than he had been even in her memory, larger and fiercer and as resplendent as a dark sun.

He strode toward her, yanking off his gloves and tossing them aside, his brow lowered and eyes burning as they devoured her. "Did you not see me coming along the road?" he demanded.

"I saw," she said. "I saw, but I didn't believe." She put a hand on her stomach and stepped backward. His body radiated tension. She could feel it battering against her, trying to break her down. She scrambled for her defenses, but they had melted away. "Why have you come?" And, almost in the same breath: "Why didn't you come before?"

But then his arms were around her, crushing her against him, his mouth on hers, taking it, taking everything. She gave a little sob and surrendered—to him and to the roaring need for him that throbbed through her body. His tongue moved in her mouth, stroking it, his lips moving in rhythm with hers as he laid her gently upon the damp leaves of the ground, her shawl slipping off her shoulders to lie beneath them.

"My breath," he said harshly as her mouth moved from his lips and roved hungrily over his face and neck. She kissed the crease between his eyes, his hawklike nose, his hard cheeks and rough chin, down the strong pillar of his neck. "My breath, my life, my soul—you took them from me when I wasn't looking. Olthwaite was right: You are a witch."

She let go of him, dropping back limply against the leaves as she tried to take that in. "What have you done to me?" she accused, the question that had been beating inside her head for the past two months. "All I wanted in the world was a little place for myself, and now that I have it—you've ruined it for me."

He began to unfasten her bodice, yanking the buttons through their holes in his urgency. "Good," he said, a trace of viciousness in his tone. "We have at least tortured one another in equal measure."

Her hands fisted in the fabric of his overcoat. "Why? I don't understand. I didn't ask for this."

His smile was almost bitter. "This isn't the kind of thing one asks for."

Then what am I supposed to do with it? she started to ask. But she already knew. "It's the kind of thing that one must hold on to with both hands," she whispered. "Because it gets its hooks in your soul, and if it flies away, it will leave a husk behind."

He stilled, his face tight, eyes closed, rocking slightly above her. "What we have is the truest thing I have ever experienced."

"But so much was lies," she said.

"Souls don't lie. I am sorry I had no faith in your last promise—sorry despite every excuse, despite all reason and logic, even."

Em's breath caught on a hiccough, and she realized she was weeping. She dashed away the tears. "I didn't deserve your faith. I had done nothing to earn it and everything to destroy it. I am sorry, too, for everything, the entire cursed mess. I have forsworn lying. I can't make myself do it anymore. The words come to my brain, but my tongue won't say them."

He opened his eyes at that, and she could not miss the glint of ironic humor in his eyes. "And when the neighbor's roast is dry and tough?"

"I tell them how nice it is not to be served raw meat," she said, a sudden giggle making her hiccough.

"You will make a terrible MP's wife," he said.

She froze. Even her heart seemed to stop beating for an instant. "Oh, God, Thomas," she said. "Do not mock me."

"I have never been so serious about anything in my life." His eyes burned into hers.

"I don't know that I even love you," she said. "Much less whether you love me."

He shook his head. "I was dying without you, Merry. Do you believe that?"

"Yes," she whispered. "Only because I was dying without you. What is wrong with us? Have we lost our minds?"

"If we have, I don't ever want mine back," he said. "You shall marry me, Emmeline Dunn. And then we can both live forever."

Then his mouth was over hers again, his hand sliding into her corset to cup her breasts and nudge her nipples above its hard, boned line. Anticipation coiled in her center, making her gasp even before his mouth came down hard on one. He took it into his mouth, rasping the fabric of her chemise across it with his tongue. Hot flames shot into her core, making her buzz with it and rock to the rhythm of his mouth. His hand was on her thigh, pulling up her skirts and sliding up to the slit in her pantaloons. She opened to him, thrusting her hips into his hand, whimpering with the need that made her skin prickle and burn, that made her ache with emptiness low between her legs.

He raised his hand to her lips even as he moved to her other breast with his mouth, leaving the first suddenly, shockingly cold against the linen of her chemise. She understood what he wanted, and she took his fingers in her mouth, moving them to his rhythm as she ground her hips against his erection that she felt through his clothing. She thought of how his tongue had felt inside her, and moved hers between his fingers like he had done between her folds. He hissed in reaction, his breath making her nipple even tighter. Sensation spiraled through her, driving her onward in search of the ultimate climax.

He took his hand away and slid it down between her legs, separating her folds in one smooth motion as he thrust a finger deep within her and began to stroke, his thumb finding the hard nub of flesh above it. She was still so empty. Even as the wave built within her, she longed for more of him, inside of her.

"More," she begged, pressing her hips hard against his hand. "Now." She dropped her voice. "Love me, Thomas. I'm not sure what love is, but I believe we can find out together."

He moved from her breast to look into her face, and half of her wanted to close her eyes, to reject the searing intimacy of that gaze, but she could not. She lay there, helpless, as he read her soul. Then he smiled, an expression of feral victory she had never seen before.

"I think you already know," he said. "Just as I do." He pressed her onward to the peak, where the sharp spears of pleasure jerked through her. But it only made her emptiness worse, her body clamoring in its dissatisfaction even as he held her there, shaking and panting.

"Thomas," she said, barely able to form the word.

"I shall make you my wife," he ground out. "No one else will ever have you like this." He thrust another finger within her, pushing the peak higher. Bright, hot surges shot through her, but it was not enough.

"I don't know," she said, weeping the words.

"You do." His words were almost swallowed by the buzzing explosions of light behind her eyes. She could not hold on much longer. She felt herself breaking apart, dis-solving, every piece of her circling the red-hot void in her center that threatened to suck her in until she drowned.

"Agree to marry me," he said, the words coming as if from far away, as dark and terrible as a storm.

She tried to think of all the reasons that she should not marry him—their different backgrounds, the insanity of their relationship . . . But they were torn from her in the maelstrom until all that she was left with were the blaze of her body and the single, aching need that she knew only he could fill—the need in her body and the need in her life merging until she could not tell one from the other.

"I will do it," she cried out. "I will marry you."

"Good," he said.

Then he was there, at her entrance, sliding into her with a smoothness that was like a homecoming. She sobbed with relief as he thrust into her, filling the emptiness, joining the sharp, bright clang of pleasure with a sensation that was as deep and as ancient as the sea. It drowned the brightness with its deeper surge, taking over. She could feel every cell in her body individually, could feel his, too, against her, merging with her, until she could not tell where one of them stopped and the other began.

Forever.